Praise for Mardi Oakley Med...

WITCH OF T...

"In her debut novel, *Death at ...., Mardi Oakley* Medawar proved a Cherokee can bring the Kiowa of another epoch alive for us. With *Witch of the Palo Duro* she does even better. Another great storyteller is emerging."

—Tony Hillerman

"Mardi Oakley Medawar has created in Tay-bodal one of the most interesting and fun detectives in the history of the genre. What's more, she has gone way beyond that by placing him in a historic context that is utterly realistic and totally convincing. That's an almost unbeatable combination. The Tay-bodal novels are wonderful."

—Robert J. Conley, author of
the *Real People* novels

DEATH AT RAINY MOUNTAIN

"More than a mystery, Medawar's novel is a beautifully written, life-affirming, heartwarming story full of adventure, humor, and tears . . . a cunningly plotted story that is as devilishly funny as it is charmingly told. Masterful and moving." —*Booklist*

"A mystery set in 1866 in the Kiowa nation, with mostly historical figures, and no whites? A preposterous idea, but a wonderful result. Medawar really captures the personalities of the individuals in her story, as well as the culture itself." —Don Coldsmith, award-winning author of
Tallgrass and the *Spanish Bit Saga*

"Tay-bodal and the other characters never fail to ring true as human beings . . . Medawar creates not only an unusual backdrop with her observations about Kiowa life but also a real puzzle and an entertaining read."

—*San Jose Mercury News*

PEOPLE OF THE WHISTLING WATERS

"Mardi Oakley Medawar has a feel for the Crow and the incoming whites as few other writers could. Her characters, white or Indian, are *people* . . . This is our history."
> —Don Coldsmith, award-winning
> author of *Runestone*

"Rather than emphasize two cultures' diversities, Mardi Oakley Medawar celebrates their similarities with poignancy, wry humor, and precise characterization."
> —Suzann Ledbetter, award-winning author of
> *Nellie Cashman*, *Prospector*, and *Trail-Blazer*

"Ms. Medawar has an astonishing talent for turning mere words on a page into characters so vivid and real, so deliciously human, you'll swear they can't possibly be fiction."
> —Penelope Williamson, author of
> *Heart of the West*

Also by Mardi Oakley Medawar . . .

Remembering the Osage Kid (Bantam)

And coming soon . . .

Rainwater on the White Road (Signet)
Brothers of Thunder (Bantam)
Murder at Medicine Lodge (St. Martin's Press)

MORE MYSTERIES FROM THE
BERKLEY PUBLISHING GROUP...

THE HERON CARVIC MISS SEETON MYSTERIES: Retired art teacher Miss Seeton steps in where Scotland Yard stumbles. "A most beguiling protagonist!"
—*New York Times*

by Heron Carvic
MISS SEETON SINGS
MISS SEETON DRAWS THE LINE
WITCH MISS SEETON
PICTURE MISS SEETON
ODDS ON MISS SEETON

by Hampton Charles
ADVANTAGE MISS SEETON
MISS SEETON AT THE HELM
MISS SEETON, BY APPOINTMENT

by Hamilton Crane
HANDS UP, MISS SEETON
MISS SEETON CRACKS THE CASE
MISS SEETON PAINTS THE TOWN
MISS SEETON BY MOONLIGHT
MISS SEETON ROCKS THE CRADLE
MISS SEETON GOES TO BAT
MISS SEETON PLANTS SUSPICION
STARRING MISS SEETON
MISS SEETON UNDERCOVER
MISS SEETON RULES
SOLD TO MISS SEETON
SWEET MISS SEETON
BONJOUR, MISS SEETON

KATE SHUGAK MYSTERIES: A former D.A. solves crimes in the far Alaska north...

by Dana Stabenow
A COLD DAY FOR MURDER
DEAD IN THE WATER
A FATAL THAW
BREAKUP

A COLD-BLOODED BUSINESS
PLAY WITH FIRE
BLOOD WILL TELL

INSPECTOR BANKS MYSTERIES: Award-winning British detective fiction at its finest ... "Robinson's novels are habit-forming!"
—*West Coast Review of Books*

by Peter Robinson
THE HANGING VALLEY
WEDNESDAY'S CHILD
INNOCENT GRAVES

PAST REASON HATED
FINAL ACCOUNT
GALLOWS VIEW

CASS JAMESON MYSTERIES: Lawyer Cass Jameson seeks justice in the criminal courts of New York City in this highly acclaimed series... "A witty, gritty heroine."
—*New York Post*

by Carolyn Wheat
FRESH KILLS
MEAN STREAK
TROUBLED WATERS

DEAD MAN'S THOUGHTS
WHERE NOBODY DIES
SWORN TO DEFEND

SCOTLAND YARD MYSTERIES: Featuring Detective Superintendent Duncan Kincaid and his partner, Sergeant Gemma James... "Charming!"
—*New York Times Book Review*

by Deborah Crombie
A SHARE IN DEATH
LEAVE THE GRAVE GREEN

ALL SHALL BE WELL
MOURN NOT YOUR DEAD

JACK McMORROW MYSTERIES: The highly acclaimed series set in a Maine mill town and starring a newspaperman with a knack for crime solving... "Gerry Boyle is the genuine article."
—*Robert B. Parker*

by Gerry Boyle
DEADLINE
LIFELINE
BORDERLINE

BLOODLINE
POTSHOT

WITCH OF THE
PALO DURO

Mardi Oakley Medawar

BERKLEY PRIME CRIME, NEW YORK

WITCH OF THE PALO DURO

A Berkley Prime Crime Book / published by arrangement with
St. Martin's Press, Inc.

PRINTING HISTORY
St. Martin's hardcover edition / November 1997
Berkley Prime Crime mass-market edition / February 1999

The Penguin Putnam Inc. World Wide Web site address is
http://www.penguinputnam.com

ISBN: 0-425-16735-6

Berkley Prime Crime Books are published
by The Berkley Publishing Group,
a member of Penguin Putnam Inc.,
375 Hudson Street, New York, New York 10014.
The name BERKLEY PRIME CRIME and the BERKLEY PRIME CRIME
design are trademarks belonging to Berkley Publishing Corporation.

PRINTED IN THE UNITED STATES OF AMERICA

10 9 8 7 6 5 4 3 2 1

FOR BEBE

My best friend throughout shared yesterdays,
today, and for all of our tomorrows

Although this is a work of fiction, the names of a majority of the characters are real, and this work is based on the actual lives of these very real men. I have done this intentionally. On too many occasions, their names have been misused, their extraordinary lives distorted. I am only a storyteller. As such it is not my responsibility to right a plethora of wrongs. But during the course of telling a story, I can give my people back their heroes. I can restore to these heroes their names.

Mardi Oakley Medawar

CHAPTER

1

I remember the last peaceful autumn my people, the Kiowa, knew as a free nation. Like something tangible, I hold the memory tightly in my heart, reliving each and every precious moment again and again. The Baptist preaching man talks to us all the time about heaven. To be back in those lost days of 1866, when I was a relatively young man, newly married, our nation at liberty to come and go as it pleased, to be there again with those I loved, that is my notion of heaven. I am an old man now, yet those days are more clear to me than my recollections of what I did earlier this morning. But those memories are understandably more clear because I am alone again and what I do to fill the hours is not as important to me as when my life was wonderfully crowded and busy with the ordinary activities of living. Now, in my advanced age, I confess that I appreciate that great mob of people much more than I did at the time. Still too young to fully appreciate all that I had, the business of living and the demands placed on me made my life feel, at times, a little bit too crowded.

At any rate, it was a season when I was still in the full

promise of youth. I have never been what anyone would describe as handsome. The best that can be said was that I was of good height and weight, had a thick head of hair and all of my teeth. My wife, Crying Wind, however, was beautiful, tall and slender. She also had large, round eyes. Where she got those, I don't know, because my wife was a full-blood, and full-blooded people are not normally round-eyed. Her oddly shaped eyes gained her a lot of attention, and bluntly put, she could have had any man she wanted. It was simply my great good luck that she wanted me. At the beginning of that winter we had been together only a few months, having married during the summer season. When we met, Crying Wind was a widow, and from her first husband she had a child, a four-year-old boy I adopted and renamed Favorite Son. As I said, my wife was a startlingly pretty woman, but she was of a tempestuous temperament. The combination was irresistible, and I adored her.

She was also from a higher class, being the maternal cousin of the war chief known by the whites as Satanta, the botched pronunciation of Set-tainte, which means White Bear. To his friends, he was known simply as The Bear. My marriage to his cousin Crying Wind meant that I, a man formerly denied his friendship and holding no alliance with any clan or band, became by marriage White Bear's full relative and member of his band known as the Rattle Band.

The Rattle Band was at that time the most prestigious union in our nation, the names of its members reading as a roll call of the most famous men in Kiowan history. My name, Tay-bodal, is there too, but only because of them, because they called me brother, because they found in me a worth no one before had recognized or credited. My closest brother in the Rattle Band was Ma-Man-Ti, Skywalker.

He was White Bear's closest adviser. A tall man and as thin as a reed, he was rather handsome in a lanky, disjointed way. He was an Owl Doctor, a seer, or if you prefer, a prophet. Although he was completely unknown to the whites, a thing that suited the secretive nature of Skywalker entirely, he was *the* most influential man in our nation during the fifteen years' war with the United States. There are no photographs of Skywalker, but his son, Rainy Mountain Taslie (Charlie), looks exactly like him. Whenever I see Taslie walking around, a sharp knife goes straight through my heart and tears flow from my life-tired eyes. My tears cause Taslie great discomfort, but I can't stop them. I am too overwhelmed with emotion whenever I see him because I greatly miss his father, who was my dearest friend. I think that what saddens me most is that, even among our own people, Skywalker has become a man all but lost to our history, a man even Taslie, his own son, barely knows anything about. This is understandable. The young have lost patience and now do not listen to old men as they should. They think our stories are too ancient. They're wrong. The past was just yesterday.

I remember yesterday.

It was in the previous summer, when I had been of some help in solving a mystery that had threatened our nation as a whole and had also tended a boy with a broken leg (did I not tell you I was a doctor? Well, I was), that Skywalker took it into his head that he should disciple himself to me. That a man of his prestige would humble himself to learn from someone like myself, a man of little consequence, is more telling of Skywalker's intrinsic greatness than anything I could ever hope to say. Only a genuinely superior person realizes that he or she is capable of learning something valuable from a person beneath his or her station.

Skywalker realized that about lowly me, and whether I wanted a disciple or not, he firmly latched onto me. There was nothing I could do or say to dissuade him.

So there I was in the autumn of 1866 when the Rattle Band moved away from the Rainy Mountain and set up its winter camp in the Palo Duro Canyon, with a wife I had never wanted, but married because I fell slave to my passion for her, with a son I had never dreamed I would have and was, to be honest, a bit leery of, *and* with the most influential man in our history following my every step like a faithful camp dog. For a man long accustomed to a solitary life of unbridled freedom, all of this was a bit traumatic, and I'm afraid I didn't handle it well. Especially as my wife prepared for the coming winter by making hats for me and our son.

Two items of clothing are necessary for winter: hats and shoes. With a good hat and a pair of fur-lined shoes, a person can walk virtually naked through a blizzard and feel relatively comfortable. We Kiowa were not ordinarily given to wearing hats, especially not in the hot summer season, unless the hat was a symbol of high office. But, as I said, I have never been a typical Kiowa. I love hats. Especially those wide Mexican hats. The brim of that type of hat offers excellent shade, almost for the entire body. The hat I love absolutely the best, the type I'm almost emotionally involved with, is a winter hat, a nice warm furry hat. People of the Rattle Band, because of me, came to love them too. Acting in my role as a doctor, I even encouraged people to sleep with their hats on because it is my belief that during the coldest nights of winter, essential body heat escapes out of the ears and nose. With a hat pulled down over the ears and with blankets pulled up over the nose, even when the fires in the lodge were unable to keep pace with the pervading chill, as the winter winds howled, rattling the lodge walls, a person managed to sleep comfy and snug. This notion caught on with the Rattle Band so well that my eternally competitive brethren turned a commonsense idea into a contest.

Unfortunately, my wife, Crying Wind, was overly competitive herself. She knew all of my reasons concerning winter hats, but as my new wife, making hats for me and our son that would be seen as better than anyone else's became a source of fervent pride. To my horror, she added deer antlers to the matching hats she made for me and Favorite Son. You have to appreciate the effort she went to, for she didn't stick on the entire antlers, she used only the decorative end tines. She spent hours of hard work sawing through the tough bone of the antler branches to get just the pieces she wanted. Then she spent more hours sewing them in place, making them secure. It had all been a labor of love, and I tried hard to appreciate her dedication, but that was a very hard thing to do because I had never in my life seen a pair of uglier hats. Judging from the way our son puckered his little face into a frown, it was clear that Favorite Son held the same opinion. Regretfully, Crying Wind missed the obvious as she stuck the new hats on our heads and then had us stand outside our lodge in full view of the entire village while she made a grand show of surveying her handiwork.

Favorite Son held my hand tightly as both he and I tried not to notice the startled looks of passersby. He edged closer to me, the pointed tip of the antler sticking from the side of his hat gouging into my hip.

"I was afraid of that," Crying Wind tsked.

Neither the boy nor I bothered to ask exactly what she had been afraid of, as we were both too selfishly absorbed with our own fears.

Pointing an accusing hand in my direction, she said in a

disgusted tone, "One of your antlers is slightly lower than
the other. And now I can't fix it. I've sewn it in too tightly.
I think maybe you should tilt your head a bit to the left."

I complied. Crying Wind beamed a happy smile. "Perfect!" She turned to go back inside our home. "I'm going
in to work on your new shoes now. Just walk around that
way, Tay-bodal, and no one will notice your antlers aren't
even."

The weight of the furry hat and the downward tug of the
cumbersome antler combined to create the beginnings of a
serious crick in my neck.

"I can't walk around like this!" I shouted.

"Of course you can," she replied dismissively. Then she
closed the door on my tilted, worry-riddled face.

Favorite Son looked up at me, then began to sob pitifully.
"I don't wike me hat!"

"There there," I whispered. I hated it when he cried. I
have always been inadequate in the art of soothing a child's
delicate feelings.

Favorite Son's response to my lame attempt was to un-
hinge his lower jaw and wail more loudly. I inwardly
groaned. It was still the early days in our father-son rela-
tionship, and frankly, I found Favorite Son to be something
of an anathema. I never knew the right thing to do with
him when he was sad, and when he was in a boisterous
mood, jumping around inside our lodge like a slippery tad-
pole out of water, he irritated the very liver out of me. I
had been an only child myself and, as an adult, to my
knowledge, was without issue. Therefore, I had no idea
how to be a father to a baby. Beginning my parenting skills
with a frisky four-year-old was a bad way to start. To be
utterly truthful, it was only when Favorite Son needed correcting or was asleep that I ever actually felt comfortable
in his company.

The correcting part was easy because parents never corrected their own children. Discipline was the job of aunts and uncles. This custom relieved the parents of being thought of harshly by their offspring and taught the child that his or her actions affected the clan as a whole, that behaving badly was not simply a problem for the child's immediate family. So, the first time I caught Favorite Son being naughty, I happily hauled him off to my illustrious new relative, White Bear.

"Why are you bringing him to me?" White Bear scowled. "This child has a lot of relatives."

"Yes, but he's more afraid of you."

In the face of my satisfied smirk, White Bear glowered darkly. Then he turned his attention to the little boy huddled against my leg.

Sounding impatient, he said, "Tay-bodal's Favorite Son, go home and be a good boy. If your father brings you to me again, you are to come with a whipping stick in your hand. Do you understand?"

"Yes, Uncle," Favorite Son murmured.

"Good." White Bear turned to go.

"That's all you have to say?" I cried.

White Bear looked at me from around his broad shoulder. "What were you expecting? A speech? Children never listen to lectures. All they ever hear is 'Stop that.' Which is something you could say to him yourself. Now get away from me, Tay-bodal, before I hit *you* with a stick."

My second-best time with Favorite Son was when he was asleep. All I had to do during those times was be careful not to wake him. That was certainly easy enough.

But now he was crying, and as his parent, comforting him was *my* duty. The trouble was, I could have done with a bit of comforting myself. The idea of living out the winter in that idiotic hat and being forced to walk around with my head at an oblique angle to correct my wife's less than wonderful sewing skills had my eyes brimming a bit too. The uncomfortable moment wasn't helped by the untimely appearance of Skywalker.

Skywalker was a father. He had a little girl, Red Dress, and an adopted white son known as Tehan. I felt I could trust him to know all about crying youngsters and how best to placate them. Ignoring me (but only after chuckling at the sight of me in my new hat), Skywalker knelt down and dealt directly with Favorite Son.

"What's the matter, little soul?"

"Me hat ugwy," Favorite Son squalled.

"No, it isn't. It's a wonderful hat. That's a warrior's hat, you know."

Favorite Son's bawling lessened, became hitching sobs, tears streaming his rounded cheeks, his little puckered lips twitching as his round, dark eyes sought Skywalker's.

"Big, important men wear hats like that," Skywalker crooned. "Your father is wearing one."

Therein lay Skywalker's fatal error. Favorite Son looked away from him, up to me, saw clearly with the unsullied eyes of the painfully truthful young just how ridiculous I looked. Even with a four-year-old's limited scope, he was able to work out that he most certainly looked just as awful as I. Still staring up at me, Favorite Son began to bellow.

Skywalker stood up smartly, shouting to me over my son's din, "Well, I tried!"

"You made everything worse, thank you very much."

"Is it my fault you both look like a pair of baffled deer?"

Hearing that remark, and understanding it as mockery, Favorite Son's cries became earsplitting shrieks. Crying Wind startled us all when she came flying out of the lodge.

"What are you two doing to my baby?"

"Pestering him," Skywalker replied.

Crying Wind was not amused. She gave us both sharp looks as she snatched up Favorite Son with one blurring movement. Placing him on her hip, she only just escaped having her eye jabbed by one of the offensive antlers.

"You two, go away," she ordered. "Go off and study interesting leaves or something." She rounded on me. "And I don't want to see *you* again until the evening mealtime."

She left us in a huff, her angry exit ruined when one of the hat's tines snared the side of the lodge door. She had to close the flap door and then maneuver Favorite Son around on her hip to unstick the thing.

"You might want to trim those down a little bit," I said, ever helpful.

"Shut up," she snapped. Then she was gone, the door slamming closed, Skywalker and I effectively left to our own manly devices.

His hands locked behind him, Skywalker rocked on the balls of his feet as he smirked and said, "My, aren't we having a wonderful morning."

Livid, I stared hatefully at him while plucking the ghastly hat off my head. "No, I'm not! And I wish you would go away!" Then I stormed off, a chortling Skywalker trotting after me.

Now, you might think me disrespectful or uncommonly brave to be yelling at a man like Skywalker in that way. Actually I was neither. He and I had simply grown into that kind of friendship. We were comfortable enough with each other to say anything or, in times of stress, yell anything, the other taking no offense. Although I must admit that early on in our friendship, I was offended by his less than glowing remarks regarding my physical appearance. To be specific, his very first comment was:

"I've known better-looking mud holes."

All right, it's true. Even in my prime I was never a maiden's dream. My nose is stubby, my cheekbones too prominent, my lips too full, and my eyes a bit squinty. None of this was made better by the pits in my face, scarring caused by the smallpox. But I've always prided myself on being a pleasant person, and I did have a strong, lean body. Crying Wind seemed to like this last virtue a lot, so I learned to ignore Skywalker's gibes. Besides, he was only saying how lucky I was—that it was a major victory for a man like me to have a wife of Crying Wind's worth. On that point I could only agree.

When I first saw her, she was standing in the center of a creek, her skirt pulled up and through her legs. The setting sun had been streaming down on her, the sparkling water flowing around her. She was so beautiful I couldn't breathe, couldn't move. All I could do was stare at the woman who was White Bear's widowed cousin. I fell in love with her with just that one look. Later on, he asked if I would promise to do a little something for him. When I found out what that something was, I was hesitant. Then he offered Crying Wind as a bribe, saying that my favor to him would be paid with a favor to me. His favor was his promise to consider a marriage between me and his lovely cousin. To have her, I would have done anything, and he knew it. My determination to survive long enough to have her for my wife served me well, for White Bear's "little something" nearly cost me my life.

Walking along beside me now, Skywalker continued to tease me about my looks. I had calmed down enough to quip that at least I had good meat on me whereas he was so thin I could hear his bones rattling around inside his clothing. And that always brought me back to the topic that fascinated me completely: Skywalker's impaired sense of taste.

Because he couldn't taste properly, he ate barely enough to survive. Which was why he was so thin. Since he was anxious to be my disciple, learn from me the healing craft, I knew he wasn't in a position to balk too much if I made him the subject of an experiment. And as the crisp autumnal morning was starting off badly, and as he had been a major contributor, now felt like the perfect time for the experiment. With a certain glee in my heart I took him with me to my private lodge.

Married men always maintained separate lodges. Having a place of our own to escape to when the bustle of family life became more than we could stand kept us out from under our wives' feet. My private lodge was a sad little thing really. Other married men had private lodges that were large enough to entertain the entire membership of their warrior societies. As I had never belonged to a warrior society, my needs were small. Actually, the little lodge I used as my private place was the same lodge I'd lived in as a bachelor. After marrying Crying Wind, my old lodge became the place I used to meet with ailing patients, as Crying Wind would not allow medical concoctions or sick people inside our family lodge. She said my potions stank and my patients were an imposition. She was very fussy like that. Terribly house proud. Besides, it was Kiowa custom that whenever someone came to call, the wife offered the visitor food. So many people came to me with their ills and troubles that cooking for all of them would have left her little time for normal housewifery duties. Crying Wind's answer was to throw me out, relegating me to my old bachelor lodge, which we had been using for general storage. When she kicked me out, all of my medical stocks went with me. Then she had me move the smaller lodge a good fifty yards behind our family home. Being so far away meant that technically, when patients came to see me, they weren't in my home area, and Crying Wind wasn't obliged to them in any way. But should *I* need anything, she had that problem solved as well. I needn't stick my head out the door and yell, all I had to do was tug on a rope inside my little lodge. Outside, the rope lay on the ground like a stretched-out sleeping snake, its tail ending inside our home and pegged around one of the lodge poles. A little brass bell on the end of the line jangled whenever I needed her. It goes without saying that whenever I summoned, the call had better be important.

Skywalker entered behind me and sat down. It was cold and gloomy in that cramped lodge, the only light the murky beam coming down through the smoke hole from an overcast sky. I piled kindling in the central pit and struck the flint stones. The first fragile flames caught hold of the cottonwood wadding and proceeded on to the dry sticks. As the fire heightened, I added split logs, and in no time at all, the less than spacious lodge containing packed parcels of my medical cache was well lit and cozy. As I looked across the fire at Skywalker, excitement rippled through me, previous irritation forgotten. I had formed a theory about his inability to taste properly, and I couldn't wait to try the experiment.

"Why do I have to wear a blindfold?" he protested as I tied it tightly behind his head.

"You just do."

"You're not going to feed me anything disgusting, are you?"

"Will you please sit still. This is an important experiment, and I need your cooperation."

Through a series of previous sessions, I had learned that Skywalker could taste four things: sweet, bitter, salt, and, his favorite, hot peppers. But he could not combine these tastes. When tasting sweet, he had no idea if the sweet thing was honey or mashed-up fruit pulp. He only knew sweet. His reactions were the same for the others. So in actuality, Skywalker could taste. What he could not do was savor combined tastes, couldn't identify what he was tasting. For the longest time I couldn't fathom why. Until one night it hit me, and I bolted upright in bed.

"Smell!" I cried.

"Sorry," Crying Wind said in a muffled voice.

"Not you! Skywalker."

Crying Wind sat up beside me, her sleepy tone incredulous. "Skywalker is being smelly in here?"

I grabbed her by the shoulders, shook her fully awake. I wanted her wide awake to fully appreciate the blast of inspiration. "Don't you understand? Skywalker can't smell. He hasn't been able to smell anything since he fell off that horse in the previous spring and hit his head on a rock. That was also the time his headaches started getting worse."

"You woke me up in the middle of the night to talk about Skywalker's nose and headaches?"

"Well," I drawled, "yes, I suppose I did."

Crying Wind flung a clump of hair out of her face and then glared at me. "I'm going to kill you."

Her face was all screwed up, her dark eyes glaring hard. I knew she meant it. But she didn't scare me. We'd been married long enough that I knew exactly how to handle her whenever she was in this dangerous mood.

"Would you mind very much making love to me first? It's always been a dream of mine to die happy."

Crying Wind began to sputter, then laugh. My wife was the type of woman who never responded meekly to threats of abuse, but humor knocked her down every time.

Through gritted teeth she said, "I would give *anything* if I could only stay mad at you."

Wriggling my eyebrows playfully, I said, "Really?"

Laughing even more, she grabbed my hair on both sides of my head and pulled my face toward hers, our mouths colliding. What happened after that is supremely private.

The first day I met Skywalker, he was suffering one of his headaches. I am still appalled by the ferocity of it—an ordinary man would have gone insane. Skywalker had been saved only by his ability to transport his consciousness to another place, but even so, he suffered terribly. When he was forced to come back to himself before he became eternally lost somewhere between the Forever and Earth, he came back to a torment that beggars the imagination. I was never able to cure his headaches, only control them, which for Skywalker, considering the agonies he had known, was a cure.

Because of the camp move to the Palo Duro Canyon a few days following my waking inspiration, I had forgotten all about it. But now with Skywalker again at my disposal, excitement grew inside me. Blindfolded, he sat there patiently as I scrambled around in Crying Wind's carefully packed stores. I retrieved an onion, and although the thing made me tear up as I handled it, I peeled it and held it under his nose.

"Can you smell this?"

"Smell what?"

I waved it some more, really working up the onion fumes.

"Take a deep breath, but only through your nose."

Skywalker complied, inhaling deeply, the effort straightening his body as the nostrils of his curved nose pulled in. When he exhaled, he slumped.

"That'd better not be your shoe."

"You can't smell it at all?"

"No."

I pushed the onion toward his mouth. "Bite it."

"Is it your shoe?"

"*No!*"

He bit down hard and then chewed.

"What do you taste?"

"Bitter. Slimy. It is your shoe."

I sat back and stared at him for a long time, my mind buzzing. I had proven my theory. Taste indeed involved the sense of smell. I have always believed that all parts of the body worked for a common good. That the arms and legs worked to provide for and protect the upper torso. That the upper torso shielded the heart as it supplied pure blood to feed the brain. Now I realized that even a healed injury to the brain could have long-term effects for the vital sensory components and that two of the five senses, namely smell and taste, relied heavily on each other. Ironically, in that moment of discovery, instead of feeling proud, I felt small, as if I were suddenly standing in the very presence of our Creator. I could only marvel at His infinite attention to detail, feel humbled and awed by how wonderfully He'd made this species He'd named man.

The sense of smell not only alerted man to danger, it also evoked pleasure. The aromas of good food increased enjoyment, encouraged men to eat more and thus feed the body adequately, and in turn the body cared for the brain. But Skywalker couldn't smell anything. As a result, his sense of taste was severely impaired. Another problem arose due to his faulty senses. Because he wasn't eating properly, his chronic headaches were again on the increase, and he was taking more and more of the pain-diminishing medicine I made for him. He had been almost painfully thin on the first day I met him, and since then he had lost even more weight. My diagnosis was that he was slowly wasting away. As his friend, as his doctor, I couldn't allow this destructive pattern to continue.

Pulling the blindfold from his eyes, I yelled directly in Skywalker's face. "You're going to eat more. I don't care if eating only makes you frustrated. You are going to eat because I say so. Because if you don't, I won't give you any more medicine, and your terrible headaches will be even worse."

He tilted his head, looked at me for a long moment, and then in a dead calm voice said, "Isn't that form of doctoring just a tiny bit harsh?"

"No, not when it saves your life. Have you eaten this morning?"

"Well, I've had . . ." He looked down at his hand, then looked up, sending me a crooked grin. "Oh, good! It's not your shoe. It's an onion. Yes, Tay-bodal, I have eaten this morning. I've had some of this onion."

His attempt at humor failed miserably. Cold anger ripped through me. "That's what I thought." I stood up. "You're coming with me. My wife is going to feed you until you faint."

"She won't like that."

"Again, I don't care."

"I feel sleepy," Skywalker complained as, much later, we walked out of my lodge.

"Good. That means your body is happy."

"Well, I'm not happy. My stomach is all pushed out. I look like I'm going to have a baby."

We walked through the heart of the sprawling winter camp. In the past months, the Rattle Band had become enormous, grown from its usual collection of about seventy lodges to over four hundred. The population increase was due to the election of the Nation's new principal chief. In the previous spring, Little Bluff, a man who, in his thirty years as principal chief, had held together a nation of stubbornly independent souls, died in his sleep of old age. An election was held immediately following the resolution of a nasty conflict between White Bear and Kicking Bird, two of the three candidates for this high office. Lone Wolf was the third candidate. Unfortunately, White Bear and Kicking Bird were longtime antagonists for whom the settlement of one argument merely lead to the invention of another. The Nation, weary of their ceaseless wrangling, elected Lone Wolf.

Lone Wolf was a good man. As I voted for him myself, I can hardly say otherwise. Like the majority ruling in his favor, I too thought that by choosing him, White Bear and Kicking Bird would settle down and the Nation would get on with healing its differences. The majority and I badly misjudged all three men. White Bear and Kicking Bird became even more locked in their personal war, and Lone Wolf's personality simply wasn't strong enough to force either of them to make peace.

Because Lone Wolf wasn't able to pacify White Bear or Kicking Bird, the Nation shifted dramatically, the strongest war chiefs, *to-yop-kes*, and their clans coming over to White Bear, the peace proponents and their families going over to Kicking Bird. Lone Wolf, I'm afraid, got what was left, which sadly wasn't much because, in those days, everyone was of a strong opinion on the best way to deal with the steady increase of Blue Jackets in our country.

White Bear wanted to wipe out all of the Blue Jackets. Kicking Bird believed the best way for the Nation to survive was for all of us to become A-me-cans (Americans). Shortly after he was elected, Lone Wolf's first decision as principal chief was that all of us would simply live around the intruders, in effect, continue going our own way, pretending that the Blue Jackets weren't there. I couldn't imagine just how he believed any of us could possibly do that. Keenly disappointed with this judgment, had I not already been aligned to White Bear by marriage, I would have chosen him as my chief on my own. I have never been the kind of man able to close my eyes as a murderous bear lumbered toward me at great speed. Besides, if White Bear was going to war, he and his warriors would need a practical doctor. Buffalo Doctors, slashing additional wounds in a shot-up man hoping to bleed the bullets out, or Owl Doctors, striving to chant the bullets away, would be no good to him. I, on the other hand, would dig the bullets out, patch up the wounds, and treat against blood fever. Clearly, I was the very man White Bear would need most. And, being the type of man he was, had I not willingly chosen to come over to his side, White Bear would have had me kidnapped.

Skywalker and I walked through the bustle of the village. The size of it stretched beyond the norm. One individual family camp met and then gave way to another. It felt odd to me, walking through one private sector and then into another without first asking the band chief's permission. But, because these bands squatting so close to White Bear's were chiefs he'd declared to be his personal favorites, no one stopped us or seemed to mind our blatant trespass. The various bands were busily preparing for the hard winter that we knew, by the sharpness of the autumnal air, was almost upon us. As we walked, I glanced around at the activity. Women sat outside their homes, sewing new winter clothing for their families and pounding up pemmican to store away in containers. The new warmer clothing would soon be needed, because we could already see our breath in the air.

Pemmican was a vital food. Not only did it taste good, it contained all of the essential nutrients. Crying Wind had a special recipe consisting of nuts, dried fruits, rose hips, and a small amount of honey. When all of these were added into the pounded-into-powder dried meat, it made pemmican, a concoction that was not only delicious but stored well throughout a winter season. All of the women had their own recipes and each believed hers to be the best. However it was prepared, pemmican was still considered the last resource during the lean days when it was either too cold for the men to hunt or game was scarce. As well as pemmican, vegetables, fruits, nuts, and herbs that had been gathered by the women throughout the growing seasons were stored, all of these packed up in separate cases along with bundles of slabs of dried meat. I am told that ours was an ingenious way to live. Possibly. What I do know is that when our winter camps went unmolested, there was always enough food to see our families through the cold season we called When the Dogs Go Hungry. We called it that because during hard winters, there was no food to spare. Camp dogs had to survive on their own, any way they could.

All around us, campfires burned brightly, vainly trying to cheer the gloom of the iron-gray overcast day. Black kettles suspended from tripods over the fires bubbled with stews and soups that would be ready for the evening meal. The aromas of cooking food and burning wood were both tart and delicious. If I hadn't just recently eaten, the scents would have made me ravenous.

I exhaled deeply, blowing a steamy cloud of breath from my mouth, and my gaze traveled past the busy women to the men sitting in separate groups on buffalo blankets. Each group represented a different warrior society, but the men of these societies had not gathered to tell stories of past victories or amuse themselves with gambling games. For the most part, they were gravely silent as they worked on weaponry, producing impressive stockpiles of lead bullets or tying down arrowheads to shafts. One man we passed barely noticed us as he bent a bow frame, diligently smoothing the green wood with a polishing stone, working to make certain that, when the bow was finished, its pull would be just right, flexible enough to launch an arrow capable of bringing down a man or a horse without the bow cracking in half. I was distinctly reminded by the concentrated industry that this was a wintering war camp and these men were preparing for war. An icy chill went through me that had nothing to do with the unseasonable cold.

Skywalker stopped abruptly, and I stopped along with him. He tilted his head back and appeared to be listening. As his friend, I had become used to this. Skywalker always heard voices I couldn't hear, heard them so clearly that had I yelled directly in his ear, he would not have reacted. His unblinking eyes half-open, Skywalker listened to the voices of spirits or, as he was completely capable of doing, listening to the voice that came to him from deep inside another living person's mind. When his eyes glazed over and he became statue still, I did what I had gradually become used to doing. I waited.

During the wait, I pulled my robe more tightly around me, for I was shivering and my teeth lightly clattering. I had to fight down my impatience and envy of Skywalker's warm hat. Knowing we were going to pay a call on White Bear, I'd purposely left my hat in my doctoring lodge. It was one thing for me to hate my new hat, quite another to endure White Bear's wild humor regarding it. You'd have to know White Bear to understand my diffidence.

White Bear, even in his own lifetime, was the stuff of legends. He was a huge man, but if he were even half as big as his personality, the Palo Duro Canyon would have been too small to hold him. As terrible as he was to have as an enemy, that's exactly how strong he was in his friendships. But for both enemies and friends, he had an uncontrollable sense of humor that we all dreaded. Because of his love for practical jokes, White Bear could be just as frightening with his humor as he was with his notable temper. Seeing me in my hat would have set him off in ways I did not even care to consider. Being cold all the way to my bones was an infinitely preferable alternative, but being cold made me irritable.

"What?" I shouted at Skywalker, the shivering and waiting finally getting the better of me.

Skywalker came out of his trance looking bewildered.

"What?" I shouted again. I became worried when his expression changed and became fixed with worry. Concerned, I reached out and grabbed hold of his arm. "Are you all right?"

He shook his head as if to clear it. "There is something hateful here," he rasped.

A violent shiver swept through me. Skywalker and I began to turn slowly, and then we stood defensively, back to back, as we scanned the valley and then the high walls of the canyon itself. In those moments, I felt that if we looked hard enough, whatever hateful thing had made its impression on Skywalker would be revealed. And my trust in Skywalker's supernatural abilities was so complete that I know that had we been anywhere other than the canyon, he would have been able to pinpoint the source of malevolence reaching out to him.

But we were in the canyon, and because of the previous evils that had taken place here, Skywalker's second sight was impaired. As you know nothing about the canyon, I must give you a brief accounting.

First, the Palo Duro Canyon is the biggest hole in the ground I ever saw. I'm told that, over in Navaho country, there is an even bigger hole, but as I have never seen the

Navahos' canyon, I find all the tales concerning it hard to believe. But the canyon of the Kiowa and Comanches, called the Palo Duro, is located in the north of Texas. The canyon was the traditional winter retreat for generations for both nations. The canyon floor is an amazing size and is protected all around by a maze of high walls. In the center of the wide valley, a runoff section of the Red River provides water, and even in the worst winter, the valley grasses are plentiful for our grazing herds. Tall trees we called lodgepole pines grow in abundance, supplying wood for our fires and buffering our homes from driving winds. There is only one trail along the northeast cliff face amenable for people on horses. The other trails are steep and narrow and must be used on foot and then very carefully.

The thing most surprising about the canyon is that it is perfectly hidden in the middle of flattened plains. In that endless and treeless country, a man could virtually stand on the back of his horse and see tomorrow being born. What he would not see, not until it just appeared directly in his path, was the canyon. The Palo Duro was so hard to locate that white men only ever found the canyon when Indian guides took them there. Without guides, white men just wandered around. That was why we always felt so safe there.

My gaze became fixed along the high surrounding walls and then ventured horizontally along the canyon's steep rim. I tried to take heart in the fact that guards were up there somewhere looking out for all of us. Only in the last years were camp guards necessary. Their unseen presence made me feel that I knew what hateful thing was suddenly concerning Skywalker, causing him to go pale in the face.

Ghosts.

Skywalker, a man close to spirits, was hearing the torment of uneasy spirits, both white and red, who had died violently only two winter seasons ago when Kit Ca-Son (Carson) and his army of three hundred men, led by Utes and Jicarilla Apaches, invaded the sanctuary of the canyon. The Palo Duro, until that winter campaign, had always been inviolate. We had felt so secure then that there were no camp guards. Ca-Son's winter war against us changed all of that. Thanks to Little Bluff we defeated Ca-Son, drove him out of the canyon and almost all the way back to New Mexico, but a lot of men died doing it. In the two years since that battle, a major portion of the Nation avoided the canyon, believing it a haunted, evil place.

White Bear said his living army could defeat even a dead army and, following his defeat for the office of principal chief, chose to winter in the canyon as a way of thumbing his nose at Kicking Bird, knowing full well that Kicking Bird wouldn't go back to the canyon even if dragged. But White Bear had something Kicking Bird didn't have. White Bear had Skywalker. And, in turn, Skywalker's preternatural skills. Choosing the canyon as his winter camp, White Bear was making Kicking Bird look the coward.

"Are we in danger?" I asked worriedly.

"Yes."

A tight knot formed in my throat. I wasn't afraid for myself. My concern was for Crying Wind, for our son.

Hopefully, I asked a stupid question. "Soldiers?"

"No."

The answer had been expected, but it was no less terrifying. Like Kicking Bird, I wasn't fond of the idea of ghosts. My teeth began clattering so noisily that I didn't hear Skywalker move off. When I noticed he was gone, that he was walking steadily for White Bear's lodge, I nearly tripped over my own feet in my jumping rush to catch up with him.

He brooded as he walked, would say nothing, not even

as I trotted beside him, pestering him with questions. He pulled his robe tightly around his body and kept his head down, his face averted. I really hated Skywalker during the times he went all quiet, because every time he did that, it meant something bad was coming.

Something very bad.

CHAPTER
2

A lot of noise was coming from inside the massive red-painted lodge. So much noise that it would have done us no good to slap the wall and announce ourselves. Ordinary lodges, or tepees if you will, were of a good size, supported by about a dozen lodge poles more than twenty feet in length. White Bear's private lodge (meaning exactly that—all of his wives and children lived separately from him and from one another), was thirty lodge poles, each pole set about a foot apart. To be precise, this meant that the interior of his personal lodge was about thirty feet in circumference. White Bear, a robust individual, needed every bit of that room to shelter the large groups of men always in attendance. Hearing arguing voices wafting from his lodge was never unusual, so I was unconcerned as I lifted the flap door, then stepped aside to allow Skywalker to precede me. Skywalker was still stony faced and remained unresponsive even after we entered, walking straight into a shouting match.

White Bear and his favorite nephew, The Cheyenne Robber, were going at it, standing toe-to-toe, yelling with such enthusiasm that each had gone quite dark in the face. Three of White Bear's wives surrounded them and were yelling too. But I'm afraid their voices were not equal to the volume of White Bear and The Cheyenne Robber. The women sounded more like small sparrows chirping fussily at two bellowing bulls. On the western side of the lodge, I noticed Big Tree sitting beside his younger brother, Dangerous Eagle. They were seated among several other warriors, and every man present was a member of the Onde class.

The Kiowa Nation had family clans, which were entirely different from bands. A clan was something a person was born to. Membership in a band was strictly voluntary. If a man became disenchanted with a band chief, he was completely free to join another band. The one rigid system the Kiowa Nation had that set us apart from most was our strict class system. The Onde class was the highest. Women could also be Ondes, gaining this rank either through birthright or by marriage to an Onde. This class was considered so high that out of about four hundred people, only forty might be Ondes.

The second class was Ondegup'a. This class, while still high, had a much larger number. The men of this class were considered the lieutenants of the Ondes. They were very proud of themselves, always strutting around and talking loud. Their wives could be even worse, always pushing their husbands to strive for further advancement. Personally, I found it very trying to be in the company of Ondegup'as. They always did all of the talking, and any listener was expected to hold an impressed expression.

The third class, of which I have always been a member, is the Kaan. More than half the population were Kaans, so I have always felt myself to be in good company. I was never driven to rise higher in rank, and fortunately for me, I married a woman who wasn't pushy. For me to rise in rank, I would have to be a daring warrior. Crying Wind knew how inept I was with weapons, and she wasn't anxious to be a widow for a second time.

The last class were the Dapom. Now I know you have heard all of the stories about the Noble Warrior, and while I hate to disillusion you, I feel it's only fair to remind you that Kiowa people are just that, people. And with every group of people there are the no-accounts, men and women you wouldn't particularly care to meet all on your own, especially if you happened to be unarmed. The Dapom were those kind of people. Even their children and their dogs were mean. Fortunately, we didn't have very many of them, and the threat of banishment, for the most part, kept them in line. But no one wanted to live near them, so the Dapom camped on the fringes of our villages, squabbling happily among themselves.

Since my induction into the Rattle Band, even though I was of the Kaan class, I found myself continually in the company of the Ondes. Too many Ondegup'as forgot I was their inferior and began currying my favor, hoping, no doubt, that I would put in good words about them with the Ondes. I never did. Jumping rank was a game I refused to play. My keeping company with the Ondes was by White Bear's whim, and he could withdraw this favor just as easily as he gave it.

Big Tree waved to us, and Skywalker and I sidestepped the family drama and joined the others, who made room for us as we sat down. During that season, Big Tree was in his early twenties. Despite his tender years, he was a proven war chief, a *to-yop-ke*. Deceptively pretty, Big Tree was one of the deadliest men I have ever encountered. Skywalker sat directly beside Big Tree, the latter closely examining Skywalker's faraway expression. Then Big Tree leaned across him and spoke to me over the hubbub.

"What's the matter with him?"

"I don't know. He won't talk." More interested in the present situation, I asked, "What's happening here?"

Big Tree lifted his chin toward the confrontation. "White Bear's trying to coax The Cheyenne Robber into taking a second wife."

My head snapped back in surprise. The Cheyenne Robber hadn't been married to his first wife for more than four months. His wife was the love of his life and was heavily pregnant with his child. Although it was our custom for a man to have as many wives as he could afford, taking on a new wife when a man was still enamored with the one he already had, by anyone's standards, rude. The Cheyenne Robber's wife was called White Otter, and though she was a lovely person, White Bear bore her a grudge. His favorite nephew's love for the girl had almost cost The Cheyenne Robber his life, and for as long as she lived, White Bear would never forgive her. Even so, I had a sense that his pushing The Cheyenne Robber into a second marriage had nothing to do with his ill feelings toward White Otter.

"Who is the woman White Bear wishes The Cheyenne Robber to marry?"

Big Tree leaned farther across Skywalker and spoke to me in a hurried tone. "Her name is Shade. She is the daughter of He Goes Into Battle First, of the Little Horse Society. White Bear wants a closer alliance with He Goes. Kicking Bird himself has offered for Shade. He Goes is said to be considering this. That's why White Bear especially asked He Goes to come to our winter camp. But He Goes thinks he may go back to Kicking Bird in the spring. White Bear doesn't want that to happen. If the woman, Shade, is married to an important relative of White Bear's, He Goes will no longer have a choice. He will have to stay with White Bear, and as He Goes is the leader of the Little Horses, that society will be with White Bear too."

"You're an important relative," I pointed out. "And you have no wife. Why doesn't White Bear ask you to marry the woman?"

Big Tree lifted his shoulders in a shrug and offered me his pretty girl's smile. "I presented myself, but He Goes wants The Cheyenne Robber."

"Strange," I mused.

"Yes, it is."

We both fell silent. I was only half listening to the verbal brawl as I considered the nature of our women. Despite misconceptions, we Kiowa have never demeaned the importance of our women. I find it depressing that people insist on believing that we thought of our women as slaves. We most certainly did not. In the beginning time, women were given to man as a reward for pleasing our Creator. Because they were a special gift and because they brought with them miraculous talents, such as the ability to create more humans inside their bodies, women were treasured. They are different from us, but this difference did not make them less than us. A man's having many women added to his wealth and was benefited in ways too numerous to count.

The Cheyenne Robber and I had married our wives almost at the same time, The Cheyenne Robber and White Otter marrying first, eloping actually, Crying Wind and I marrying two weeks later. In effect, we were two couples still considered to be in the honeymooning stage. I couldn't bring myself to imagine what Crying Wind would do if I came home with another woman and announced this woman to be her sister wife. Having a sister wife so soon in our marriage would have been mortifying for her. The only right time to take another wife was when the first wife herself made the request. If the request was never made, it wasn't uncommon for a man to remain monogamous. Many men (I was of their number) preferred monogamy. Monogamy is a more economical form of marriage and, to my way of thinking, saves undue stress. I strongly suspected that The Cheyenne Robber felt exactly the same way. Before he married, he'd had many sweethearts. Now that he was married, he wanted only one. White Otter.

Unfortunately, White Bear failed to see his favorite nephew's point. Monogamy was not something White Bear could understand or tolerate. He was a lusty male and a demanding husband. To be blunt, White Bear was a lot of work. Whenever White Bear took a new wife, his other wives celebrated. Their unbridled joy was a bit embarrassing for him, but they didn't care.

"Take my word for it," White Bear declared. "Your marriage with White Otter is rapidly changing. Children change everything. Women always put their children first, and on very cold nights they even put them in the bed between themselves and their husbands. And you can beg and you can whimper all you want, but she'll only hear the needs of that baby."

The Cheyenne Robber turned his face away, struggling not to laugh. When he regained himself, he countered, "My wife has a servant. If after the baby comes she says she needs more than one servant, I'll get more. I will give her anything she wants, because she is the only woman I want."

"You are such a hard head!" White Bear thundered. "Why won't you listen to good advice?"

Angry now, The Cheyenne Robber pushed his face nearer to White Bear's. "If ever the day comes for me to take another woman, both White Otter and I will do the choosing. We will decide. That is the way of our fathers, and it's a good way."

The women surrounding them heartily agreed, nodding their heads and patting The Cheyenne Robber on the back.

Knowing he was defeated, White Bear threw up his arms and bellowed, "I give up on you!"

"Good." The Cheyenne Robber rounded, spotting me. "Tay-bodal, I want you to come with me."

Still worried about him, I glanced in Skywalker's direction. As if coming out of a mental fog, he looked to the side, our eyes meeting. "I'll see you after a while," he said just above a whisper. The Cheyenne Robber was looking at us both, his impatience and rising temper evident. "Go ahead," Skywalker urged.

Just as The Cheyenne Robber opened his mouth to yell at me, I hurried to stand. Within seconds and with a parting glimpse to reassure myself that Skywalker was becoming himself again, I was following The Cheyenne Robber out.

Compared to the Comanches, we Kiowa are a tall people. I suppose it's because we Kiowa were created differently from other men. Every nation has its own genesis, this is ours. Our beginning name was Kwu'da. It means pulling up or out. Our religion, like our life structure, is complicated, but the basis is this. The Creator, Saynday, called the Kiowa out of the below world by striking a stick against a huge hollow log. With each strike, a Kiowa person emerged. We are forest people, literally born from a tree, which is why trees are sacred to us and why we were much taller and more fairly complexioned than our friends the Comanche.

The new white men say that we are tall because we are cousins with the Crow and children of the Mandan. These men who say all of this say they know this to be true be-

cause of bones. I will not listen to men who are grave
robbers. I will only believe my fathers. And my fathers say
that when Saynday brought us to life, he gave us the only
timbered place in a vast ocean of grasslands. The Black
Hills. We lived in those hills for a long time, but we had
many enemies there. Once we gained the horse, we began
to move south.

In the south, the Comanches were our enemies. Then the
Comanches began having trouble with the Mexicans and
the white men they called Tehans (Texans). Divided, the
Comanches and Kiowa were ineffective against the Tehans.
That's when the Kiowa and the Comanches became allies.

When the new white men came, Am-e-cans, we liked
them pretty well even though the peculiar thing about Am-
e-cans was their love for making treaties. In 1840, after the
Comanches suffered a brutal punishment at the hands of
the Tehans, our then new principal chief, Little Bluff, called
a great council. At this council, he used the Am-e-can trick
of making treaties. Little Bluff's Treaty of the Nations was
the confederacy of the Comanches, Kiowas, Kiowa-
Apaches, Cheyennes, and Arapahos. We stopped making
war against each other.

I said all of this in order to describe The Cheyenne Robber to you. To help you understand not only his splendid
height, but the origin of his name. His full name was He
Will Steal From The Cheyenne and Make Them Cry. This
name was given to him by his uncle, the first The Cheyenne
Robber, before that man died. This was the only way a
name could be inherited. It had to be given away by its
owner before death. Otherwise, when a man died, his name
went with him and could be said no more. The second The
Cheyenne Robber had never stolen anything from a Cheyenne because he hadn't even been born during the time
when the Kiowas and the Cheyenne warred against each

other. But his uncle had, and he had been greatly feared
and hated by the Cheyennes. And that man, vindictive to
the end, hated the peace between our nations. Giving his
name to his nephew meant that whenever a Cheyenne ad-
dressed the innocent youth, that Cheyenne would be remembering the first man, who had hated the Cheyenne
people so much. It was especially irksome for the Cheyennes that the second The Cheyenne Robber grew up to be
a formidable warrior, that his name was the subject of stories and songs.

Equally depressing for them was that he was so magnificent, standing well over six feet tall, made of solid bone
and muscle. We Kiowa, in my life's memory, had begun
wearing our hair as long as it would grow. My hair stopped
in the middle of my back. The Cheyenne Robber's hair
hung down to his legs and was so thick that, to keep it out
of his face, he wore the sides tied, the rest left to hang
behind his shoulders. He was an impressive sight and so
handsome in the face that even Cheyenne maidens were
known to faint at his feet. He was a renowned lover, able
to woo away wives from rival warrior societies and coax
maidens out of the lodges of their fathers. It was said that
all The Cheyenne Robber had to do was crook his finger
and the singled-out female would run to fling herself at him.
In the brief months I had known him, I knew that to be
true. But other women were a game to him. He only had
one love in his life, and that love was named White Otter.

All of this brought me back to the moment, to the subject
of the woman called Shade. Knowing what I knew about
him, the nagging question was out of my mouth before I
could stop it.

"The woman called Shade. Was she, perhaps, a long-
ago dalliance?"

The Cheyenne Robber stopped. His hands on his hips,

he looked down at me, his expression furious. "No!" Then his expression shifted, became worried. "At least, I don't think so." He started walking again and I jumped to keep pace. "Anyway," he said angrily, "it isn't important now. If she is someone I once knew, I don't remember her."

The Cheyenne Robber became quiet. I guessed that he was worried about his wife. Cold weather is a dangerous time for birthing mothers. Which is why The Cheyenne Robber requested my services instead of trusting his wife and child to the care of midwives.

His enormous gray-blue tepee came into view. In the olden days, the paints we used to decorate our lodges came from the earth. After a long association with Am-e-cans, paints came to us by trade or as a gift. The paints were in powder form and in a wide variety of colors. We learned that if the powder was mixed only with water, the paints didn't set. The colors flaked off. However, if melted tallow was added to the paint mixture, then the rich colors stained the prepared hides. Another coating of the normal hide treatment made the paint waterproof. It wasn't long before Am-e-can powder paints became extremely popular.

White Bear loved the color red. Even though red was considered the Comanche Nation color, he liked it, so the outer walls of his lodge were stained the color of a fiery sunset. The traditional color of the Kiowa Nation was blue. Why, I don't know, it just was. The color blue dominated nearly every aspect of our lives, stained into our clothing, woven into blankets, baskets, decorating weapons and especially cradleboards, as blue was regarded as good luck. Once steady trading began with Am-e-cans and women were given great supplies of tiny glass beads, white and blue beads decorated our clothing but most especially our shoes, and in particular the ankle flap, which was a trailing piece of rawhide so long that it dragged behind our shoes.

Having that bit of extra was peculiar to our nation and made for difficult walking, but that was all right. A Kiowa male would never walk when he could ride, and the flowing ankle flap, especially when it was decorated with grand designs and surrounded by the long fringing from leggings, made for an impressive presentation—most especially when the Kiowa male was on horseback, his feet in the stirrups. At those times, the longer and the grander the ankle flap, the better.

Soon after The Cheyenne Robber and White Otter married, he had their new lodge built. From one of the soldiers at the new fort situated near the Wichita Mountains (Fort Sill), a young man known to us as Haw-wee-sun (Harrison), The Cheyenne Robber was given enough powder to mix up a large amount of gray-blue paint. Haw-wee-sun was a foolish young man deeply in love with The Cheyenne Robber's younger sister. Wanting to make a good impression on her family, Haw-wee-sun always gave her family costly gifts. The Cheyenne Robber took the paint, but he still didn't like or approve of Haw-wee-sun. My wife wasn't too happy with Haw-wee-sun either. We had just married and our new home was being built at the same exact time The Cheyenne Robber was building his. When Haw-wee-sun came to call at the place of our last encampment, he made a great show of giving The Cheyenne Robber the paint.

I knew of course that Haw-wee-sun had no idea why he was giving paint powder. He was just doing it because Billy, his interpreter and my friend, a half-caste Kiowa who had been raised white, told Haw-wee-sun to give the paint. What made me upset with both Hawwy and Billy was that they hadn't given me or my wife any paint. Crying Wind tried to make me promise to speak to Haw-wee-sun about paint, yellow paint, her favorite color, the next time he and

I met. I couldn't make the promise. For all I knew, the next time I saw Hawwy, he and I might be shooting at each other. What, I asked her, was I supposed to do? Stop in the middle of a big fight and ask the man if he happened to have any yellow paint powder with him? Crying Wind just gave me a withering look and I had to walk out. Sometimes my wife angered the breath out of me, and in order to catch my breath again, I had to retreat from her presence. But as The Cheyenne Robber and I neared his nicely painted blue lodge, I felt more than a twinge of anger against Hawwy.

What Hawwy had done without realizing it was he had shown favoritism. He had favored The Cheyenne Robber's wife over mine. Now, mind you, I was the man he went around saying was his true and great friend, but his words meant nothing after he gave White Otter expensive paint powder and my wife a hand mirror. I knew Hawwy was ignorant, but ignorance did not excuse his having embarrassed our friendship. The only thing that had kept me from taking that mirror and throwing it back in his face was that he had, not long before, saved my life. But like my house-proud Crying Wind, I too was becoming more and more sullen about the paint. I determined in my heart, right then and there, that before any big war began with the Am-e-cans, I was going to make Hawwy give me all of the yellow paint powder that there might be in that new fort's house Hawwy always called Supply.

His hand on the heavy door flap, The Cheyenne Robber turned and whispered to me, "Don't say anything about my argument with my uncle."

"Do I look a fool?"

The Cheyenne Robber's stare was lengthy. "Well, now that you've asked, yes, you do. Your face looks a bit green and sour. What ails you, Tay-bodal?"

I looked again at the accursed blue lodge walls and remembered my very plain-looking lodge. Another wave of jealousy rolled through me.

"Nothing," I snapped. "Nothing at all."

I knew The Cheyenne Robber had a servant, but until the moment I entered his lodge, I had never seen his servant. As I said, The Cheyenne Robber and I were of different classes, he of the highest, I in the middle. He liked to keep it that way. I had never been invited for a visit, and this was my very first entrance into The Cheyenne Robber's lavish home. I had seen White Otter twice during her pregnancy, but The Cheyenne Robber had brought her to me, to my doctoring lodge, thus keeping both occasions strictly professional. The only means I have of comparison is to say that both The Cheyenne Robber and Skywalker were princes. Skywalker and I could be close friends because he did not stand on pomp, whereas The Cheyenne Robber thrived on it.

On my first step inside The Cheyenne Robber's home, his servant grabbed my complete attention. A very healthy young Navaho manservant. Normally, servants were captive females, although it wasn't unheard of for captive males to be servants. However, for a captive male to be a servant to women, he first underwent the harsh treatment of castration. As cruel as this sounds, it guaranteed that our women would remain safe and the servant would not keep looking to escape. Taking away a captive warrior's male pride meant he was no longer a threat.

But the young Navaho busily preparing the evening meal while his lady amused herself sewing baby clothing did not have the look of a eunuch. Even though the young man was fully clothed, I could see that he did not have the typical softness of a sexless male. I hadn't realized my lower jaw was hanging until The Cheyenne Robber placed a finger under my chin, closing my mouth for me.

"I call him A Good Friend To Have," The Cheyenne Robber said mildly. "I bought him two seasons ago from High Backed Wolf. We were still in enemy country then, and the Tehans surprised our camp. I couldn't get to my horse and this one"—with a lift of his chin he indicated the Navaho—"grabbed me up onto his, saving my life. In return, I saved his manhood. Which is a good thing. No-sex males won't fight. Because this one is still whole, he will help me protect my family."

While I digested this, questions nagged. If this servant was such a good friend to have, where had he been during the time of The Cheyenne Robber's troubled days? Why was this my first sight of him?

The Navaho looked up and offered me a somewhat friendly smile. Then he looked away, speaking to The Cheyenne Robber. "Mistress don't eat," he said in broken language. "When I try like you say, she say me go way."

The Cheyenne Robber frowned at his wife while he spoke to me. "She's doing that all the time now. I'm worried she is starving the child."

White Otter, putting away her sewing, made a move to stand, and the Navaho was immediately there to help her to her feet. "Thank you, Good Friend," she said softly. "Now please serve our guest."

"He's not a guest!" The Cheyenne Robber said, staying the Navaho. "He's only the doctor."

Firmly put in my place, like the servant Navaho, I went about my duties. The Cheyenne Robber sat down, making himself comfortable. White Otter stood before me and I placed my hands on her stomach, feeling, through the heavy garment of her dress, the weight and placement of the unborn child.

"Why aren't you eating?" I asked in a low tone.

White Otter ran a hand from her throat to her breasts.

"Aways after eating there is a burning here. Sometimes the burning is so terrible I can't sleep."

Even under her clothing I could feel the child squirm. It was lively and felt to be a good weight. Still, it needed nourishment. "I will prepare a mixture of herbs to be brewed in a tea. That should take away the burning, but for a while, you should only drink meat broth." Next I examined her legs and ankles. They were swollen. "Very plain broth," I amended. "No spices of any kind. Especially salt."

When I stood, I saw White Otter pulling a face.

I smiled broadly.

"Thank you for coming, Tay-bodal," The Cheyenne Robber said.

Hearing the curt dismissal, my smile began to fade.

As I stepped out, two riders approached at a gallop. The Cheyenne Robber came out of his lodge and stood before the mounted men. I would have stayed if the Navaho hadn't encouraged me with a push. His hand firmly against my spine meant that his master's business was none of mine. Still, I managed to hear some of what was said.

"White Bear says you are to come right now. He says you are to go with him to He Goes's camp."

I chanced a glance backward. The Navaho appeared nervous. He took this out on me, roughly pushing me forward. When I neared the stand of pines, I heard the Navaho turn and run back to where The Cheyenne Robber argued with the messengers sent by White Bear. Taking refuge in the trees, I watched unseen as the riders turned their horses and rode out of the private homesite. As they went far around the small stand of trees, they didn't notice me. I returned my attention to the Navaho and The Cheyenne Robber. The Navaho did all of the talking while The Cheyenne Robber listened. Then, the two of them walked toward the smaller lodge off to the left and disappeared inside.

Moments later, a highly incensed Cheyenne Robber came out dogged by the anxious Navaho. Together they retrieved The Cheyenne Robber's favorite horse, which was picketed out in the small field behind his group of lodges. Once it was saddled, The Cheyenne Robber rode hard for the central camp, leaving his dejected servant to stare after him. I didn't move until the Navaho turned and went inside the large blue lodge to attend his mistress. The Cheyenne Robber's campsite became quiet. With a shake of my confused head, I turned away and made for home.

CHAPTER

3

Once I made it home, Crying Wind served me a hot meal and I enjoyed it just as much as I enjoyed being safe and warm inside our home. In some homes, the floor was bare dirt. Not ours. Crying Wind hated dirt. Our floor was completely covered with smoothed hides. Around the lodge, between the ground and the bottom of the lodge walls, rolled hides acted as draft excluders, and the inside lining of the walls was packed with insulating, sweet-smelling sage. Thanks to her, our home was snug and perfect.

While I ate, she set my boots close to the fire and then hung up my robe. She didn't ask what had happened to my hat, and I didn't volunteer the information. I concentrated on the delicious stew.

"I have so much to tell you," she said. Then she started in on the latest gossip she'd heard.

In many ways Crying Wind reminded me of my long-dead mother. My mother had been a talker. My father was such a self-contained person that had it not been for my chatty mother, there might never have been any conversation in our home. As I grew older, I began to notice that whenever my mother talked, a vacancy came into his eyes. We are nothing more than a blending of our fathers before us, and that night I proved to myself just how like my father I was. My mind wandered off while I ate and Crying Wind talked. Almost with a start, I realized she had stopped speaking. I looked up to see her staring at me, her expression expectant. Within seconds she caught on that I hadn't been listening. Immediately I began to apologize, but she turned her disappointed face away. And then our son bustled in, his arrival giving Crying Wind the excuse to turn completely away from me.

In his winter clothing, Favorite Son looked like a tiny bear, and I noticed his hat was missing its antlers, that the holes where they had been were patched over. Still feeling guilty about the way I had treated my wife, and knowing that her feelings were hurt, I was so deep in the throes of remorse that again I didn't hear her. Her temper snapped and she yelled at me.

"What?" I cried. When I looked, she and Favorite Son were all set to go, Crying Wind bundled in her coat and holding drying cloths and a packed parfleche. Favorite Son was wrapped up in a big robe.

"I said it's time to bathe," she said crossly.

I hurriedly undressed and started for the door.

"Tay-bodal," she said, thoroughly annoyed. "Don't you think you should cover yourself with a robe?"

Holding his mother's hand, Favorite Son rolled his eyes and giggled. Crying Wind gave the boy a corrective tug. "Your father," she said, "is a great man. Sometimes his greatness muddles his mind. Now is just one of those times."

Families always bathed together. Not only do we believe regular bathing is a healthy thing to do, but a man and his wife bathing together was a sign of a good marriage. Many

families were all moving to the riverbank at the same time
I tagged after my little family. Crying Wind veered away
from the others, choosing a more private spot just for us.
While she unpacked the soap container and washing cloths,
I gathered wood for the fire. I was striking flint against
kindling while Crying Wind carried our son on her hip into
the water. I had to look away. Even in the growing darkness
I could see splinters of ice floating on the water's surface.
I have always deplored winter bathing. Woefully, it just so
happens that winter bathing is about the healthiest thing a
person can do. But, dreading those first bone-jarring steps
into the indescribably cold water, I took my time making
the fire and tried, to the best of my ability, to ignore Favorite Son's screams.

Finally, the fire was just right, high enough to still be
burning warmly when our bathing time was finished. Unable to stave off the inevitable, I disrobed. The instant that
cold water lapped my feet, my teeth began clattering. Hugging myself, I entered the water. Crying Wind was almost
waist deep, and Favorite Son was crying more loudly. Being a little boy, he never seemed to remember the previous
terrors of bathing in the cold evening air or the particular
torture cold water had for males. He only remembered the
better part of the evening, being dried off by the fire and
then given a tasty treat. It wasn't until he was taken into
the water again that he remembered the weakness all males
share.

Themselves strangers to this form of weakness, women
didn't understand it, and so Crying Wind was less than
patient with our nearly hysterical boy. Crouched as far as
he could climb on his mother's chest, Favorite Son looked
back to me, tears streaking his little face. I wanted to save
him, but there was no way I could go any farther than my

knees because even then I was feeling everything I owned drawing up into myself.

"My darling," I yelled to her. "I believe you and I should have a long, long talk."

Her tone, over the wails of our son, was exceptionally irritated. "Talk about what?"

With a turn of my head I saw other families stretching along the small river. Women and children were, like Crying Wind, deep in the water. Cowardly men ventured, like myself, no farther than the knees.

"Not now," I yelped. "Just remind me before we go to sleep that I have something important to explain to you."

My wife made good soap. It wasn't made into hard little cakes like white people's soap. Her soap was liquid and wonderfully fragrant. She kept it in a special stoppered container. Other than beginning with the yucca plant, I don't know how she made the soap because soap making was another specialty women guarded. To my mind, Crying Wind's soap was the best. Hers smelled like new grass. I loved it. Unfortunately, so did my horse. Whenever I went near my horse after bathing, it always tried to graze from me. But, as I wasn't going to be riding anywhere that night, I used as much of the soap as I pleased, giving myself a good scrub and washing my hair, the suds in my ears lessening the awful sound of Favorite Son's bawling.

As we were toweling off by the fire, Crying Wind produced another of her specialties: mesquite-bean cakes. She collected the beans and dried them, then pounded them into a meal, allowing the meal to ferment. When the meal was just right, she made little cakes, which were so flavorful that both Favorite Son and I begged for them all the time. But because the cakes were so time-consuming to make, they were only given as rewards. So, all nice and clean and bundled against the frosty air, we made a game of placing the cakes on sticks and toasting them over the fire.

My little family finished our treats and then trundled home. As Favorite Son was still cold, we allowed him into our bed. Like three peas in a warm, cozy pod, we were quickly asleep.

The next thing I knew, I was hearing the voice of my old friend Hears The Wolf, father of White Otter and father-in-law to The Cheyenne Robber. Hears The Wolf was shouting for me to wake up. Our home was insulated against the cold, but the sage packing inside the walls was not enough to keep out the sound of a loud voice. Hearing the shouts, Crying Wind, Favorite Son, and I popped up in the bed at the same time.

"Tay-bodal!" Hears The Wolf shouted again. "Wake up! Now!"

"Come in, friend," I shouted in reply. Before I could blink twice, Hears The Wolf was inside my lodge.

Hears The Wolf was at one time a man known for eccentric and highly comedic dress. What saved him from ridicule was his unquestioned valor and generous nature. However, lately, Hears The Wolf found no purpose in continuing to wear clownish garb. In the last months he had changed, reverting to a more conservative style, which he wore well. His new dress sense added a regal dignity to his smooth looks and robust good health. In all, he was a splendid individual with an even more splendid spirit. I thought a lot of him, and seeing him in an agitated state alarmed me considerably.

"Whatever is the matter?" I cried.

"Skywalker! He's disappeared. He's vanished without a trace. We need more men for the search party."

Because she was naked under the blankets, Crying Wind couldn't help me dress. I had to hobble around, dressing myself, and all the while Hears The Wolf followed after me yelling the entire story.

"The Bear was worried about him on account of Sky-walker's being in one of his dark moods. When he left The Bear's lodge, The Bear sent Big Tree and Dangerous Eagle to follow him. First they thought that everything was fairly normal because he went home and stayed in his lodge so long that Big Tree and Dangerous Eagle were becoming bored. Their interest picked up as one of Skywalker's wives entered his lodge and they heard sounds of arguing. Then Skywalker came out carrying a heavy-looking bag, and his wife was still yelling at him. He ignored her, walking away."

"He walked?" I hadn't meant to interupt him, but I believed I knew Skywalker better than most. If his intention was to travel a great distance, he would not have walked.

"Yes, he did," Hears The Wolf answered. "And his walking greatly upset Big Tree and Dangerous Eagle because his walking meant they would have to walk too. But they didn't believe he would be walking very far, so they carried on following him as White Bear had ordered them to do. Imagine their distress at having to follow him for miles and with darkness setting in. They walked for hours, always believing that they heard him just ahead because by then they couldn't see him at all. In the end they couldn't keep up with him, not without a rest. That was how they lost him. They couldn't find one sign of him. They searched as long as they could on their own and then came for help."

I gave him an encouraging nod to continue as I sat down to pull on my knee boots.

"The Bear questioned Skywalker's wife, the youngest one. She was still angry, and what she had to say to White Bear was not comforting. She confirmed that Skywalker packed up a bag but all he put in that bag were containers of his special powders and large amounts of cedar chips."

I stopped suddenly, the second tight-fitting fur-lined boot only half on as I looked up at Hears The Wolf. "Cedar chips?"

"That's right. No food, no extra clothing, just his power medicines and cedar."

"He means to fast," I said more to myself than to Hears The Wolf.

"Yes, that's what his wife said. And this is a bad time of the year to starve the body. His wife tried to talk sense to him, but Skywalker wouldn't listen. He told her too many were depending on him, that he had no time to talk to her. While she spoke to White Bear she became very distraught, begging him to find Skywalker before the cold weather and his fasting combined to kill him."

I could understand White Bear's anxiety. The only reason so many bands had followed him to the canyon was because he had convinced each leader of Skywalker's powerful medicine.

My desire to find Skywalker was for an altogether different reason. He was my best friend. The best I'd ever had. I knew The Bear loved Skywalker like a brother, but in times of great stress when his temper got the better of him, The Bear tended to forget tricky things such as love and concern.

All I could think of, as I hurriedly followed Hears The Wolf out of my lodge, was that Skywalker had fallen again, that he was lying unconscious in some dark cove and near death. The bad fall from a horse only months before had left him with crippling headaches, the loss of his sense of smell, and something else: a weakness in the skull just along the front left side.

During my first years of doctor study, I would buy the brains of game animals. In dissecting the brains of animals

that had died instantly and comparing them to those animals
that had been clubbed, I found that severe blows to the head
bruised the brains and caused blood eruptions, which could
clearly be seen in the gray tissue. This suggested to me that
a crack in the protective bone mass surrounding the brain
induced the tiny blood eruptions, which while they seemed
so small, were enough to cause death. Even after so long
a time after his bad fall, there remained an unnatural con-
cavity in Skywalker's skull. In that area, no bigger around
than my thumb and forefinger really, a steady pressure
would build, eventually becoming one of his terrible headaches. Now I was worried even more. Worried that, in the
darkness, he had slipped and hit his head again. If he had,
Skywalker could be dead.

Hears The Wolf led me away from the cluster of separated
villages. From a distance, I could see a great number of
small, moving fires. These I knew to be the torches of
searching men. When we reached one group of men,
torches were given to us, and after that Hears The Wolf
and I became separated.

It was the coldest night we had known so far that season.
So cold that, ordinarily, men would have to be pried away
from their fires. But, because Skywalker was so valued,
every available man suffered the cold and the winds that
came up now and again. I didn't see White Bear, but I
heard him somewhere up ahead in the murky distance. He
sounded the way a wounded bull sounds when it calls after
a herd that is moving off, abandoning it to a lonely death.
Owl Doctors, men of Skywalker's society, were also
searching, and all too frequently I heard their rattles, which
were made from buffalo hooves. I wanted them to quit that.
The rattling was a grim reminder that the night was fraught
with evil. Which was why, of course, the Owl Doctors

shook the rattles. They were driving the evil away. In theory. The occasional rattle of the medicine hooves gave no one comfort. I felt the nervous tension running silently through the lines of men. Evil seemed to be all around us, its touch colder than the night itself.

The full moon was all the way up and white-blue. The night was so clear that every hole in the moon seemed unnaturally close. The searchers, all of them wearing robes against the bitter cold, looked like shuffling hulks. The flames of so many torches gave the patchy-snow-covered earth a strange glow and backlit hoarfrost forming on barren tree limbs. Until my friendship with Skywalker, I had considered myself only mildly superstitious. After we became good friends, mild superstition took a severe turn. Intentionally, I never thanked him for this.

According to our belief, darkness is the home for ghosts. And this night was a perfect ghost night. I kept my eyes sharp and my ears perked, trying to ignore the nervous whisperings coming from the other men belonging to my search line. The men were not happy, and I tried not to listen to the muttered worry about bad spirits. I kept my eyes on the ground as we walked in a steady line, glad of the presence of the men beside me and the muted sound of their voices.

Then a new voice reached me.

"Why are you walking back here all alone?"

The instant I looked up, my mind went blank. And I sincerely mean that. In the time it takes to blink, I realized that somehow I had fallen behind the last search line. This flash of knowledge combined with a huge jolt of fear. The revelation that the men I had walked with could not have been as human as they felt sent me into a daze. Small slaps to my face brought me out of the trance. My brain began to labor, seeking a logical explanation. I knew I'd heard

the voices, felt myself to be in human company. Except, I
hadn't been. I had been alone, and now, with the exception
of the person hitting me on the face and talking to me, I
was still alone.

"This is bad," the croaky voice said.

Bringing my torch in closer, I realized that person was
Owl Man, the leader of the Owl Doctors. When I was a
boy, Owl Man had been tall, at least five inches over six
feet. Now he was very old, his face heavily lined, his body
shrunken and bowed, his hair the color of gleaming white
snow. I knew him to be a good man, possessing great wisdom and power, but in that moment, I didn't appreciate
him much.

A breeze began to play with the flames of my torch, and
the flickering light did unflattering things to Owl Man's old
face. The deep wrinkles looked like black worms crawling
from his eyes down to his chin. Whenever the flames
moved, those black, wormy lines moved.

"I know your heart," he said in his gravelly voice. "I
know your love for your friend. White Bear loves him too,
and that is good. Skywalker needs that pure power. I think
maybe you should tell these things to The Bear."

"Tell him what?" I asked in a raspy voice.

Owl Man lowered his head. "Just what I told you. That
we are wasting valuable time walking around looking for
something we won't find." Owl Man looked off to the
distant moving lines of torchlight. "Coming to the canyon
was not Skywalker's doing. He spoke against it, but The
Bear wouldn't listen. His faith in Skywalker has always
been too full. What he fails to remember is that Skywalker,
while he is a man of power, is what he is—a man. The
power that has been entrusted to him comes from The Man
Above. Skywalker is not, nor will he ever be, The Man
Above. White Bear conveniently forgets that Owl Doctors

are only servants. If a servant is too weak to fight alone, that's the way it is. The Bear should remember that whenever he sets impossible tasks. This canyon has been for Skywalker an impossible task. There is too much lingering evil. Only the Man Above, over long seasons of time, can wipe it out and make it a good place again. But for now, this is a place where the things that live in darkness thrive. Now, you must tell The Bear.''

I waited for Owl Man to speak again. When he didn't, I knew it was my turn. "I believe you should tell him all of these things."

"No," Owl Man said sadly. "Right now he will only listen to a practical man, for he is seeking a practical solution."

"How do you know?"

Owl Man laughed softly. "Wouldn't you say that searching for a precious lost thing is a practical thing to do? Would you listen to anyone who said to you, 'No, what you should do is wait and pray for it to come back on its own'?"

I understood his point, but still I lacked the courage to approach White Bear. Owl Man said nothing more and we began to walk. With Owl Man and me far behind, the search group gradually made its way from the rim of the canyon back toward the broad meadow through a thick stand of spruce and lodgepole pines. As the first line of the searching party stepped out of the trees, large bonfires glowing against the murky predawn sky came into view. Then I heard White Bear's roar.

"They've found him!"

The distant forward line of searchers broke and began to run with torches high over their heads. Then the men in the following lines let go their hollers as they began to follow. Soon all of the men were running across the open plain,

heading for the faraway fires. As my ancient companion
was not what one would describe as fleet of foot and I was
mindful of Owl Man's frail body working harder than it
should on such a cold night, I stayed with him as we lagged
farther and farther behind. But as I wrapped an arm around
the old man and helped him run, the joy in my heart felt
like a live thing bursting out of me. Skywalker was found,
he was safe.

"No, he isn't," Owl Man wheezed as he stumbled beside
me.

I had to stop before he fell on his face, and when I did,
making certain that he was all right, Owl Man's dour expression in the subtle torchlight killed my joy.

"Listen," he whispered harshly. "Now, tell me what
you hear."

I listened. The voices of the searchers began to die out.
After a momentary lull, a lone holler went up.

"I hear . . . rage."

"Well done." Owl Man chuckled. "Your stupidity less-
ens. Now, we must hurry."

Helping an old man dodder over frozen ground, made
slippery by ice covering dead grasses, is not an easy task.
But letting go of that old man and running ahead of him
was something I didn't even consider. This man was Skywalker's teacher. He loved him. I knew whatever physical
handicap I endured by keeping Owl Man close to me would
be appreciated by Skywalker. By the time we reached the
groups of men around the fires, the dawn had extinguished
any further need of our torches. The sky was cloudless and
the sun rising out of its sleeping place, hovering just over
the prairie, a prairie high about all of us in the deep canyon.
The new sun burned red but without heat. If anything, this
new day had begun to feel much colder than the fading
night.

The bundled-up Owl Man and I were behind everyone. We were unable to see over the taller masculine forms. Owl Man seemed content with this place. I wasn't. I wanted to know just what was going on and I wanted to be close to the fires. Especially now that I could see bits of ice in my eyelashes. I tried to steer Owl Man around, but it was like trying to maneuver an unwilling child. He refused to budge, and all of my tugging was to no avail. For whatever reason, he liked being exactly where he was. When I resorted to pleading, he quickly told me to shut up. He tapped the shoulder of one of the warriors in front of us and whispered to him.

"Who started this bonfire?"

The warrior looked back in annoyance. "The fathers of the herders. They made this fire as a signal for all of us." The warrior turned away.

Owl Man tapped him again. This time when the warrior looked back, he was struggling to control his temper. Talk was still being made somewhere up in the front, and Owl Man's pestering prevented him from hearing what was being said.

"Do you know who reached the fire first?"

"The one called Red Bird!" the warrior shouted in a whisper. Then that warrior edged himself forward into the crowd, letting Owl Man know that he would answer no more questions.

Owl Man was not offended. He stood quietly beside me as he and I listened. Listening, I learned, as we all did, about the boys seeing a woman transform into a raven. Seeing that, the herders ran off to their homes. At first light, the fathers of the boys came back to check on the abandoned herds. Many voices spoke excitedly, and I quickly discovered that when one is robbed of sight, the other senses immediately hone themselves to a fine edge. The air was so crisp that it carried every voice. I easily recognized each speaker as if that person were speaking directly to me. But the most incredible thing was that visualizing the speaker helped me hear through what was being said. I was able to read the tone much more precisely than I would have been able to read an expression.

"The herders saw a witch?" That was White Bear, his booming voice incredulous.

"Yes. They saw a woman turn into a raven and fly over the canyon. The raven ran them off."

"And then the raven killed these horses!" another cried.

When the crowd shifted, Owl Man and I shifted with it, looking, I'm afraid, like a pair of feeble old women encumbered by heavy winter robes. Only our booted feet were visible as we puttered along behind the crowd surging like a tide in the direction of a new speaker.

I heard the rage and the disbelief in The Cheyenne Robber's tone. "Ravens do not have knives to cut the throats of horses. A human being did this. Now, what I want to know is the name of that person. I want to know just who would have dared do this! To me!"

"This is vile," White Bear snarled. "Your finest horses . . . slaughtered."

"It was a sacrifice," the new speaker's voice said.

I quickly looked to Owl Man, but he wouldn't look at me. All I saw was the tip of his nose protruding through the folds of the blanket and the frozen droplet of water hanging from its tip. He was listening intently as the unknown speaker continued.

"What I am telling you is true. Shape shifters need a powerful sacrifice before they can work the Dark Way power. The killing of the two horses belonging to The Cheyenne Robber gave this evil person the power he needed to change into other creatures."

White Bear's voice again, this time his tone bothered. "But didn't the boys say they saw a woman? And didn't they see her become a raven before they ran away? Before The Cheyenne Robber's horses were killed?"

"Logical questions," Owl Man muttered.

But the unknown speaker was not thwarted by logic. "Shape shifters can be male or female. In the light of day, he or she must return to their true identity. It is in the light of day when a shape shifter is vulnerable and can be destroyed."

As a buzz went through the crowd, I heard Owl Man say, "That one always has an answer, but you'll notice not for a direct question. He talks the way a shotgun shoots, with a lot of lead pellets going everywhere all at once."

"You know him?"

Owl Man turned his head inside the robe and I saw the flat look of one eye. "Yes." He squirmed inside the robe. "I'm cold. I want to go to my fire. Come with me, Taybodal."

"B-but," I stammered, "we haven't—"

Owl Man turned and moved off. As we walked away, he told me all there was to know about the man who had done so much talking, the man known as Red Bird.

At this time in our history, the Kiowa Nation was overrun with foreigners, mostly women, who had been taken captive and had either married into the Nation or had been adopted. The largest portion of adopted women were Mexicans. The second-greatest number were Navaho. The last group were made up of Tehans, young white women married to warriors or children who had been adopted into families. We used to have Cheyenne and Arapahos, but those captives had been returned when the League of Nations was formed. There were even more captives among us who had

not been adopted or married. Those captives were servants.
Again, these captives were Mexicans, Navahos, with only
a trace of white servants. To my knowledge, there wasn't
a single Pueblo man, woman, or child living among us, and
it was widely known that only the Pueblo people practiced
the Dark Way of witches.

Owl Man looked like a large mole as he made his way
inside his lodge. Following after him, I didn't imagine I
looked much better. From Owl Man, Skywalker learned
and then taught me that body, soul, and spirit were separate
things just as skin, blood, and bone are separate things, but
that all of these things worked in unison to contain life. As
a practical doctor, I could easily accept this concept, and
in teaching me this, Skywalker opened my mind to the
workings of the unseen world, a world he existed in just as
much as he did the physical world. If true Dark Way magic
had found its way into this canyon, I wanted a talisman.
Even in his shriveled state, Owl Man seemed to me to be
a good-sized good-luck charm.

It was dark and bitterly cold in Owl Man's lodge. My
teeth were clattering badly as I stood near the entrance waiting to be asked to sit. Owl Man was too preoccupied both
with his private thoughts and building up a fire to notice
that I was standing, waiting a sociable invitation. The fire
caught and then he stood, beginning to disrobe. I was
shocked to find that he was nearly naked beneath his robe.
That old man was wearing only his boots and breechcloth.
He had endured an entire night of biting cold without a
single complaint. And there I had been, fully clothed under
my robe and decades younger, shivering and mewling like
a babe. Owl Man finally beckoned me forward, pointing to
the sitting place nearest the fire. Gratefully, I sat down and
held my palms close to the flames. Owl Man sat down on

his bed, keeping his haggard face in profile. His jawline worked, muscles bunching under loose skin.

"I've been thinking about The Cheyenne Robber's horses," he said grimly. "Two horses were killed. Two. Both with their throats cut. That's bad business."

"Yes," I agreed. "Do you know why it was done?"

"Unfortunately," he sighed, "I do not hear minds. My talent is, has always been, discernment." He looked at me and smiled slightly. "All Owl Men are different, each of us having separate gifts. Our real power comes when we combine our gifts. The most powerful of us is Skywalker. He is truly gifted. He is the only one of us with the ability to work alone."

"Do you think that's what he is doing?" I was beginning to thaw, the warming fire draining my reserve. This was the first occasion I could recall of feeling halfway comfortable in Owl Man's presence. Throughout our shared past, professional animosities prevailed. For years he'd thought of me as an upstart, stopping just shy of calling me a blasphemer. Only during the passing of this strange year had he began to reconsider his opinion. Then my recent friendship with Skywalker seemed to have decided the old man. If Skywalker thought I had worth, then possibly I wasn't a blasphemer. But I was still something of a meddlesome upstart.

"I have no idea what Skywalker is doing or where he is," Owl Man said slowly. "But I do know he is alive and that no one will find him until he is ready to be found."

My head shot up. "How do you know this?"

Owl Man chuckled softly. "I know because he is the son of my heart. If his heart no longer beat, my heart would know."

I brushed what he was saying aside and said with an impatient shout, "But is he in life-threatening trouble?"

Owl Man blinked quickly, surprised by my rudeness.
"We are all in life-threatening trouble, Tay-bodal."

He lapsed into stony silence, his gaze fixed on the fire.
Taking his silence to mean my dismissal, I rose and left his
lodge. I was only a few feet away when I was almost run
down by men on galloping horses. I jumped clear barely in
time. None of the riders paused to apologize for the near
miss. White Bear and The Cheyenne Robber, riding at the
head of the group, didn't even look back. A cluster of boys
excited by the fast pace of the mounted warriors whooped
and cheered the sight. When the warriors were gone and
the boys had settled down, I asked where the riders were
going in such a hurry.

"He Goes's camp," one answered.

I considered that briefly, wondering why White Bear
would need to visit He Goes a second time in the space of
less than a single day, then redirected my attention to the
boys. "Would any of you happen to know the names of
the boys who were the herders last night?"

The same boy who answered the first time now nodded
energetically. "One of them is my cousin. His name is
Comes From Far Away. He is the adopted son of Takes
Many. Their family lodge is over there." The boy pointed
to the far western cluster of lodges, about a half mile from
where we stood.

After I thanked them, the boys scampered off, leaving
me to trudge in the direction of the lodge of Takes Many.
I was cold to the bone, coherent thought an effort, but the
sight of the man known as Takes Many snapped me into
full awareness. He was outside of his lodge, and hearing
me ask his neighbor which lodge belonged to Takes Many,
the man himself bellowed, "Here! My lodge is here. Who
are you and why is this information important to you?"

For a full moment I couldn't speak. Takes Many seemed

a giant, much bigger even than White Bear. But his size
wasn't the thing that stunned me, it was his hair. It was
very long and untied and so abundant that he appeared to
have more than the expected allotment of three ordinary
men. There were more gray hairs than dark and as the wind
tossed his hair, swirling it behind his shoulders, it added to
the effect of a large, brooding deity.

"Well?" he shouted again. "Are you going to answer
or have you come only to stare like the others?"

At last I found my tongue. "My name is Tay-bodal. And
I—"

"I've heard of you," Takes Many said gruffly. One hand
waved me forward, and as I moved to obey, he opened the
door of his lodge, knelt down and entered. He held open
the door for me to follow and I did.

His young son was bundled up and in the arms of his
mother as she crooned to him and rocked him like an infant.
Feeling like a dwarf, I stood quietly beside Takes Many.
The older man spoke to me in a softened, sober tone.

"He's frightened half to death. So many have come to
pester him about what he saw, that he's worse now than
when he first ran home."

I felt guilty, for I had come to pester the boy myself.
Takes Many turned to me.

"It was good of you to come. White Bear trusts your
skills as a doctor. Because I trust White Bear, I will trust
you. If there is anything you can do to ease his mind, help
him rest without bad dreams, his mother and I would be
very grateful."

"May I examine him in private?"

Takes Many nodded. With a hand he beckoned his wife,
who left her son grudgingly. When I was alone with the
boy, I went to him. He was wrapped up in blankets and the
first order of business was to get a good look at him. Cap-

tive children were not a rarity. Skywalker himself had an
adopted son, a little boy with bright red hair and eyes the
color of spring grass. Therefore I was not too surprised to
find hair so light that it looked almost white and eyes as
blue as a cloudless sky. This boy had indeed come from
far away.

They say our women don't breed well. This isn't true.
In the final years of our civilization it was the sicknesses
introduced into our countries and eventually the loss of
hunting grounds creating constant hunger that struck our
women especially hard, making too many of them barren.
But as it was the understood duty of a good husband to
provide his wife children, a man did so the only way he
could. He brought them to her. Children—like the almost
twelve-year-old boy before me with blue eyes, white hair,
and golden skin—were becoming too common a sight. The
people Takes Many was angry with hadn't come to stare
at his son because of the child's coloring. No, they had
come to stare at the boy who had seen a woman turn into
a raven, the boy who had seen the witch. Because he was
shaking like a frightened little dog, I knew this boy hadn't
made up the tale to draw attention to himself or stand as
an excuse for his abandoning the herds. He had seen something frightening, and that something continued to terrify
him.

"The way to throw off bad memories is to talk about
them to someone. Someone like me. Take your time, tell
me everything you remember, always keeping it in your
mind that you are safe. No harm can come to you here."

"But witches can fly," the boy whimpered. "I know it's
true. I saw it. And that witch can fly down the smoke hole
and take bites out of my spirit while I am sleeping. The
witch will keep taking bites until my spirit is all gobbled
up."

"Who told you that?"

"I heard my auntie saying it to my mother. She said that no one is safe as long as we are in this canyon. That the witch will gobble up all of our spirits and leave our bodies dead on the ground."

I ran a weary hand over my face, then looked at the boy. His chin was quivering as he fought against the tears trying to form in his sky-blue eyes. I was beginning to feel a bit skittish about the witch myself, but I reminded myself that I am a man of reason and such a man requires solid proof of a thing before believing in it entirely.

"Tell me about this witch," I said gently. "You have nothing to fear. You have a powerful father and he will not allow any bad thing to fly down the smoke hole and harm his precious son."

The reference to his extraordinary father pleased him. The boy's spine straightened and he beamed with pride. "My father is stronger than anything. Even a witch."

I smiled and nodded, envying Takes Many all the way down to my toes. I lived in hope that Favorite Son would say something like this about me. It was a dim hope because I was not a large person like Takes Many or a famous warrior like The Cheyenne Robber. There was very little about me that a boy-child could claim in boast, other than I was . . . nice.

The boy began to talk, slowly at first, then as I listened, his speech speeded up and he used his hands, then wide sweeps of his arms as his tale became more and more fantastic. I blocked out the fantastic, hearing the truth that lay somewhere in the middle. While the boy talked, I examined him, finding bruising on his feet and raised scratches on his arms and legs. These marks were indications that the terrified boy had been oblivious to rocky ground and sharp branches during his run for home. As he finished speaking,

I bundled him up and told him that I would send his parents back to him. Outside I spoke to his mother, asking her if she had a store of the small fruits of the horse nettle and perhaps some mint and honey. She assured me that she had these things, and I explained how to make a thick, sweet tea.

"But that's for stomachache!" she cried.

"Not always." I smiled. "It's been known to make agitated little boys calm down. I learned about it from my mother. For half my life I thought the tea was a special treat. Then when I was grown, I realized it's what my mother gave me when she'd had enough of my noise."

She returned my smile, her eyes warm with amusement. "Those women who have gone away from us were very smart."

"Yes," I agreed. "And their wisdom is greatly missed."

Bone tired, I made my way home. Crying Wind looked up from her sewing as I entered. I was a bit stunned to notice what she was sewing. She had my hat, the new one I had intentionally hidden. The antlers were missing. She was covering the holes where the antler tines had once been with white doeskin patches. From these patches came long, twisted fringes. Against the dark fur of the hat the new adornments were quite pleasing to the eye. Instantly, I loved my new hat. But mostly, I loved her. Relief filled her lovely eyes as we gazed at each other.

"Sit down," she said softly. "I made hot coffee. From the look of you, you need it."

I couldn't get enough of the coffee, drinking cup after cup. I rarely overindulged with coffee because it made me too nervous and wouldn't let me sleep. But it was all right to drink coffee that morning. I didn't want to sleep and I was already nervous. Crying Wind toweled my hair dry as

I told her about the search, about the mysterious killings of The Cheyenne Robber's two best horses, and of my discussion with Owl Man. To my delight, and guilt, Crying Wind listened attentively. She did not shut me out as I had done her the previous evening.

"So," she said, giving my hair a final rub with the towel, "Owl Man believes that Skywalker has just taken himself off somewhere, to be alone?"

"I really don't think he knows what to believe. I think what he said is merely what he hopes. If he's worried about anyone, he's worried about your cousin The Bear. And this is what Owl Man had to say in regard to him." I turned to face her. "Owl Man says that White Bear has too many things pressing him. He says that now is a very bad time for him, and Skywalker's being gone, even for a little while, is enough to drive White Bear half out of his mind."

Crying Wind settled down beside me, taking the cup from my hand and taking a sip of the remaining coffee. Over the cup's rim, her eyes remained locked with mine. When she spoke, her voice echoed slightly inside the metal cup. "Tell me again about the man who spoke of witches."

Folding my arms around my knees, I rocked back as I stared at the distant wall. "I don't know him. I didn't even get a look at his face. All I know about him is what Owl Man said." When she set the cup aside, I took her hands in mine. They felt cold. Instinctively, I rubbed her hands as I spoke.

"Years ago, this man, Red Bird, petitioned to become an Owl Doctor. He brought with him three witnesses to his type of power. The Owl Doctors were very impressed with what they heard and voted to induct him into their society. This happened while Skywalker was away, off somewhere with White Bear. Skywalker came back just in time for the induction ceremony and promptly called everything to a halt, saying the man Red Bird was a fraud, that his witnesses were liars.''

Crying Wind's remarkably round eyes rounded more. ''Oh, my goodness! What happened then?''

''The man called Red Bird hotly refuted this, but as Skywalker has the gift of knowing minds, the Owl Doctors believed him. Red Bird was sent away, and guess where he went?''

''Where?''

''To old Bent's Fort over in the Colorado. I was about sixteen in the year of the first Stomach Cramp Illness (1849), when a great number of white people passed through our country leaving behind them their killing sickness. Before that, Bent's Fort was a big walled city open to all the Nations for trade. When the sickness came, the white man known as Bent blew up his trading city and left, never to be seen again. Now, ruins are all that is left of the old fort, but it is still used as a gathering place by practical doctors like me who seek to trade knowledge instead of hides and furs. Red Bird knew all about this and, wanting to build his power and knowledge, I've no doubt he would have gone there.''

I waited, but Crying Wind hadn't caught on to the full import of what I'd said. I would have to be more clear. ''Last summer, before receiving word about our great chief's death, I was at Bent's attending a great gathering of the wisest men of all the Nations. Not knowing what this man called Red Bird looks like, I can't say for certain that he was there, but from what I understand from Owl Man, the chances are that he was. It was at this last gathering that I first came to hear of the new spiritualism called the Dark Way. The way of witches. A religion that has begun among the Pueblos.''

Placing a hand to her mouth she said weakly, ''And you

believe this man Red Bird learned the Dark Way?''

"I think it's more than possible. I could have learned it if I had asked the right men. I didn't. There are some things even I have no curiosity for. The Dark Way is one of those things. But because Red Bird has presented himself to White Bear as a man who possesses this knowledge, I can only conclude that he learned about it at Bent's.''

We both thought for a moment, then I went off on a different tack.

"I spoke to one of the herders, and that boy said that he and his companions saw a woman. He said that they all saw her shape quietly clearly against a bright full moon as she transformed herself into a giant raven.''

Crying Wind blanched, drew away from me. I saw fear in her eyes. I reclaimed her cold hands and rushed to assure her. "They were frightened boys and it's very dark out there. So dark that even while I was searching for Sky-walker, I became unnerved enough to think something was one thing when actually it was another. So maybe the boys saw what they claim and maybe they didn't. But whatever it was, it was enough to cause them to desert their duty. It was because they did that, that something else happened. Something horrible.''

During my slight pause for breath I noticed that Crying Wind's gaze never wavered. Her expression was fixed and intent.

"The Cheyenne Robber's herd was attacked. Two of his best horses were killed, their throats slashed.'' Crying Wind gasped and I gripped her hands more tightly. "But don't you understand?'' I cried. "That was not magic.''

"How can you be certain?'' she asked with a tremor in her voice.

Actually, I couldn't be. The memories of my experience while out searching for Skywalker were still a bit too fresh, raising the hairs on my neck whenever I allowed myself to think of them. I shoved the memories as far away from me as they would go. I had to keep my mind free of fear in order to think rationally, and I certainly didn't want my wife to be frightened any more than she was. I could feel the rapid beat of her pulse, and her unusually large round eyes were becoming glazed. These were signs that my wife was on the edge of hysterics. I had to calm her down, so I said with an insistent tone, "Think, Crying Wind. Think hard. When have you ever heard of a spirit carrying a knife?"

"B-but," she said in a small voice, "the witch?"

She was very afraid, and this discussion was the root cause of her fear. Even though I wasn't all that convinced there was nothing supernatural to be afraid of, especially now that Skywalker wasn't around to lend us the power of his protection, I said a bit too dismissively, "You're forgetting that the witch had become a raven. Ravens have talons, not knives."

My wife's pluse began to slow. I timed it as I became lost to my own thoughts. I made another mistake with her when I voiced these thoughts out loud. "This man Red Bird says he will look for the witch. That he will know her when he sees her. He says this is his power."

A very odd look came over Crying Wind's face. I didn't question her about what she was thinking then. Later on, I would wish I had. Wrapping my arms around her, I held her against me, kissing the crown of her head.

She wrapped her arms around my waist as she sniffled. "I don't like this talk about Dark Way magic. I don't care how reasonable you try to make it all sound, this man Red Bird makes me afraid. I wish he had stayed at Bent's and never come back to us."

It took me a while to calm her. When she returned to

her sewing, I stretched out on our bed, and lulled by her nearness and the comforts of home, I drifted off to sleep. This deep, dreamless sleep held me unconscious for hours but felt like only the passing of a few minutes once I was startled awake. All around our home there came the unmistakable sounds of keening. Then there was the flurrying of people racing by our lodge. The keening meant only one thing: the death of a human being. Terrified all the way to my soul that the dead person was Skywalker, I scrambled out of bed. At the doorway, I grabbed my frightened wife by her shoulders and yelled, "Where is Favorite Son?"

"With my sister."

As I opened the door, the keening sounded louder, and I could see all of the people running. Quickly closing the door, I dressed in fresh clothing as hurriedly as I could. My boots were still soaked through, but I could do nothing about that. And then I spotted my new hat. I grabbed it and slammed it onto my head. Because my robe was still soggy, I took a blanket off the bed, wrapping it around my shoulders. When I looked back, Crying Wind was still standing where I'd left her.

"Sweetheart!" I yelled. "Go to your sister's. Now!"

"I hate this terrible place!" she wailed. "And I hate White Bear for making us all come here!" Weeping uncontrollably, she ran out.

I went to retrieve my best horse. Because that horse was my favorite of my small herd, I never picketed it out in the pastureland. I kept it in a small shelter I built for it inside a clump of trees. Crying Wind liked to keep her little pinto mare in there as well. Doing this meant that both she and I had to bring our horses food and water, but as I said, it was my best horse and her horse had been a wedding gift, so neither she nor I trusted their care to the herders. As I

eased my horse out of the shelter, I noticed that my wife's
horse was sweaty. I took the blanket off my horse and
placed it on top of the blanket already on hers. I hoped her
horse wasn't becoming ill, but I didn't have time to examine it. I made a mental note to do that just as soon as I
could. Crying Wind would be upset if that little mare was
developing lung sickness.

When I arrived at the distant camp, the death lodge was
surrounded and the wailing was awful. Dismounting, I tied
my horse to a scrub and joined the crowd, trying to push
my way through. It was an unforgiving crowd, and I was
jostled so roughly that my new hat slid around on my head,
settling almost over my eyes. Beside me a man muttered
that this death was on account of the witch. Intentionally,
he kept his voice low, his expression guarded as if he
trusted only the person he spoke to. When he caught my
eye and realized I had heard, he moved away from me,
trying to loose himself in the crowd. His abandoned companion was looking at me with unabashed suspicion as
White Bear's voice began to shout my name.

My arm went up as straight as a lance. "I am here!"

Seeing my hand peeking above the heads of all of those
people, White Bear began throwing bodies left and right.
The others, out of a fine sense of self-preservation, volun-
tarily gave way and I was able to worm through. When I
was almost at the front, White Bear caught my hand and
yanked me the rest of the way.

"Is it Skywalker?" I asked while pushing my hat off my
eyes.

White Bear wrapped an arm around my shoulders. "No.
This is a personal tragedy for He Goes. And He Goes
blames me." White Bear's features tightened.

My heart went out to The Bear. Not only was he nearly

sick from worry for Skywalker, he looked ragged from exhaustion. The last thing he needed was for his judgment as a leader to be called into question. But that's the way of chiefs. Rightly or wrongly, a chief is ultimately responsible for the welfare of all who follow him. It's a terrible obligation. I've always been amazed by those who wanted this responsibility.

I had seen the man called He Goes Into Battle First many times, but from a distance. Now, I was seeing him in close quarters and at the lowest point in his life. He was a big, barrel-chested man with vulpine features that were slightly obscured by the black paint smeared over his face. Sitting with his legs crossed, he held in his arms the body of a young woman. Tenderly he brushed her hair with his curled fingers as he rocked her and wept. The lodge was filled with people, and the only two I knew were White Bear and Owl Man. By their dress, I knew five men to be Owl Doctors. The remainder of the people I safely assumed to be immediate family.

Owl Man came to me, placed his hand on my shoulder, and led me forward. With him I sat down on the backs of my legs before a heartbroken He Goes.

The girl in his arms was startlingly pretty and quite obviously of mixed parentage. I instantly assumed her to be He Goes's issue from a captive wife. I quickly realized my error as I listened attentively to the flow of conversation between the grieving He Goes and Owl Man.

"You must give her over to us now."

He Goes moved his mouth, but words would not come. Finally, he managed to speak in a trembling, tear-choked voice. "I can't bear this. I—I can't."

Owl Man placed his hand on the man's head, drawing the head toward him and kissing He Goes's temple. "My son, this woman you loved best, the woman who was your favorite wife, is gone now. There is nothing any of us can do to bring her back. Please, for the sake of her spirit, to help her find peace, you must give her over.''

He Goes's voice was a weak croak. ''S-she's only little. You must promise to hold her gently. I-I always . . . had to remember . . . to be gentle.''

I had to turn my face away. The realization that the man was grieving for his adored wife made everything worse. Thinking of my own wife, tears began to sting and I closed my eyes. Softly, I heard Owl Man speak my name. Looking up, I saw two men lifting the girl from He Goes's arms. Her body was limp, which meant, in my experience, that the death had been very recent, most likely no more than an hour ago. The two men handling the body walked carefully, carrying the dead woman near the fire, laying her down on a blanket.

His arms empty of the one he loved, He Goes became even more distraught, falling sideways, his knees drawing to his chest. The heels of his hands pushed against his eyes as he wailed his unbearable grief. Not knowing how to comfort him, or if he would even appreciate a stranger's attempt, I quickly moved away. The lodge, fairly humble in size, was overly crowded. I had to dodge around the Owl Doctors, who had begun to dance and sing while broadly waving feather fans. The breeze of the fans would lead the dead woman's spirit toward the flames of the fire, and there the spirit would mingle with the smoke. Once this was done, the Owl Doctors would then wave the smoke and the woman's spirit up to the smoke hole, directing it toward the Sky Road, where dead ancestors would take her into their keeping. While the Owl Doctors were doing this, Owl Man motioned for me to come and sit across from him, the small female form between us. Owl Man leaned over the body and spoke to me in whispers.

"I need your special knowledge to tell me how this little person was killed."

I looked back at He Goes and immediately felt Owl Man's hand on my face, steering my attention back to him.

"Don't look at him, look only at me and listen carefully. With Skywalker gone, I have only you to turn to."

"B-but what if I can't help you?" I stammered.

"You must!" Owl Man whispered bitterly. "I cannot understand the minds of those around me, but I do understand hearts. Evil feeds in the heart of someone close. I don't know who this person is. I only know this death pleases that evil heart."

For a long moment, his eyes bore through mine, then I tore mine away, examining the young dead woman as much as I was able in these circumstances. There are signs I have trained myself to look for in cases such as these. A woman this young and well nourished had no reason to be dead. But she was, and given that there was still as much warmth in her body as there was in mine, and that she was limp, she was like someone merely asleep. I knew by these signs that her death had happened less than an hour ago. No marks were on her neck to indicate she had been choked. Bringing my face close to hers, I saw tiny red points around her eyes, nose, and along the hairline. Those tiny points were quite vivid against smooth, pale skin, and the starburst patterns told me that this girl's death had been caused by lack of air. Owl Man did his best to protect me from the view of others as I turned the pretty head more toward the light of the fire. The delicate nose was perfect, that little middle line between the nostrils completely straight. No bruises were on her face, nothing to indicate that the shortage of air had been caused by a hand placed firmly over the nose and mouth. I was guiding the head back to its proper position when I noticed the lips.

This girl, wife to a man twice her age, had the look of a pampered woman. Her dress was fine and costly, her wealth of dark hair decorated with small but expensive silver disks. And, this girl had something else that ordinary wives did not have—face paints. An art practiced among the women from the south, primarily Mexican women. These paints accentuated the eyes and the mouth. Even the captive Mexican women tended to be flamboyant, outlining their eyes unnaturally and staining their mouths bright red. It was an art they jealously kept to themselves. To her credit, this girl used a greater degree of skill, merely smudging her eyelids to lend a flattering shadow and faintly staining her mouth a more natural hue. Alive she must have been stunning. Looking at her mouth more closely, I saw a faint blue color outlining the lips. I knew by this that underneath the false mouth color, her lips were actually blue. Her long neck was smooth, unblemished. Her head was not wobbly.

I looked up at Owl Man. The noise of the singers and the steady thudding of the prayer drum throbbed inside my head. As I had eliminated the obvious, I was left with only one other possible way this woman could have died. But I couldn't even be sure of that until the body was removed for further examination.

CHAPTER

4

When the Owl Doctors finished with the spirit-leaving ritual, the body was covered for removal, and He Goes fell into a second bottomless hole of grief. His cries were hideous and set off a chorus of mourning that was deafening, particularly when the women raised their voices in high-pitched tremolos. The body was lifted and carried by two beefy males. Owl Man and I followed them, making for a small but somber parade. The other Owl Doctors remained with He Goes to see to the purification of his lodge. The body was destined for a smaller lodge, one that could more easily be sacrificed to the ultimate purification, being set alight and burned down to ashes. During the exit of He Goes's lodge, I noticed a girl about the same age as the victim. The only reason I noticed this girl was because she broke from the comfort of an older woman, attaching herself to me, taking my hand as if I were a brother or an uncle. She clung on tenaciously as I ducked and passed through the door. Outside the lodge, she stayed with me, refusing to let go of my hand. In the too bright light of approaching noon, I eyed my companion. As I said, she was close in age to the dead woman, but she was slightly taller, her body too slim, the outline of her breasts no larger than twin bumps. This young woman could easily have passed for a boy. Her hair was thick, and almost white from the ashes of mourning. Matted strands blew across an oval face with delicate features.

I had no idea who she was, but I wished she would let go of me. Because she was crying, it would have been cruel of me to shake her off. So, I endured her as we followed after Owl Man, who followed after the men carrying the corpse through the wailing village. Because I needed relief from the little person holding on to my hand so tightly that she was all but glued to my side, I looked around, noting the familiar faces of those we passed. And then, as if a light in heaven suddenly shone on him, I saw the face of The Cheyenne Robber's Navaho. His despondent eyes locked with mine for an instant, then skittered away. Navahos have an extraordinary fear of the dead, most especially the newly dead, for they believe in Ghost Sickness, an ailment that can ruin the health and fortune of a living person believed to have been contaminated by a dead person's spirit. The Ghost Sickness purification rite requires days and nights of fasting and the expensive services of a Ghost Way healer. Because Ghost Sickness cleansing is such a harsh and costly ordeal, no sane Navaho would risk ghost fever. Instead, he would run as far as he could from the body of a newly dead nonfamily person. Yet here was The Cheyenne Robber's Navaho servant.

My eyes remained on the Navaho, my head turning on my neck, lining with my shoulder as the procession walked forward to the designated death lodge. I was so intent on him that on our arrival at the death lodge, I bumped into one of the men carrying the body, treading on his heel. He looked back at me with unveiled disgust. The girl who had been holding on to me finally let go. The procession entered the lodge behind Owl Man while I remained outside, standing with my back to the lodge.

Women, who had been inside the lodge preparing it as a final shelter for the dead, streamed out, carting away items they didn't want destroyed when the lodge would be burned. While their heads bobbed past me, I saw the distant Navaho turn away, walking out of the camp in the direction of White Bear's camp. I heard Owl Man inside beginning the death chant. His low, gravelly voice was joined by a clear soprano that could belong only to the girl. The two body carriers made a hasty exit, passing me without a word. I was still in deep thought about the Navaho when I heard Owl Man break from his singing and bark, "Tay-bodal! Get in here."

The body was laid out and my former companion was preparing the gourd lamps that would encircle the dead woman. The light would keep away body-stealing demons until the body was properly buried. Owl Man was ignoring the living girl, on his knees as he hurriedly removed the shroud from the dead woman.

"We haven't much time," he said crisply. "Those other women will soon return." When he looked up at me, he saw that I was nervously looking in the direction of the young woman still in our company. "Don't worry about her. She's our lookout."

I sat down, once again opposite Owl Man with the body between us. After the last lamp was lit, the young woman scooted out, planting herself in front of the opened door. There she took up a wailing cry, intentionally loud to discourage the comforting company of others. It was then that I knew the girl's inconsolable grief was false.

"Who is she?" I yelled in a whisper.

"Her?" Owl Man grunted. "Oh. She's He Goes's daughter, the woman they call Shade."

My eyes doubled in size. "The woman White Bear is insisting The Cheyenne Robber marry?"

"The very same."

"Why would she help us examine her father's second wife's body?"

"I have no idea. I asked her just now if she would keep watch for me and she said yes. But that's enough about her, fix your attention on this little person."

Although he kept his expression blank, I sensed his shock at how thoroughly I did as he asked. Being an Owl Doctor, a man of spiritual persuasion, he rarely saw his patients undressed. With my kind of doctoring, a naked patient is the best patient. Not because I am perverse, but because symptoms, spots, or rashes hide inside clothing, particularly in the armpits, under the breasts of a generously endowed female, or inside the upper thighs or between the buttocks. My task was made easy because this woman was of modest proportions and her skin was exceptionally fair. I didn't have to search for the blotches, they were right there, on her chest, like hundreds of explosions. Again a sign that the body had been starved of air. Examining the hands is also necessary as a troubled heart can cause the palm of the left hand to be more blue than the right palm. The crescent whites of the fingernails change a variety of colors, and knowing how to read these colors reveals all sorts of things going on inside a sick person. The whites of the eyes change colors too, but mostly, these colors are yellow or orange, both colors telling me about the liver. Orange is the worst color, meaning death is imminent. When I see orange eyes, I typically kiss the patient, tell him or her that I will miss them.

The mouth, in particular the gums and tongue, also provides valuable clues. Tilting the head back, I pried open the mouth. As my face was close, a sharp odor, almost masked by a familiar odor, assaulted my nostrils. Then, the under odor was gone, leaving just the masking odor, which I knew to be coffee. Whatever the second property was, it had been deliberately given, mixed up inside strong coffee. Which was clever, for coffee on its own is brackish, able to cover a second, less harsh flavor.

Poisoning is a rare occurrence among Indian peoples, but it's not unknown. This should hardly be surprising when you consider that poison follows the thrown rock in being the oldest murder weapon known to all of mankind. The poisoner's skill was learned by watching which plants and berries birds and animals avoided. With a bit of experimenting, early peoples soon learned why birds and animals avoided such plants and berries. The second type of poisons that became popular came from animals—poisonous snakes, lizards, and toads. Death by poison always occurs two ways, accidental or intentional. When intentional, poisoning has an effectiveness matched by no other weapon. For one, the sophistication of it allows the victim to be killed from a distance. Yet, if the killer is completely cruel, he or she has the option of just sitting back and watching the victim die. But the most insidious thing about poison is that unless it is suspected, the actual cause of death goes undetected.

The thing that puzzled me most was the absence of flush—the vibrant color that comes to the skin when the plant poisons I had knowledge of stopped the heart. I knew too by the absence of locked jaws that whatever this poison was, it was not animal. Venom always causes the victim's jaws to lock during the death throes.

This young woman must have died from a fast-acting plant poison that left no identifiable sign on the body. It was a poison I knew nothing about, and if I didn't know about it, then neither did the practical doctors of five other nations. Practical doctors, a title we'd given ourselves, were at that time a small community transcending national ties. We all knew each other and eagerly shared our knowledge. We did this to help all people and because it was so exciting to learn from one another. I had been with many of these doctors the previous spring, and not one of them had shared the knowledge of a fast-acting plant poison able to kill almost without a trace. Knowing these men as well as I did, I knew for a certainty that this knowledge hadn't been shared because it wasn't known.

"What is it!" Owl Man demanded.

I closed the victim's mouth and sat back. "Tell me exactly how this child died," I said.

Owl Man looked uneasy. "All I was told was that she was standing, talking with her husband, then she was on the ground. He thought she'd fainted. It was while he tried to revive her that he realized she was dead."

"Was she drinking coffee?"

Owl Man thought for a brief second. "No one said."

I tried to be patient. "When you arrived, did you see a coffee pot in He Goes's lodge?"

"No. But there could have been. I think these questions could better be answered by Shade."

Before I rose to leave, I asked him one last question. "Just who was this girl?"

His face, as deeply cracked as the floor of a sun-baked dry riverbed, twisted with anger as he threw up his hands. His tone was even more angry as he shouted, "She is the wife of He Goes!"

"No," I said, fighting for calm, "I mean, who was she really? What was her clan? Who were her parents?"

"She didn't have parents or a clan. She was a mixed-blood Tehan. Her mother was a Mexican and her father was a white man. She came to us after He Goes kidnapped her when she was a child. He brought her home, and then, when she was old enough, he married her. That's all I know. Why is that important?''

''Knowing about the dead person's life is important. Now, tell me about the girl called Shade.''

Owl Man calmed down, scratched his head. ''What little I know is that she is a good and caring person. She was always friendly to this little girl here, but in the last year the friendship became strained.''

''How so?''

''Because this one replaced Shade's mother as first wife. And, because as you might imagine, there was a fair amount of scandal when He Goes married a girl-woman who had been treated almost like a daughter. His marriage to this child, in some minds, was considered incestuous. Only the fact that he hadn't formally adopted her prevented this being said to his face. But people talked behind his back.''

Owl Man quietly studied me the whole while I thought about the girl-woman outside.

''It would seem,'' I said in a low tone, ''that the woman Shade had many reasons to despise this dead woman.''

''Maybe.''

Now, I threw up my hands.

With patience in his voice he said, ''I've heard her heart. I've detected no real malice there. What I did detect was that she is a woman deeply in love.''

''But The Cheyenne Robber doesn't even know her!''

Owl Man lifted his shoulders in an indifferent shrug. ''Why do you believe that matters?''

Enigmatic Owl Doctors have always infuriated me blind. In a deep sulk I didn't say anything more as he added cedar chips to the small fire and used both of his hands to purify me with the smoke. Then he covered up the dead woman and lost himself in his prayers for her spirit. I stood and left. The dead woman's soul was his business now, and I was happy to leave it with him. Once outside, I knelt down and concentrated on the living woman, speaking to the little person known as Shade.

Her small, delicately lovely face was completely open, without guile. I always rejoice when I meet a person like this, for lying is beyond them. Now, you must realize that, in our culture, asking questions was considered rude. If a person wants you to know anything personal, that person will volunteer the information without prompting. Ordinarily, I was a singularly polite man, but these were extraordinary times, plus I was physically exhausted and in emotional upheaval. All of this left me without tact. I am afraid I wasn't as considerate of the young woman's pride or feelings as I should have been.

"Girl, do you know me?"

"Yes," she replied evenly. "You are a friend to the man who will be my husband."

I looked away as I squatted before her, my arms resting on my thighs, and my hands, fingers entwined, hanging in the middle. Mildly, I shook my head, wondering if I should tell her the truth, that her marriage was at present being hotly contested by The Cheyenne Robber. It was not my place to say such a hurtful thing and I had no wish to wound her. She seemed nice. Too nice to allow her further embarrassment. When I next opened my mouth, I heard myself recommending Big Tree. All of which was untoward because Big Tree had not once asked me to be his representative. But there I was, pressing his suit anyway.

"I have a good friend, a man of high office and many

honors, that you should consider ahead of The Cheyenne Robber.''

She looked at me with that open expression of hers, her head tilted as she listened with interest. Bolstered by this, I continued on hurriedly.

"His name is Big Tree. Possibly you've heard of him. He is a young man without a wife. He would appreciate you in ways The Cheyenne Robber wouldn't. And he is a young man pretty in the face. I believe him to be a man of gentle nature where women are concerned. And, he loves to laugh. He would be a fun husband to have.''

Her mouth twisted to the side. "How kind of you to speak for him," she said softly. "But I must marry The Cheyenne Robber.''

"Why?'' I barked.

"Because my parents have decided this. My mother started the talk first, and then after a while, my father came to agree with her. He has always been a great admirer of The Cheyenne Robber.''

"But what about you? What are your feelings?''

Her shoulders lifted as she looked at the hands lying still in her lap. Her ashy, matted hair partially concealed her face as she continued to speak in a soft, near toneless voice.

"I have seen him. He is a beautiful man. And I understand he is kind to his wife and that she is a good person. I have no objection to becoming part of their household.''

Impatience welled inside me. My voice took on a hard edge. "But what if both The Cheyenne Robber and his wife object to you?''

Again the subtle lifting of her shoulders. I was getting nowhere on this subject and reminded myself that none of this was really my business. If this girl was content to allow her mother and father to make a fool of her, there was really nothing I could do. I switched subjects.

"Did you perhaps notice if your dead second mother was drinking coffee before she fell dead?"

"Yes. She was drinking coffee."

Excitement began to grow like a worm inside me. And then Shade stepped on the worm.

"We were all drinking coffee. White Bear and The Cheyenne Robber had come to visit my father. And they brought friends. My mother and my auntie and I served everyone food and coffee. There couldn't have been anything wrong with the coffee. No one complained about it, and no one else died."

"What was done with the leftover food and coffee?"

"Oh, to make room for the many people rushing in to console my father, my mother and I took everything out and threw it away."

I went blank for a moment, finally saying, "I'm very sorry for your family's loss."

A tear began to streak her face. Her chin bobbed as she muttered, "Thank you."

This young woman's grief was real. But how could that be when it was common knowledge that the mixed breed had been placed above her own mother? I could not resist the question.

She sniffed back another tear and the hands in her lap became slightly active, thumbnails clicking one off the other.

"I know what was said, that I was her servant. I wasn't. If anyone was the servant, it was my aunt, my father's widowed sister. It was my mother who allowed the talk against my father to continue. She can be like that, vindictive. She isn't really a mean person, but she has great pride and she carries grudges. I suppose she had good cause for the grudge against my father. She felt betrayed and humiliated."

I placed a hand on the young woman's shoulder. Whether she wanted to admit it or not, her life of late had indeed been especially cruel. And now I saw behind her mother's notion of marrying Shade off to The Cheyenne Robber. If her daughter was married to a man of The Cheyenne Robber's celebrity, then Shade, a girl everyone pitied, would instantly be catapulted to the position of envy. And if White Bear's influence could be used to secure the match, it hardly mattered that The Cheyenne Robber was less than enthusiastic. His reticence would be forgotten on the wedding day when a mother's pride in her only child was restored.

The benefits to He Goes went without saying. Any verbal alliance between the two bands could easily be set aside by one chief or the other. But an alliance made with the seal of marriage, making relatives of the two chiefs in question, would not so readily be forgotten. He Goes, a man prone to the war road, would naturally want to be related to White Bear. But using the threat of his going over to Kicking Bird was enough for White Bear to push for the marriage between He Goes's daughter and his nephew, The Cheyenne Robber. In all of this motherly and political maneuvering, the tender feelings of the one person crucial to everyone's plan were callously set aside.

I considered what Owl Man had said. That he'd heard her heart, that she was a young woman in love. Hoping for the best, I questioned her again.

"I believe we both know there is someone else you would marry if given the opportunity."

Her head shot up and fear-riddled eyes searched mine. She uttered a cry that became muffled under the palm of her hand as she scrambled to her feet and ran off.

•   •   •

My home camp was busy. A steady wind was changing the
outlook of the day, lowering the already cold temperature,
gathering in dark gray clouds. The wind pulled at my hair,
tossed the decorative fringes on my hat as I rode at a walk.
Homes were guarded by armed men, women and children
peering out of the door holes watching me both fearfully
and intently as I passed by. When I came near the home of
a man I knew quite well, I nodded a greeting. His response
was alarming. Instead of acknowledging the nod with one
of his own, he stood and stationed himself between me and
the doorway of his home. Hugging the rifle to his chest, he
bared his teeth at me and issued a warning growl. With a
cold lump growing in the pit of my stomach, I averted my
eyes and kneeing my horse to a trot, moved hurriedly on.
Only yesterday that very same man had waved and smiled
at me. Now he was treating me like an enemy. I tried not
to take it personally. When people are afraid, they trust only
the members of their own blood family and even those with
a watchful eye. I kept that in my mind as I dismounted
behind White Bear's cluster of family lodges. Before
rounding the lodge used by his eldest bachelor sons, I heard
the sound of his fulsome voice that could be clearly heard
over the winds washing through evergreen pines and barren
branches of cottonwoods and elders. Fogging clouds
steamed from the mouths of men and horses as White Bear
gave directions for a new search party. Desperate now to
find Skywalker, White Bear was sending out mounted
teams of searchers. The freezing ground under my feet was
crunchy; I made a lot of noise as I walked in White Bear's
direction. I stood behind him as he bellowed his last instructions to the mounted men. Still shouting, he turned his
head.

''There you are! I was beginning to think you were lost
too.'' His eyes narrowed, a single eyebrow lifted, and his

voice dropped. "That's a good hat. Where did you get it?"

"Crying Wind made it for me."

His large hand went for the long, pale, and twisted fringes falling from a patch. "This is a chief's hat. I'll give you mine and you give me this one."

The hat on his head was a good hat, made of beaver fur. It also sat low on his large head, which meant it would be far too big for mine. Placing a hand on top of my hat to prevent its being snatched away, I said, "And just what will I tell my wife?"

He chuckled deeply in his fulsome chest. "You tell her a powerful man now wears the hat she made. She will be honored."

With a grunt I replied testily, "I don't believe that and neither do you."

He glowered at me. "You're not going to trade?"

"No."

The muscles in his strong jaw bunched, relaxed, bunched again. "A lot of bad things have been happening to me. A new hat might have cheered me up. You are a selfish person, Tay-bodal."

"No, I'm not. I am merely a man afraid of his wife."

White Bear tipped back his head and laughed. Still laughing, he waved his mighty arms, dispersing the search teams. Watching them ride off in five separate directions, White Bear became pensive; he gnawed at the corner of his mouth.

The sun overhead was feeble, able to give light but little else. Soon, it wouldn't even give that for the brisk winds were carrying in ominous dark gray clouds. Before the day was out, there would be snow. Worrying about the worsening weather, my anguish becoming acute, I said I was ready to join another search team.

"Enough have gone out," White Bear said flatly. "And

every man my best tracker.'' His quicksilver mood changed
again. Wrapping an arm around my shoulders, he guided
me toward his lodge. "No offense, but you are not a
tracker. There's a vicious rumor going around that while
you walked the search lines last night, you got lost and
Owl Man had to find you."

"Who told you that!" I cried.

"Owl Man."

I was in a sulk when White Bear ushered me through the
opened door of his lodge. After he stepped through, he
closed the door. Tying it shut, he said gruffly, "We need
to talk. But in private. Build up the fire."

I was doing exactly that as he sat down, removing his
boots and robe. Warming his bare feet and the palms of his
hands before a now lively fire, he said lowly, "Tay-bodal,
the people are anxious. You know how they get when unex-
plained things begin to happen. They've begun working
themselves up into a panic with all of this witch talk. I see
it in their faces before they turn away from me. The one
person able to calm them down is missing, and it's being
said that even this is my fault."

I turned a stunned face toward him. "Who told you
this?"

"The man known as Red Bird. He says that I am under
a curse. That until the curse is lifted, terrible things will
continue to happen to those closest to me. I believe this
man knows what he is talking about. I think he has the
power to know these things."

"I disagree."

White Bear studied me at length. Then his gaze returned
to the flames of the fire. "I'm not as simple as you might
think," he said in a low tone. "I know better than you
Skywalker's opinion of Red Bird. But Skywalker isn't here
and Red Bird's talk about witches is working the people

up, making them fearful. So fearful that they've begun accusing each other of witchcraft.''

"What?" I cried.

The corners of White Bear's mouth lifted in a humorless smile. "Oh, it's getting very exciting around here. While you were still over at He Goes's camp, I was home breaking up a fight between two families who have been content to camp near each other for years. Now, they've begun accusing each other of all manner of ridiculous things. And their attitudes are spreading. Fear is jumping from one household to another, and there doesn't seem to be any way to stop it. At least not with reason."

We both pondered for a moment as he warmed his hands before the flames. I don't know what he was thinking, but my thoughts centered again on the homes I had passed, the open hostility on the faces of the protective men.

"The people want magic," White Bear said bitterly. "Magic against the witch. Without Skywalker, Red Bird is all I have."

"And just what is Red Bird doing to make the people calm?"

"He's supplying charms."

"And selling them?" I asked with a sneer.

White Bear's broad face tightened. "Well, of course he's selling them! What doctor doesn't sell his craft? And that includes you."

I felt a wave of pure anger. True, I charged fees, but there were many warriors still walking around after I'd removed bullets or cured blood fevers on the promise they would pay me when they could. So far, only a few had kept their word. White Bear knew all of this, which was why his lumping me in with a charlatan made me furious.

"How opportune that Red Bird has on hand enough good medicine charms to sell to so many people!" I shouted.

"Before another day passes, he should be a very wealthy man."

"Tay-bodal!" White Bear thundered, "you don't have any religion."

"I have just as much as you. But I also have a healthy skepticism. Red Bird is not an Owl Doctor. His authority in this matter is no better than mine, or yours. But it's by your authority he profits from the fears of our people. If you withdraw that authority, Red Bird's good magic dies in his lying mouth."

White Bear's expression was murderous. "You speak as if I have a choice."

"You do. If you concerned yourself less with witches and curses and more with what you know to be true, the problems besetting you would all fall away."

Anger began to drain from White Bear's broad face. Encouraged, my own anger began to dissolve. My tone became less loud, more reasoning, as I held up my first finger. "One, Skywalker left camp on his own. We both know that he sometimes does this, goes off alone to meditate or whatever it is he does when he's off by himself. If it weren't for this place and the usually cold weather, neither you nor I would be worried."

My second finger joined the first. "Two, The Cheyenne Robber is a man of great conceit and there are too many who envy him, would like to see him suffer. Killing two of his finest horses would make him suffer, and the opportunity for this petty vengeance neatly presented itself when we were all out looking for Skywalker and the herders had run home frightened of what they supposedly saw."

"A woman changing into a raven."

"Precisely. I questioned one of the herders. I'm convinced he saw something all right, but what exactly is the issue you should pursue. When the body is cold and tired, the mind plays tricks. I myself believed I saw things that in the cold light of day I know weren't real. The boy I spoke with is highly impressionable and now added to his tale are the fears he has heard being aired by the females of his family. Were I you, I would look for the hard truth lurking somewhere behind that boy's original claims."

I raised a third finger. "Lastly, we have the death of He Goes's wife. You have my complete assurance that she was not killed by any curse."

"How do you know?"

"I examined her."

His brows shot up his forehead. "You did? How did you accomplish that?"

"Owl Man helped me." I lowered my hand, placing it on top of my knees. I leaned in, bringing my face close to his. When I spoke, I intentionally kept my tone to just above a whisper. "But how we managed that isn't important. What is important is that the girl was poisoned."

He sucked in a ragged breath.

"A true curse," I continued, "would not need a fatal aid, and I know of no charm able to ward off a human murderer."

White Bear turned his face away, staring blankly into the fire. When he turned to me again, he was seething. "If what you say is true, then you are going to have to prove it."

"Me!" I shouted. "Why do I have to be further involved?"

"Because it's as you said—until Skywalker is found, I have no one I can depend on."

"You have Owl Man."

"No, I don't. Unlike you, I am not a great respecter of age. I want a man able to duck and hide while he learns the truth. Can you really imagine Owl Man going about ducking and hiding without being noticed?"

He had me there. Even the mental image of Owl Man trying to dodder out of the way of watchful eyes was highly comic. What White Bear wanted was another man like Skywalker, a man in the shadows, a man he could depend on to whisper truths in his ear when all others spoke lies to his face. With a hard cringe, I realized that this person was . . . me.

"You're perfect," he said bluntly. "And this, after all, is what Skywalker has been training you to do in his place."

"Hold on!" I cried. "Now you have everything back to front. Skywalker is *my* student."

White Bear shook his head as he smiled faintly. "Please don't make me laugh. I'm not in the mood."

While I sat there feeling wounded to the core, White Bear began to speak more urgently.

"Red Bird is useful as a front. Don't take that away from him. Skywalker wouldn't, and from this point on, you must think like Skywalker. I want you to find me the person responsible for killing my nephew's horses. And while you're at it, solve the murder of that poor unfortunate woman. It's quite possible that both things were caused by the same hand."

"No, I don't believe that," I said dispiritedly.

"Why not?"

I took a deep breath and expelled it. "One crime was brutal, the other, subtle. I've never known a brutish hand to be subtle."

He considered this. "Now that I think about it, maybe you're right. But it doesn't really matter what you or I think. What's needed is proof. So, your task is to find the two criminals. And once you do, maybe all of this talk of witches and curses will end."

I retreated into deep thought. He brought me back to the

moment with yet another upsetting statement.

"I think you should know too that the talk is that Kicking Bird is the one behind all of this."

I must have looked as stunned as I felt.

"It's true," he said glumly. "I heard it with my own ears. The gossips are saying that Kicking Bird is responsible for sending the witch against me. If this trouble isn't sorted out before we leave this canyon, it means that the next time Kicking Bird and I meet, I will have no choice but to kill him."

The enormity of what he said struck me like a fist. If White Bear killed Kicking Bird, the council would have no choice but to demand White Bear's death. That would mean the loss of not one but two of our strongest leaders. Then there was something else. White Bear was the greatest life force I have ever known. He wasn't simply a magnificent warrior and leader, he was a man who lived each day beyond its measure. His talent for winning against our enemies was only equaled by his ability to love. To be a person loved by The Bear can only be compared to being placed on top of a mountain and given everything within view for hundreds of miles, in all directions. How crushingly empty this world, my own life, would be without him.

Now I knew I could not let go of his hand. Not without a fight. A fight I first leveled against him.

"Have you lost your mind!" I raged. "You can't make a threat like that! Kicking Bird is an innocent man!"

"No, he isn't," White Bear answered flatly. "Not until you make the people believe it."

Before I was able to recover from this awful statement, we heard men beating on the tied-shut door. The sounds of their pounding competed with the sounds of wind whipping the walls of the lodge. White Bear left hurriedly, going to the door and untying the straps. The men who entered reported the latest progress in the search for Skywalker. Their news was not good. During all of this highly excitable talk, I felt the last of my strength leaving me. I was tired and I couldn't remember my last meal. Turning to speak to me, White Bear noticed my pitiable condition.

"Tay-bodal, you look terrible. Go home."

For a second, my legs wouldn't cooperate. A man known as Little War rushed to help me to my feet. Even more helpful, he quickly offered to see me home. I was greatly embarrassed by his fussing over me. Everyone has a favorite person in their life; it was no secret that I was Little War's favorite person. He thought I could do anything, which is only understandable. I had saved his life, but despite my best efforts, he still bore the terrible scars of his life-threatening misadventure. But he didn't care about that. He only cared that he was alive, still able-bodied.

Before he became known as He-Showed-His-Courage-In-A-Little-War-Against-The-Tehans, he had been a well-built and handsome young man of a careful nature. So careful a nature that a year ago the brothers of his society teased him unmercifully, all but calling him a coward. Although outwardly he laughed at the jokes made at his expense, inside he was deeply disturbed. In a fight against the Tehans, to prove his bravery once and for all, he did a reckless thing. Shouting "Now is my die-day!" he charged ahead of the war party chasing the Tehans. He rode far ahead of the others, his horse drawing alongside one of the white men. At this galloping speed, the white man turned at the waist and fired his handgun. The bullet, at such close range, not only struck Little War in the face, but it threw him off his racing horse.

The others allowed the Tehans to get away, for when they reached their fallen brother, interest in pursuing the Tehans vanished. Their brother needed them more than they needed war honors, for this young man of careful nature was in a bad way. The bullet fired from the Tehan's gun had taken out his left eye and had somehow traveled down his throat, becoming stuck in his shoulder bone. Because of the nearness of the blast, half of his teeth had been knocked out. The man everyone considered pleasant looking would never be considered so again. His lost handsomeness hardly mattered for, as you might imagine, his recovery was in grave doubt. Two Buffalo Doctors were with the group. They did their best, calling on Buffalo Woman, the creator of their society, to intervene and have mercy on the impulsive young man.

Now the Buffalo Woman was at one time a real person, but she lived long before my grandfather's grandfather. As a young girl she had been caught out in a blizzard. Lost and nearly frozen, she came across an almost completely decomposed buffalo. She took shelter inside the buffalo's ribs, and the hide left on the bones kept the snow out. Soon, in this unlikely shelter, she was warm enough to go to sleep, and in sleep, the buffalo providing the haven spoke to her in her dreams, giving her special songs to sing in times of trouble or illness. The next day, she awoke to find the storm had abated. She took the hide from the bones, wrapped it around herself, and walked many long miles until she made it safely home. She kept that robe for the rest of her life, and when she became the mother of two sons, she taught them the Buffalo songs. Those two sons became the first Buffalo Doctors. The doctors who came later customarily called on those two when they prayed for a patient. Buffalo Woman's power was reserved for patients as bad off as the patient known as Little War. But no matter how much the Buffalo Doctors beseeched the Old Woman, Little War's condition steadily declined.

I heard about him after they brought him home. I did not

intervene in any way until his brother warriors came for me. According to what I was told, this man now known as Little War had been shot three days prior and they had tied him in the saddle to bring him home. This did not sound good, as bullets left inside the body for more than a day fester the blood. Not only that, but filth and flies get in the open wounds, and during and after three days of travel, this type of damage would have been considerable. All I could say to the warriors asking me to take over Little War's case was "Are you prepared for him to die?"

"Yes," they said. "But we would appreciate his dying more comfortably, as it is because of our teasing that he suffers so."

I said I would do what I could to save him, but if this was not possible, I promised he would not feel any more pain, his passing would be peaceful.

They said, "That's all right. That is enough."

With these terms agreed to, I became Little War's doctor.

Little War was the biggest mess I have ever been asked to clean up, and considering the plagues of smallpox and cholera I've had to deal with, this says a lot. I treated each wound as best I could, taking care of the eye first, then probing for the bullet and digging it out. Little War didn't feel anything. I had knocked him out with a strong mixture of the same medicine I make for Skywalker to dull his crippling headaches. In Little War's case, I brewed the medicine into a tea, but to give it to him, I had to place my hand firmly over the hole in his throat or the tea would come out each time he swallowed. This force-feeding was a task neither Little War nor I enjoyed, but eventually enough of the tea got inside him, and when the brew took effect, he passed out.

While he was unconscious, I seared his wounds with punk wood to prevent festering and applied soothing tallow.

Bandaging is lengthy process because I'd learned long ago that it is best to boil the bandages with various roots. When this is done the scaring is lessened. Little War's scars are admittedly horrific but, on the whole, far less than those he would have had had I not first infused the goodness of the healing roots into the bandages.

Four and a half days, that's how long I stayed with him, feeding him soup, draining away the putrid fluids building up in his wounds, then purifying the wounds with melted tallow. When he was finally on the mend, I made him a special patch to wear over his empty eyehole. Even though I had sewn the eyelid to the cheekbone, he looked better with the patch, and I instructed him on the importance of always wearing the patch and keeping it clean. Little War recovered, and because of his scars, no one ever again dared question his bravery, not even in jest. As for me, I was paid quite well, but Little War refused to call the debt even. Whenever I needed anything and he heard about it, all I had to do was turn around and there he was.

His unfailing gratitude was becoming increasingly annoying, but because I felt weak, I swallowed my pride and leaned on him. Outside, the winds that had been whipping the lodge walls and howling around the high smoke hole hit us with full force. After being so long inside the warm lodge, the cold air made me dizzy. I hand-signed to Little War that I needed to stand still for a moment. Patiently he stood with me until the dizzy spell ended.

I took in great gulps of frozen air, my lungs protesting the frigid assault. I kept it up anyway and my brain began to clear enough to understand Little War's muttered statement.

"It's really too bad about that girl. Her life in this last year was not happy."

I turned on him. "You knew her?"

"Oh, yes. I knew her very well."

My hands grabbed for the front of his robe and I pulled him close to me. "Tell me everything you know!"

I let go of him when Little War began to jabber rapidly.

"I-I was with him when He Goes first found her. She was little, but she was almost near the age of full womanhood. Anyway, the men wanted to use her. He Goes kept all of them off of her, saying she was his to use. But he didn't. Instead, he brought her home to his wife. He Goes's first wife immediately loved the girl and wanted her for a daughter. He Goes said he would have to think about it. While he was thinking, the girl was treated as a daughter. She was a good girl, always cheerful. She had a good mind, learning the language of the people very quickly. I know that her manners were impeccable. I remember one time when she came upon a woman crying and she asked what was wrong. That woman didn't want to tell her, saying that she only felt a bit unwell. This was not true, but that girl pretended to believe the lie, doing that woman's chores for her until the woman felt better in her spirit. He Goes's first wife knew this to be the sign of a worthwhile human being, and again she asked her husband to adopt the girl. He Goes's answer was that he was still thinking about it.

"By this time, even his own daughter, Shade, tired of her father's indecision, took it upon herself to take the girl by the hand, lead her through the village and tell everyone they met that the girl was her true sister. After that day, the two girls were very close, doing everything together. When you saw one, you saw the other."

When Little War paused, I rudely put a question to him. "Was the girl Shade, to your knowledge, jealous that this new sister was . . . prettier?"

Little War rocked back on his heels. "*No!* The girl's loveliness was Shade's pride. She wanted to look just like her, and that girl taught Shade the use of Mexican face paints for women. Being an unselfish person, she taught other girls too. It became a game among them, all of them finding just the right roots and berries needed to make the paints and—"

I raised a hand, stopping him in midsentence. "This dead girl knew a lot about the uses of plants?"

Little War nodded enthusiastically. "I am told she brought this knowledge with her from the Mexican Tehans. That her former mother knew all about strange plants and how to use them. It was on account of this knowledge that the foods served at feasts given by He Goes taste so much better than ordinary foods. Anyway," Little War continued as if this aside were meaningless, "for a time the wife of He Goes had a lodge filled with young girls giggling and playing with their faces. He Goes's first wife was a very happy person. She began calling herself Mother of Many. She was even more happy that her blood daughter, Shade, for the first time in her life, was an extremely popular person. Her new sister kept Shade's hair oiled and brushed until it shined, and with the face paints, Shade still appeared too skinny, but she turned out to be surprisingly pretty."

I recalled the girl I met today. She had worn no paints and her hair was in disarray. It was fairly easy to imagine her delicate features as pretty, but her boyish body would still be viewed as a critical flaw. As for such a timid person's being popular, all I could do was take Little War's word for it. None of that actually concerned me; what I dwelled on as Little War continued was the dead girl's extensive knowledge of plants.

"Then one day," he said, "He Goes called his women and his band together, saying that he'd reached a decision. The women were all very excited about this, certain that the adoption would take place, that there would be days of

feasting and dancing. Instead, He Goes announced his intention to marry the girl. Everyone was surprised. Many
women were instantly angry, saying that He Goes was doing a terrible thing. But, anger and disapproval would not
stop him. He said that the girl was not his daughter, that it
was his right to claim her as a wife. In front of everyone,
he tore the girl from the arms of his wife and daughter. All
three women were crying, begging him not to do it, but he
would not listen. He took the girl inside his lodge. The
whole time he was in there with her, his first wife and his
daughter lay on the ground weeping and pouring ashes on
their heads. It was a terrible sight. Out of respect for them,
people turned away, allowed their shame to be private. To
this day, no one has spoken of it, keeping the wrongness
committed against the three women a confidence shared by
the entire band. I know that since then, others have learned
a bit of what happened, but no one outside of the band has
been told the full details. If you repeat any of this, I would
consider it a favor if you failed to mention just who it was
that told you."

"You have my promise." Having received all of this
new information, my brain suddenly seemed revitalized. I
wasn't tired at all. Indeed, I seemed to have received a bolt
of energy. "I think maybe I would like to see where that
woman changed into a raven."

Little War's one eye rounded in surprise. "That's a long
way from here."

"I don't care. I'm going anyway. I need to see this place
for myself."

Little War hesitated, then said, "I think maybe I better
go with you."

We left our horses at the base of the canyon wall. Even
with a sheen of ice on the rocks, it was an easy climb to

the outcropping that jutted from the wall midway to the top rim and open prairie. This easy path was known to us as a false trail, meaning that it looked like a good way out of the canyon in an emergency, but actually ended at the midway shelf. Anyone using this trail would quickly find themselves stranded on the outcropping with no place to go but down. Of course, one could always hide and wait out the danger, but we Kiowa have always had a fight-or-flight mentality. As Little War and I climbed, I pointed out to him that the pathway had been well used. He didn't seem to appreciate this knowledge much. I knew he was nervous, thinking this a witch's place, but he said nothing and stayed with me. It was easy to transfer from the path of hand and foot holds of the wall face onto the flat-surfaced outcropping. I went first, testing the strength of the midway ledge. This cliff was larger than it appeared from the ground. It was wide and receded into the wall, almost like a cave, but not deep enough to be an actual cave. I was so involved with examining this little territory that I forgot about my companion until he was with me, his big feet almost trampling out the tracks I studied.

"Stand still," I ordered. My voice echoed all around the canyon, and when it came back to me, the words had become gibberish, sounding more like a caw than a human voice. Little War's unpatched eye bulged with fright.

"The witch is talking!" he shouted in a whisper. When his fearful mutterings came back to us, they sounded like a warning hiss.

To prevent further echoes, I hurriedly took Little War by the robe and spoke directly into his ear. "Those are our voices. Be calm. This is not a bad place. I don't believe a witch was ever up here. I don't dispute the existence of witches, I just don't believe we have a witch with us in this canyon."

His large hands grabbed my face, almost yanking me by my head off my feet as he frantically spoke into my ear. "Tay-bodal! You shouldn't say things like that. You will bring evil on yourself. Besides, your own wife believes there's a witch—that's why she bought charms from Red Bird."

"What!" I shouted. As my voice boomed again and again, Little War let go of me, hunkering down, his hands going to his ears to block out the sounds. That small burst of energy responsible for bringing me to this place was nothing compared to the explosion of angry energy I now felt.

I left Little War quaking on his haunches. I tried to keep my anger against my wife at a minimum as I examined the cavelike recess. Many signs were captured in the fine layer of frozen dust, signs that had been protected from the winds passing over the ledge itself. I could see an imprint of where a blanket had been spread. I could also see footprints, one set man-sized, and by comparison to the prints of one of my own feet, a large man. The other set were definitely feminine. Squatting down next to the prints, I held my hand directly over one of them, setting the print in my mind in relation to the heel of my hand and the tip of my middle finger. The narrow ball of the foot came to that point, and moving my hand again, measuring from the first knuckle of my middle finger, the tip of that finger neatly reached the imprinted big toe.

Then I sat back on my haunches, my brows meeting at the bridge of my nose as I frowned. I tried to remember the size of the dead girl's feet, but I couldn't. All I had done in that area was look between the toes and note the color of the toenails. Which meant, of course, that I would have to go back before the funeral took place. Some families buried their dead at sunset, some at sunrise. Not knowing the traditions of He Goes's band, it was imperative I return at once. Whatever the time chosen for burial, I knew that, right about now, the dead girl was undergoing final preparations, being bathed, dressed, and then guarded in turns by mourners. Going back into the death lodge for a quick peek at her feet would not be an easy task. But I knew that I must succeed. Once she was buried, it would be too late to prove or disprove He Goes's young wife had been the mystery woman of the ledge, for even I drew the line at digging up the dead.

I looked away from the feminine prints, closely studying those left by the man. From the size of the print, he was a big man. From the depth, he was of considerable weight. I put him to be about two hundred pounds. But all of this was not what intrigued me most about the male's print. I stared at it until I had a fixed mental image, then I stood and walked the few paces to the place where Little War sat huddling under his robe. In the dimming light he looked like a big lump; even his head was covered. Were it any darker, I would have mistaken him for a boulder perched in the center of this cliff shelf.

The instant this thought occurred I stopped and stared. Excitement kicked up in my stomach, and on the move again, passing the huddling Little War, I came to stand dangerously close to the edge of the rock shelf. From this place I had a good view of most of the canyon floor, but a better view of where the herders had been and a broad scene of the picketed herds. Each herd had its own grazing area marked off by the owner of the herd. From my lofty vantage point, I clearly saw the various lances stabbed into the ground, each lance bearing feathered markings. Even from this distance I could easily pick out the lances I recognized as belonging to White Bear and The Cheyenne Robber. Their herds were close together. If the slayer of

The Cheyenne Robber's horses was the same man who left the footprints on this ledge, then he had most probably done this very thing, stood just where I now stood studying the positioning of the herds. But how much would such an overview help him once he was on the ground and moving around in the blackness of night?

This gave me something to ponder as I went back to Little War and bumped his form with my foot. His one eye peeked out at me from under his robe. He was clearly afraid. Relief washed over his ruined features as I knelt down beside him and told him what I wanted him to do. Then he all but ran to the wall face and, like a hurrying squirrel, made his way down to the canyon floor. It took him several minutes to make his way to the herders' abandoned night camp. When he was in position, I went back to the spot he had previously occupied, squatting down.

"Do you see me?" I shouted, again raising the responding echoes.

"No!" he hollered.

That was when I stood and opened my arms the same way the woman would have done to greet her lover. From the valley below, I heard Little War cry out. When he realized it was only me, he calmed down, even laughed at his foolishness. In the meantime, I scanned the top half of the canyon wall. It was craggy and dipped at a sharp angle. The rising full moon would have hung just there, forming a backdrop of silvery light for an impetuous young woman.

This was a good meeting place, yet there was a second problem with it.

Sound.

The slightest mutter carried. Because this young woman had felt happy about meeting her lover, she had compounded one mistake with yet another. For one, she forgot to stay low, and then she'd cried out, probably an excited

Oh! The answering echo would promptly have been mistaken for cawing. This being too much for the already frightened boys, they let out a few cries of their own as they tried outrunning each other in the race for home.

Many things pestered my mind as I made my way down from the ledge. One theory was certainly strong but deeply dependent on the foot size of the dead girl. Before making up my mind on this set of events and presenting them as fact to White Bear, I had to get at that woman one more time. But I told Little War only that I wished to pay my last respects, and he agreed that this was a good thing to do. He rode with me to He Goes's camp.

I was mildly astonished by the welcome we received. Within seconds of our dismounting outside He Goes's lodge, the man himself came out, warmly embracing Little War. He Goes did not know me beyond recognizing my face. We did not exchange personal greetings. We merely nodded and felt uncomfortable with each other. His face was no longer painted black. I could now see his features clearly. His eyes were closely set and hooded. Twin creases ran from the corners of his nose to a chin that, because of a V-shaped jawline, was like a point. The creases around his mouth were quite deep for a man of his middle years. This told me that He Goes was either a concentrated thinker or that he continually scowled.

He turned away from me, giving all of his attention to Little War. Then when He Goes realized how cold both Little War and I were, he profusely apologized for his bad manners, offering us the warmth of his lodge fire. Our acceptance of his generosity was instant. Once inside his lodge, we made ourselves comfortable. I experienced a pang of alarm when a woman entered carrying a jug. Wisps of steam rose out of the narrow opening of the jug, and I imagined the contents to be hot coffee. The woman placed

a partially filled bowl in my hands, and I sat looking at the
dark liquid contents as He Goes and Little War swallowed
their bowls of brew right down. I was waiting for one or
both to die when Little War spoke.

"Rose hip tea is my favorite. May I have some more?"

Rose hip tea? The woman refilled Little War's bowl
while I sniffed at mine. It was rose hip tea, and after a
cautious sip, the tang of honey was sweetly on my tongue.
It was delicious. Because I was relieved, I spoke out of
turn.

"I was expecting coffee."

He Goes looked at me, his expression a mixture of rage
and loathing. It is bad manners for a guest to speak before
he is formally recognized by his host, even worse to question the offered food or drink. On both counts I had broken
the rules of proper conduct. I thoroughly deserved He
Goes's churlish reply, but I had done nothing to warrant
such a terrible look.

"You want coffee, go home."

Little War leaned against me and whispered in my ear.
"He Goes is not allowed to drink coffee until this time
next year. Coffee was his dead wife's favorite drink, and
so he has given it up out of respect for her."

Nothing more was said to me by either man. He Goes
spoke only to Little War, talking about his wife and what
a joy she had been. Little War listened sympathetically. My
attention came to rest on the woman in the lodge with us.
This woman greatly favored He Goes. Being so similar, I
could only assume her to be Shade's auntie, the widowed
sister of He Goes. She looked a bit older than my wife, but
only just. She had an agreeable face and her figure was
even more agreeable, breasts and hips straining taut her
plain work dress. I couldn't help but notice the way she
continually glanced at Little War, and that now and again

he glanced at her too. Now I knew why Little War was so welcome in He Goes's lodge. Obviously He Goes was looking at Little War as a possible husband for his widowed sister.

He Goes waved a dismissive hand and his sister set aside the jug of tea, going to sit off to the side. While I listened with half an ear to the talk between He Goes and Little War, I watched the sister. She placed a finely made buckskin glove on her hand and spread a little apron across her knees. After dipping a dry tobacco leaf in a pot to dampen it, she quickly rolled the moistened leaf against the apron with the gloved hand. She repeated this process, adding two more leaves, making a fine and firmly shaped cigar.

I smiled. I loved cigars. The trouble was, none of the cigars I ever made burned evenly or held together. Crying Wind didn't know how to make them either. Now I was being treated to a firsthand lesson.

I slowly inched my way toward her, away from my place near Little War. The woman's twinkling eyes watched me as her gloved hand deftly began yet another cigar. When I was near enough, I whispered to her. Her smile widened. She had such a pretty smile.

I whispered to her as loud as I dared. "I admire the way you do that. I've never seen anyone make a finer cigar."

She glanced nervously at her brother. He Goes was interested only in talking to Little War. Her sweet smile began to fade. "The woman who went away"—meaning the dead girl—"taught me how to do it."

"And you miss her?"

"Oh, yes." She was about to say more, but our whisperings had caught He Goes's angry attention. I went back to my proper place and she returned to her work, her head kept low.

My exhaustion was catching up with me again when Lit-

tle War finally embraced He Goes. As we were leaving, He
Goes said to Little War that he was always welcome to
come back and share his fire. He Goes said nothing to me.

Outside the lodge, I bullied Little War into one last favor.
He didn't want to do it, but relented when I said, "We will
be even for the rest of our lives. You will owe me nothing
more for saving yours."

Little War rolled his one eye toward the lead-gray sky
and heaved a great sigh.

Getting into the death lodge was a lot of work. He Goes
had hired professional mourners, aging widows in need of
the gifts He Goes provided for their services. They were
doing an exemplary job, keening shrilly and covering themselves with filth as they kept watch over the dead girl. In
the end Little War promised them each a gift if they would
allow us a moment of private prayer. I suppose even professional mourners need a break from grief, for the women
took Little War at his word and hurried right out. The instant we were alone, I went for the feet.

"What are you doing?" Little War gasped. Touching a
dead person wasn't something a normal person would rush
to do, and Little War's one eye was wide with horror.

"Just watch the door!" I shouted in a whisper. The girl
was stiff. Trying to move a body around during this stage
of death will break bones. Knowing a corpse with a broken
leg would be noticed, I crouched down and measured my
hand against the sole. And what I discovered ruined my
hard-won theory. The dead girl's foot was small and wide.
She could not possibly have made the foot marks discovered on the ledge.

I covered up the body, a thing I had to do quickly because Little War was highly agitated. Then I lapsed into
deep thought. I must have thought for much too long be-

cause a frantic Little War hauled me to my feet and pro-
pelled me out of the death lodge.

My home was dark and cold and there was no sign of my
wife. Judging by the frigid ashes in the firepit, she had not
been home for many hours. I made a fire and, after it
caught, added cedar chips. I bathed myself with the purifying cedar smoke, crawled into bed, and passed out.

CHAPTER

5

An annoying tinkling would not be ignored. The sound pulled me from a leaden sleep, and when I pried my eyes open, unfamiliar objects, shells and large beads strung from cords, dangled above me, suspended from the crossing lodge poles. The updraft from the fire caused the shells to twirl and dance, clank together. When I sat up, the movement of throwing back the blanket increased the tinkling. Crying Wind was sitting near the firepit with her back to me, cooking the morning meal.

"Crying Wind," I croaked. "What are these things?"

She turned her head and looked back at me, her expression fearful. "They are charms," she said, her tone a whine. "Charms against evil."

It was then that I remembered what Little War had said, that my own wife had been seen buying good-luck charms from Red Bird. My anger must have caused me to go red in the face, for she came to me and placed a hand against my brow.

"You have a fever. You were out in the cold much too long."

I took hold of her hand. "Crying Wind, I love you with all of my heart. But your buying trash from a faker upsets me greatly and—'' Everything just stopped when I saw that the top half of her breasts, the place where her necklace normally lay, was bare.

It is called a river necklace because it is made of fine strands of beaten silver. Only the most skilled craftsmen are able to make such a necklace. Crying Wind's necklace had five delicate strands, all of them connected to a central strand. When worn, the fine flattened silver moved with the normal body rhythms of the wearer, undulating and shining like gentle waves of a river. Skywalker had given the expensive gift to honor our marriage. Crying Wind loved the gift so much that she never took it off. But now it was gone and I knew why. I fell back on the bed; Crying Wind came after me, weeping and speaking in a rush.

"Everyone is afraid. It's all on account of the evil in this place. And Skywalker . . . it's said that the evil got him too. That he's dead somewhere, that this is how the searchers will find him. I had to protect my family. There was nothing else of mine that Red Bird wanted. I had to sell the necklace. I didn't want to but I had no choice.''

I sat up again, taking her in my arms, holding her as she wept. And each tear she shed caused my heart to harden. Red Bird had taken away not only my wife's necklace, but he had stolen the honor of the one who had given it.

Skywalker.

Crying Wind tried to hold me back, but I was enraged. I tore down the awful charms, shoving them into a bag, and as I left, I heard my wife's sobs. It was snowing hard, tiny, sharp flakes that came down sideways. More than a foot of snow had fallen during the night, which would mean slow going.

My favorite horse and Crying Wind's pinto mare were

sleeping in the warm, dry shelter. When I entered, Crying Wind's mare eyed me, stepped to the side. My horse nickered, glad to see me, nudging me for food. But when I came at it with blankets and saddle, it changed its mind about being friendly. On this type of day horses in the fields turned their backs to the wind and huddled close. My horse, spoiled by the cozy shelter, was doubly resistant to the idea of travel. I was fighting with it when my wife entered.

"You can't go!" she cried, her tone more pleading than angry. "You'll get lost, like Skywalker."

"He isn't lost," I growled.

"If he isn't lost, why is my cousin still sending out searchers?"

"Because your cousin is a stubborn man. Just like you."

Crying Wind placed her hands against her face. "I'm sorry." She wept. "I'm sorry I traded away the necklace. Please, please don't leave me."

Hearing the fear in her voice, I turned to her and took her in my arms. "Sweet woman, my anger is not with you. My anger is for the man who stole from you." I raised her chin and kissed her mouth. "Where is our son?"

"With my sister," she said, her voice trembling.

"Keep him with you at all times. I'll come home as soon as I can."

I'd slept with my hat on, but beneath the shoulder robe I wore only my sleeping clothes, a thin shirt, leggings, and a pair of light moccasins. Because of my anger I didn't feel the cold as I rode for the camp on the other side of the little river. During Owl Man's telling me all about Red Bird, he'd said that Red Bird was currently with the band ruled by the subchief Crow Foot. His was a small band, and Crow Foot was generally considered an amicable fellow. But because he continually curried White Bear's favor, Crow Foot was accused, rather crudely and behind his back, of having rough lips—meaning his lips were overworked from the kissing of White Bear's backside. I, a man known to be close to White Bear, would be welcome in Crow Foot's camp.

It began snowing harder—so hard that it was difficult to tell the earth from the sky. The few dozen lodges of Crow Foot's band seemed more like dark, fat trees. I might have passed the campsite had I not smelled the smoke of lodge fires. Entering the small camp, I headed for the largest lodge, the lodge that would belong to Crow Foot.

A visitor on such a morning, when anyone with a shred of sense would be snug in his home, could only mean bad news. Hearing me calling out his name, Crow Foot hurried from his lodge. One sight of me, a man of White Bear's camp, Crow Foot assumed the worst.

"How many soldiers?" he yelped.

"No soldiers!" I answered hotly. "This is personal business. I am here to confront Red Bird. I would take it kindly if you pointed out his lodge."

The blood left Crow Foot's face. "H-he is here. In my lodge." Crow Foot turned and opened the lodge door.

Red Bird emerged and was not at all what I'd expected. I had never seen him, only heard his excited voice as Owl Man and I stood behind the crowd. I had formed a false image of him, one of a man of small stature and perhaps owning the face of a weasel. What he was, in truth, was a supremely tall, arrogantly handsome man. He straightened to his full height, and his obsidian eyes that held a trace of instability bore into mine. There was a primal aspect belonging to this man that drew rather than repelled. He was exactly the type of man whom otherwise sensible people would turn to when frightened. A wry smile tugged at the corners of his mouth as he adjusted a splendid robe about his broad shoulders.

"Perhaps," he said, his tone amused, "I am not what you had expected." Three other men had come out with him, and he paused for effect, turning his head, smiling at the men, who came to stand beside him. Then he directed his attention back to me. "You are known to be a great friend to Skywalker. Have you come to see for yourself that I, Red Bird, stand ready to face the dangers of the Dark Way, while Skywalker . . . hides?"

That was the final thing I needed. Jumping from my horse, I walked straight for him, bumping my chest against his, knocking him back. Surprise first came over his face and, for a second, a flicker of fright.

"You cheated my wife," I raged. "You took from her a precious thing and gave in return meaningless trinkets. I've come for her necklace. I demand you give it to me."

His eyes became hard, his mouth a tight line. A stronger wind whipped by, pelting his profile with tiny flecks of snow. The winds ruffled the fur of his robe and threw around the eagle feathers hanging from the side of his hat.

"Your wife came to me," he seethed. "She sought me out and begged the protection of my power. Our trade was fair. That is all I have to say."

I threw down the bag containing the worthless beads and shells. It landed between his feet, and horrified, he stared at it. "You have defiled the power," he gasped. "You are a foolish man!"

I placed my fist close to his nose. "Give back the necklace or we will fight, you and I."

Red Bird took a step back, gathering his dignity. "A man of my rank," he sneered, "does not brawl with someone so . . . common."

I was still at the ready when he raised his hands, put them behind his neck. He unclasped my wife's necklace and flung it to the ground. I stooped to grab it up just as it was disappearing like a sliver snake into the deepening snow.

"You have what you came for," he said grimly. "I tried to save you, but you wouldn't allow it. I am no longer responsible for your family."

Hearing this veiled treat, I lunged for him. Crow Foot and another young man stepped in just before my fist connected with Red Bird's highly startled face.

"Take him to your home," Crow Foot hollered to the young man holding onto me. "Make certain he is fed and dry before you send him back to White Bear."

Of course, even in a dire moment, Crow Foot would think of hospitality toward a friend of White Bear's. It was the very thing a man with rough lips would worry over. But I didn't want his hospitality, and I tried to shake off the young man taking me away by the scruff of my neck. Behind me I heard Crow Foot yelling about someone seeing to my horse. He was making certain, you understand, that I would have nothing bad to say about him to White Bear. What I might say about Red Bird didn't really disturb Crow Foot all that much. Like me, Red Bird was merely a guest, not a member of Crow Foot's band, therefore any trouble between Red Bird and me was not Crow Foot's fault.

The name of my host was Bear Shadow. His lodge was of good size and his wife was as pretty as a flower. Her smile of greeting was met by Bear Shadow's sullen glare. Her smile faded as her gaze locked with his. The silent tension between the two quickly became a palpable thing. Bear Shadow looked away first. Then, without a word, she left.

A bit discomfited that my presence might be the cause of their marital strife, I began to babble. "I apologize for the intrusion. I need only a moment by your fire and I will leave."

"You are not intruding," Bear Shadow said stiffly. With his hand he indicated the place of honor before his fire. "Please, you are welcome to stay however long you wish."

"B-but your wife is outside in the cold."

Bear Shadow sat himself down, removing his protective robe, boots, hat, and gloves. "She went home to her mother. She always does that."

He made a disagreeable sound in the back of his throat and stared hatefully into the fire. As I didn't have a mother-in-law, his was a problem I did not share but fully understood. In our culture, a man is forbidden to speak to his mother-in-law. This restriction came down to us through the Bear Women Society, a group composed of the most honorable older women belonging to the nation. This highly secret society of women, has, from its inception, made the moral rules we live by.

A man's being overly familiar with his mother-in-law was considered incestuous. He was not allowed to speak even if the sole purpose was simply to request his wife's return from her mother's house. All he could do was wait for his wife to come home. If she didn't, then they were divorced. Evidently, because he'd said she ran to her mother's all the time, Bear Shadow's little wife liked to make him wonder a lot if they were married or divorced.

Again, I felt uncomfortable being a witness to something so personal, but I was also feeling every minute of the cold I had endured during the ride to Crow Foot's camp. I badly needed the warmth of Bear Shadow's fire before making my way back home. Sitting down in the place indicated, I furtively noted the surroundings as I warmed frozen hands before the fire. It was a tidy home but markedly lacked the womanly clutter Crying Wind had brought with her into my life. If I hadn't known Bear Shadow was married, I would have guessed him to be a single man of fastidious nature.

"I am a newly married man," I said. "Have you been married long?"

"No," he grunted. "I have been married only as long as The Cheyenne Robber."

Feeling vaguely relieved that we had something in common—The Cheyenne Robber—in an attempt at friendly conversation, I stretched the point. "I'm well acquainted with The Cheyenne Robber myself. In fact, on account of my wife, he is my relative. I am pleased to be in the company of one of his friends."

He tilted his head, hard eyes meeting mine. "I am no longer his friend. You tell him if he wants to challenge me, I will come out and fight."

Decidedly uncomfortable now, I tried warming myself as quickly as I could as we sat in painful silence. But when I secured the necklace to my breech string, he spoke again. "You must think a lot of her, your wife."

"Yes, I do. Being married to her is the best part of my life. But I don't have to say this to you. As a newlywed yourself, you know the joy in my heart."

He looked levelly at me. "No, I'm afraid I don't. I thought I would, but I was wrong." He turned his face away, once again looking forlornly into the fire. He kept his voice so low, almost talking to himself, that I had to strain to hear. "I went to him and told him everything in my heart. He listened and that was good. Then he said he had a charm that would fix everything. I paid a good price for that charm, and to make it work, I did everything just as he said." He looked at me again, his expression intent. "I am glad you got your wife's necklace back."

He fell into a deep absorption with the dancing flames. Using a trick I'd learned from Skywalker, I didn't move, didn't speak, as this troubled man's mind went deeper and deeper into a trancelike state. Then I leaned in and whispered softly in his ear.

His response was one word.

"No."

The ride home felt longer than the ride out. I had left Crow Foot's camp before I was warmed up enough to endure the cold again. I'd left in haste because I simply couldn't stand Bear Shadow's sulky company. In the slog for home, I came to regret that decision, but as the journey back to Crow Foot's was now the same distance as the journey to home, I continued on.

My near frozen appearance must have been terrible because when my anxious wife spotted me, she screamed. The odd thing about freezing to death is that you have no idea that it's happening. As strange as this may sound, other than being a bit groggy, I felt just fine. However, had I been on foot, not on a horse determined to take us both home, I would most probably have sat down for a rest and died.

Because I treated my horse the same way I had seen soldiers treating theirs, during the brief time I had lived among the soldiers at the new fort (Fort Sill), I'm still here. Since I'd pampered my horse, it headed straight for its shelter.

I had endured a lot of teasing about the way I treated my horse, but on that day, the overindulgence was repaid. My horse took me home. After members of my wife's family dragged me from the saddle, one of my wife's male cousins, a young man named Elk Cry, took my horse to the shelter. Elk Cry was a fine young man and I thought a lot of him. He was quiet and rarely spoke out loud because he stuttered badly. Instead, he talked with his hands. His affliction was beneficial in that it taught him to be a good listener and a highly observant person. Having seen the way I cared for my horse, he simply did what he knew I would do.

Inside our lodge, there was chaos. Many hands roughly tried to warm me up while my wife poured hot soup down my throat. None of that seemed to be working for my teeth were badly clattering.

"We need to get him in the bed," Crying Wind said shrilly.

Again, I was grabbed up and hauled around like a near frozen block of meat. While all of this was happening, I felt outside myself, as if I were standing off somewhere and watching the frantic activity.

Crying Wind ordered everyone out, instructing her sister to take our son along with her. When we were alone, she stripped me down to the skin, rubbing me briskly with drying cloths and calling me some unsettling names. But I forgave her when she took off her dress and climbed into the bed with me, holding on to me, giving me her warmth while freezing winds howled around our lodge and whistled down the smoke hole.

My teeth were still clacking, my voice a weakened croak. "Did you see I got your necklace back?"

"Yes," she fumed, "I saw. I put it in a safe place." Briskly, she kissed my forehead. "Tay-bodal, I'm not sure if I should thank you or hit you."

She settled down to hold me and warm me up. For the longest time, all I could do was hold her and think of Bear Shadow. He was formidable in size and a good-looking young man, whereas I was craggy faced and of modest build. Both of us had been blessed with lovely wives. Anyone comparing us would have believed that he was the confident husband and I the insecure one. Yet in my heart

I knew for a certainty that my wife loved me, whereas Bear Shadow had no idea how his wife felt about him. So happy that I was not Bear Shadow, I rolled on top of my wife and kissed her just as hard as I could.

Taken by surprise, Crying Wind sputtered and laughed, pushing me off her. I lay on my side, my head propped against my hand. She rolled over, snuggling her back against my chest. Together we listened to the falling snow tapping against the walls of our snug home. A sudden shift of wind caused a minor downdraft, the flames of the fire rising and popping.

"You're worrying about him," she whispered. I knew she meant Skywalker.

My happiness in the moment ended. For a long time she and I simply breathed together as if we shared the same lungs.

"He's never been gone this long before," I finally said. "And the weather is so bad. I just pray he's found good shelter."

"Well, of course he has," she scoffed. "Skywalker can be very strange, but I've never known him to be stupid."

I slowly let go a breath. "I wish he were here. There are so many things going on. Everywhere I look there seems to be only trouble and sadness. And your cousin says that many of the people are ready to blame Kicking Bird for all of it."

She chuckled. "That's been going on for years. If either White Bear or Kicking Bird so much as stubs a toe, the other is blamed. If you really must worry about someone, you should worry about The Cheyenne Robber."

"Why? What's wrong with him?"

She rolled onto her shoulder and meekly peeked back at me. "Now promise you won't get mad."

Why is it that this request never fails to trigger anger?

Bolting up, I yelled, "Just tell me what he's done!"

Crying Wind sat up beside me. "Why are you yelling?"

"I'm yelling because you just said the very name I didn't care to hear. In many ways The Cheyenne Robber is worse than your cousin The Bear."

"I couldn't agree with you more."

My arms resting on my knees, I looked at her and waited. And waited. "Well? Are you going to tell me?"

"No, not in the mood you're in."

My wife could be a stubborn woman, especially when she felt offended. My yelling had offended her. "I'm sorry." I hoped I sounded suitably meek.

"All right, I'll tell you. But if you yell one more time, I will hurt you." I nodded and she continued, "He Goes's dead wife was buried before dawn this morning. I was told that The Cheyenne Robber went to the funeral. He rode as part of White Bear's honor guard. Anyway, after the funeral, he claimed Shade for his second wife."

"What!"

"You're yelling."

"I'm sorry, I'm sorry. Please, continue."

"I don't really know any more than that. Bad weather drove everyone back inside their homes before the gossip got to be really juicy."

"Yes, but did you hear if The Cheyenne Robber took her to his home?"

She looked at me as if I were the thickest human being she'd ever known. "Where else would he take her? He Goes handed his daughter over, so she is now The Cheyenne Robber's lawful second wife."

With a moan, I fell back on the bed. Crying Wind came after me, lying on top of my stomach. "I know you're upset on account of White Otter, but she must have agreed to the marriage."

I glared at her. "Perhaps," I said bitterly, "as this new marriage seems so acceptable to you, I should begin considering a second wife."

Her eyes flared wide. Then she began backtracking. Rapidly. "The Cheyenne Robber is too much like my cousin. Those two need a lot of women. But a man like you—"

"I'm a man too!" I yelled, no longer concerned if my yelling was offensive. "Granted, you are the most beautiful woman I've ever had in my life, but for your information, my needs are no less than The Cheyenne Robber's or White Bear's. Now, think again, my wife, and this time answer truthfully. If you were heavy with my child, would you welcome another woman as your sister wife?"

Tears came into her eyes. Her voice was barely above a squeak when she said, "No, I would hate her, and . . . you."

Once again I was battling the weather, this time on foot as I made my way to The Cheyenne Robber's home. Perhaps because this trek seemed especially long and because I had to bend into the wind, physically push against it with each step, I noticed that The Cheyenne Robber's home was set a long distance outside the camp. Pausing for breath, it came to me that there was almost an acre between his home and his nearest neighbor's. A fine stand of pines had been maximized, blocking out not only the wind, but a direct view of The Cheyenne Robber's home ground. A nosy neighbor would really have to put him or herself out in order to spy. I was about to knock on the stiffened-hide door flap when out of nowhere the Navaho servant was beside me, staying my hand.

I couldn't believe the nerve of the man. I mean, when I tried to pull my hand free, he actually began grappling with me. A brisk wind got in the middle of our unseemly tussle, spraying us with powdery snow that momentarily blinded us both. I recovered first, pulling open the door as he scrambled behind me. He was coming after me again, but he was too late. I had already rushed inside The Cheyenne Robber's very private home, and the sight that greeted me broke my heart.

White Otter was all alone in the bed, looking, although it grieved me to think it, like an unattractive lump. She turned her face toward me, her expression tragic. Sniffling back tears, she began to haul herself up into a sitting position. I did not think nor did I hesitate. I rushed to her, gathering her up in my arms. She broke down further, her sniffles becoming fullscale sobbing as she buried her face in the frosty fur of my robe. Behind me I heard the slight movements of the Navaho as he shifted his weight from foot to foot. He was watching us, the way we held on to each other. His servant's mind knew that his master would not care for this, but he didn't dare risk putting his hands on me again. Already I had enough against him that I could take him to the council, demanding his death. I heard him go out. He'd made the only decision he could. He was going for The Cheyenne Robber. Which meant my time alone with White Otter was extremely short.

I pushed her back, just enough to see her puckered little face, and spoke quickly to her. "I would have come sooner but I only just heard. You must not let this destroy you. You must think of the child. You must—"

Her hands dug into the folds of my robe and she hung on to me fiercely. "Tay-bodal! He must be stopped before my husband places himself in terrible danger."

"What danger?" I cried. When she didn't answer, I shook her. "White Otter, you must tell me. What danger?"

"I can't! He made me promise."

"White Otter, I can't help him or you if you don't tell me. You must—"

"Let go of my wife!"

Looking back over my shoulder, I saw a thoroughly enraged Cheyenne Robber and his equally angry servant. Standing side by side, they were an impressive sight. From the corner of my eye I detected movement. At first I believed it to be only a shadow, but then the shadow became solid as out from behind The Cheyenne Robber stepped his new wife.

I barely recognized her as the young woman who had clung to me then acted as a lookout outside the death lodge while Owl Man and I inspected the corpse. She was immaculately groomed, wearing a beautiful white dress. Her cheeks held a lovely blush and her eyes were wondrous, made to seem larger than they actually were. Her mouth looked dark, full, and inviting. Somehow, she'd been magically transformed from a sweetly pretty girl into one of the most striking women I had ever seen. Then I remembered: She had learned from a dead woman the art of Mexican face paints.

Although her gaze was steady, her expression was frightened. I tore my stare away from her, looking again at the teary face of White Otter. The comparison between the two women was cruel. The Cheyenne Robber's new wife was slender, well groomed, while White Otter was a corpulent mess. And crying did not become her. Her eyes were swollen, her nose red and snotty, her poor impregnated body so bloated that she could barely stand without help. As difficult as it was for me to accept, I grudgingly understood why a man such as The Cheyenne Robber would give in to White Bear's pushing. And how advantageous for him to have as an excuse that of being honor-bound to help his uncle maintain the peace between the two bands. Instead

of being regarded as a callous husband, his taking of a
second wife so soon in his first marriage would be seen as
a near heroic act. A great personal sacrifice he had made
for the good of his family band.

All I could do was shake my head. The Cheyenne Robber
was throwing away the perfect love that not too long ago
he had been willing to die for. Worse still, as White Otter's
doctor I knew him to be endangering the welfare of his
unborn child. And the cruelty of his bringing this second
wife into the main lodge, flaunting her before his distraught
first wife, left me completely speechless.

Not so The Cheyenne Robber. He was seething, and his
words flew at me like the bullets fired from the new guns
my people called *e-pe-tas* (repeaters).

"What are you doing here? How dare you break into my
home! Is this the way of a friend? I think not. I demand
you leave. Now! And don't bother coming back. The wise
women will tend my wife from this day forward. I never
trusted your skills all that much anyway. It was only at
Otter's insistence that you were her doctor. But now I say
no."

The woman Shade neatly dodged out of the way as The
Cheyenne Robber pushed open the door, tossing his head
in the direction of the opening, indicating that I was to
leave. Ducking through the door hole, I paused to look at
The Cheyenne Robber, wondering if I had ever really
known him at all.

The Navaho followed me out, maintaining a sullen silence as he dogged my steps, making certain I left the
camp. Then, he stood and watched while I trudged on.
When I was a good distance away, I glanced back over my
shoulder. The Navaho was gone.

CHAPTER

6

Entering the sprawling main camp, I was in a deep depression. Then a hand grabbed hold of my arm, and I found myself looking up into Hears The Wolf's stricken face. I was momentarily stunned that anyone could look almost as bad as I felt.

"I've been waiting for you. We need to talk." Then he knocked me off-balance when his features relaxed and he said in an almost cheerful tone, "That's a nice hat. Is it new?"

"Yes."

"Would you like to trade?"

First White Bear, now Hears The Wolf. The appreciation for my wife's accidental skills was becoming tiresome. When I spoke, my tone was a bit more aggressive than I intended it to be.

"No, I wouldn't like to trade. Not with you, not with anyone. This is my hat and I intend to keep it."

Unfazed, Hears The Wolf gazed covetously at the fringes flowing from the patches over the holes where the deer tines had been. The fringes blended in with my hair, framing my face. His fingers lightly toyed with the twisted strands. "You know, you should put little bells on each one of these."

"If I did, then everyone would hear me coming."

"Why would you care? I've never known you to go into battle. You could wear bells all over your body and it wouldn't matter."

He was only teasing, but after the confrontation with The Cheyenne Robber, my pride was severely wounded. Slapping his hand away, I shouted, "Yes, it's true. Everyone knows Tay-bodal is a thoroughly useless person. I should admit this myself and just go ahead and die."

Hears The Wolf's chin snapped back. "And I thought I was having a bad day." He placed an arm around my shoulders. "I think maybe two moody old friends should have some coffee and talk about our troubles."

Hears The Wolf's lodge was twice the size of mine and grandly painted with designs he'd inherited from both family and absent friends. A decorative design on a lodge belonged to the original artist. The design could be shared only prior to the death of the originator, preferably with a family member. If there were no surviving family, then the design could be given to someone deemed worthy of the honor. If no one was chosen or, as it too often happened, death came quickly and unexpectedly before the artist was able to give the wealth of his design away to someone he trusted, then the design died with him. When that person's lodge was burned, his art went with him, forever lost to the people. Hears The Wolf had many designs on his lodge. Five I knew to belong completely to Hears The Wolf. He was more than a great warrior. Hears The Wolf was also a skilled artist, and the five designs he'd created depicted the five most important events in his life. The main design was my favorite and not simply because he'd publicly willed it to me. I loved it because the design explained how he'd received his name.

In the design, a strong man stood lashed between two trees. Large drops of blood falling from the man meant that he was close to death. Off to the side of the dying man there sat a wolf. The Wolf's mouth was open, its tongue out, indicating that The Wolf was talking. The dying man's head was turned toward The Wolf indicating that he was listening. And all of that is true. That's exactly what happened. The Wolf promised my good friend that he would not eat him until he was dead. Grateful, my friend promised The Wolf that if he survived, he would never kill another wolf. My friend was saved, and without a single bite mark. He became known as Hears The Wolf and he never broke the promise he'd made.

The other designs on his lodge are only important because they offer visible proof that he was very respected, deemed to be a worthy person by the artists who were no more in this life. And in my mind, even though I was annoyed with him, he more than deserved the honors bequeathed to him. This man, who was The Cheyenne Robber's first father-in-law, the father of White Otter, was someone I trusted. We had a lot in common, he and I. Hears The Wolf knew what it was to be an outsider, knew the pain of being misjudged. All of this meant that he too had suffered loneliness, and he had suffered much longer and more keenly than I, because for years I hadn't even realized I was lonely. Hears The Wolf had always known, which was why for almost half of his life he had tried hard to die in battle. Happily, his many attempts at suicide failed. Instead, he became rich in glory and plunder. Finally, during this previous summer, he was given the two things missing from his life: his wife and his child. As I had had something of a hand in this, Hears The Wolf became my stalwart friend. Which was an honor to me, for not only was he of the Onde class, he was the most decent man I have ever known.

Case in point, Duck.

The old woman known as Duck was not related to him in any way. His only connection to her was that she had once been his wife's mother-in-law. When the old woman fell on hard times, Hears The Wolf had every right to leave the old woman among the Dapom, living in squalor, fighting for scraps of food. Instead, Hears The Wolf went to that pest hole looking for her, and when he found her, I am told that she fell to her knees and wept against the earth. He picked her up and said, "Woman, I am your son. I have come to take you home."

He expected no thanks, which was good because the fractious Duck was not the type to endure being grateful for more than a day. Within days of being installed in the small lodge he had built just for her, Duck was fussing at him as if she truly were his natural mother. Hears The Wolf bore the many disturbances she brought into his life with a shrug and a grin.

When asked how he could stand the quarrelsome old person, he answered, "I am Duck's son. My mother is a good person. She's just a little bit . . . scrappy."

Duck was being scrappy again. As we neared his lodge, we heard her and Hears The Wolf's wife squabbling. It was a thing they did a lot. There was never any anger in their quarrels, arguing was just their way, a type of communication they learned to enjoy. But the sound of their arguing voices made me happy all over again that neither my wife nor I had living mothers. Carping women might not bother Hears The Wolf, but they would have bothered me. Enormously. Enough to maybe make me run away.

When the two women saw me entering behind Hears The Wolf, they went quiet. Duck scrambled to her feet and tottered over to me. Her approach made me wary. She was old, but she was built like a wall. As a doctor, I had seen the type of damage she was able to inflict when she was truly angry, and her mind, because of past tragedies, had become a chancy thing. In the recent past, when our paths crossed, she would sometimes be genuinely glad to see me, but other times, she would suddenly remember that I had caused her troubles and she would go at me with her scathing tongue while shaking her fist much too close to my nose. The way she was marching determinedly toward me now put me in fear that maybe this was another one of those times. I let go a relieved breath when she stopped and stuck her fists to her ample hips.

"There you are!" she shrieked. "All of this witch talk making everyone so nervous that they keep to their homes, and where have you been? You are no better than that rascal Skywalker!"

"Skywalker is not a rascal."

Duck shook a finger at me. "Yes, he is. He's supposed to be a powerful Owl Doctor. There's a witch running around doing mischief, butchering horses, striking dead young women, and what protection from this does the mighty Skywalker provide his people? None! He goes into hiding, causing the men who should be home protecting their own families to go out looking for him. And you stand there and tell me he isn't a rascal? Red Bird is right about that one. He has called Skywalker a coward, and that is the truth."

Livid, I looked to Hears The Wolf and said to him from behind tightly clenched teeth, "Tell this woman to take her finger out of my face."

Hears The Wolf's voice, deep and resonant, warned, "Mother . . ."

Duck backed off, returned to her place, sitting down in a huff. But for the life of her, she couldn't keep her tongue still. "It's a good thing we have Red Bird. He's providing good charms against all of this bad business and—"

"At what price?" I shouted. Duck's eyes flew wide and her mouth snapped shut. Now that I had her on the defensive, I stepped forward, keeping up the verbal attack. "I personally know that Red Bird isn't as generous as you would have me believe. The truth is, he's selling his magic at very high prices. So high that he demanded my wife's river necklace." Duck gasped, her face draining. "And what," I demanded, "did he charge you? What thing of great value did you hand over in exchange for a few shells on a string?"

Duck did not want to answer, but Hears The Wolf was eyeing her. In a shaky tone she answered, "I-it was nothing truly important. Nothing more valuable than our own safety."

"Mother," Hears The Wolf said. "Tell me what you gave Red Bird."

"My-my blue stone ring."

Hears The Wolf's temper blew. "What! Your ring?" When she lowered her old head, Hears The Wolf slapped his thighs. "I don't believe it. Woman, that was all you had left of your husband. How could you—"

A soft voice interrupted, and all attention turned to Hears The Wolf's wife. Seeing her in clearer light, I was for a second taken aback. I had always known she was remarkably lovely, especially considering that she was entering her middle years. But during our first acquaintance, she had been under considerable stress. Now, happy at last, she reminded me of a spring rose that had come into full bloom.

She did not look old enough to be the mother of a grown-up daughter. She most certainly did not look old enough to be an expectant grandmother. Within the last months I had known this woman by different names. The last name, given to her by her new husband, suited her best.

Beloved.

"Forgive us, Husband," she said in a voice so soft, so tender, that Hears The Wolf beamed. "I too am guilty of overtrading with Red Bird." Hears The Wolf's smile withered. "We, your women," she continued repentantly, "are afraid. When that girl fell dead, we became terrified. I ask your patience with us if we seem foolish to you. But you brought Tay-bodal here on account of our daughter, and that's what we should talk about."

Hears The Wolf sighed heavily and turned to face me. I saw the raw emotions beginning in his eyes. "My daughter," he said simply, "is in misery. The Cheyenne Robber promised on his very life he would never make my daughter unhappy. He's broken that promise. I think maybe I'm going to have to fight him."

No one knew more than I just how unhappy White Otter was, but her father killing her husband would not dry her tears. Putting my hands up in surrender, I said wearily, "Before you load the gun, may I please have the coffee you offered?"

Hears The Wolf was a wealthy man and lived in unrepentant luxury. When I first met him, like a miser he kept all of his valuables in his main lodge. To visit him meant that one was required to stumble through a lodge that was more a treasure trove than a home. Now that he had a wife, only the best things were kept in the main lodge. This lack of clutter made the interior much roomier, but knowing that Hears The Wolf was not the sort of man to throw anything away, I was more than confidant that the bulk of his possessions were stored in the three smaller tepees behind his home. Moving to where he indicated, I sat down on good rugs. While Hears The Wolf settled himself, the two women prepared the refreshments. Enjoying the comfort of this happy home, I glanced around at the many valuables, which were either placed in areas best able to show them off or hanging directly over my head. A hanging thing, just around the kitchen area, caught my eye. A bundle of dried tobacco leaves. I was just sitting and staring at the bundle, thinking about how marriage seemed to be agreeing with Hears The Wolf, but in my mind's eye a gloved hand rapidly and expertly rolled tobacco leaves into a cigar.

A hand touched my shoulder and Duck looked at me curiously as she handed me a bowl of hot coffee laced with honey and a large slice of bread made from dried and ground corn. The food was delicious. It didn't fill me up, but it nicely dulled the edge of hunger. After the light meal, Hears The Wolf made the fire brighter and then prepared a small clay pipe. He and I shared the pipe as we settled comfortably, preparing ourselves for serious talk. Beloved stayed by her husband's side, but Duck retreated to the corner. By the light of a gourd lamp she pretended to concentrate on her sewing, but I knew that her ears were attuned to everything being said.

"All I know," Beloved said with a breathy sigh, "is what my daughter told me. She came to me, wanting to tell me herself before I heard it elsewhere. She said her husband was taking another wife, and this was all right with her. She didn't look as if it were all right. She looked to me as if her heart had just been crushed under his heel. Her coming to talk to me did not ease my mind. If anything, her visit upset me more than the gossip I'd heard."

"And what gossip was that?" I asked.

Beloved lowered her head. "I've heard whispers that The

Cheyenne Robber and the woman known as Shade have been secret lovers.'' She looked up quickly, her brimming eyes searching mine. ''I didn't believe the talk. With a man like The Cheyenne Robber, there are always rumors linking him with women. This was the very thing I warned my daughter of before she married him. I told her that if she was ever to know peace of mind, she would have to trust her husband. But when she came to me, the sight of her wrenched my heart. I believe now that the talk was true. And now he's married Shade, which tells me that her father found out. That would explain why The Cheyenne Robber married her so quickly. He had to or there would have been a blood feud between the two bands.''

Before I could respond, Hears The Wolf's angry face filled my line of vision. ''I went to talk to him, but he wouldn't see me. That servant of his wouldn't let me pass, not even when I threatened him. There's something wrong with that one. I don't think he's right in the head. Anyway, I made a big racket, and finally, The Cheyenne Robber came out. But not out of his main lodge. He came out of one of the smaller ones, which let me know that he was in there with that new wife of his. That he was enjoying her while keeping my daughter a prisoner in her own home and under guard by that accursed Navaho.''

''Did you have words with The Cheyenne Robber?''

''Yes, I did,'' Hears The Wolf fumed. ''I had several words with him, none of them pleasant. He ordered me out of his camp. He said I couldn't come back again until I was invited, and that this restriction also applied to my wife. That's when I started yelling for my daughter to come out, begging her to come home with me.''

''And what did she answer?''

''Nothing. Not a word.''

''You heard no sound at all from the main lodge?''

A look of irritation passed over Hears The Wolf's normally patient face. "No."

I ignored the expression as I thought for a moment. Then I asked what seemed to Hears The Wolf an irrelevant question. "Where was the Navaho?"

Impatiently, Hears The Wolf slapped his knees and barked, "I told you that part already. He was in front of the doorway."

"Of the main lodge?"

"Yes!" Then Hears The Wolf said each word carefully, as if speaking to a slow-witted child. "I tell you again, that impossible servant and my son-in-law are keeping my daughter prisoner in her own home. What I want you to do is help me get her out of there."

Circumstances saved me from making a rash promise. Just as I was about to open my mouth, a great commotion began outside. I jumped to my feet and Hears The Wolf scrambled to his. I heard him warning his women to stay put as I pushed open the doorway cover and bolted out. Before I drew another breath, Hears The Wolf was beside me. We saw streams of people running in the direction of White Bear's lodge. Hears The Wolf and I joined the flight.

In the center of the village a large crowd had formed. Because of Hears The Wolf's high status, milling people parted, giving way as he and I moved to the front. In the center of this loosely formed circle, White Bear stood pulling on his lower lip while listening to two messengers from another camp. Hears The Wolf and I made it to the front just in time to hear the messengers finish their report.

White Bear's hand came away from his face and he placed both hands on his hips. "How bad is he?"

"Near death," one messenger gloomily reported.

It felt as if a cold hand had grabbed my heart. I knew

they were talking about Skywalker. It was then that I lost
the ability to think clearly. Instead of waiting for White
Bear to notice me and call me forward, I ran to him. White
Bear turned his head, looking down at me. His features
were taut. He was too overwrought by the news to be bothered by my flagrant breech of his chiefly authority.

"Tay-bodal," he rasped, "will . . . you ride with us?"

I placed a hand on his shoulder. "You don't have to
ask."

We left within minutes, riding flat out, pushing the horses
brutally over ground that was barely fit to travel. To my
amazement, we were riding in the opposite direction of the
area that had been so methodically searched, the area Skywalker had last been seen before his disappearance. It had
occurred to none of us that he would double back on himself, purposely fooling any and all certain to come looking
for him. Instead, we had done exactly what he'd wanted us
to do—searched in one direction while he went off in another. From the hard looks on the faces of the riders, men
noted as expert trackers, they were lashing themselves harder than they physically lashed their horses. As for myself,
I was too caught up with my worry for Skywalker to admit
that Owl Man had been right. The lost one had turned up,
all by himself. But, near death.

When we entered Sitting Bear's camp, we were escorted
to his lodge. At the sight of Skywalker lying in bed, the
only visible part of him a gaunt blue face, I lost control.
Before anyone could stop me, I ran to the bed, and there,
on my knees, I grasped the front of the warm sleeping shirt
Skywalker was dressed in, pulling him up, shaking him like
a toy and screaming at him.

"How could you do this to yourself! How could you?"

White Bear was there, trying to pry my hands loose as

Skywalker opened his eyes. His answer to my unseemly tirade was inside a brittle wheeze. "I'm not feeling well . . . my best friend. Scold me . . . later." With lips that were cracked and blistered, he managed a slight smile. Coming back to my senses, I assisted White Bear as together we laid him back down. He wheezed again, the effort of drawing a breath painful.

"Everything is backward, Tay-bodal. It's all . . . backward." He closed his eyes.

Sitting Bear, leader of the Ten Bravest, magnanimously vacated his personal lodge. On his instruction, the men, even White Bear, left me alone to tend to Skywalker. I did not have my supplies with me, but Sitting Bear's wives were prompt to bring anything I requested. I was happy to notice that before going off into extreme weather for an extended period that he had applied tallow to his face, hands and feet. But I knew too that he'd done so most probably out of habit, a thing we have all learned from infancy, more than as an objective to his personal comfort. Even with the protection of tallow, frost burns littered his body. His feet and hands were bad, but his face had suffered the most damage. One of the women brought a jar of sappine resin and I applied it to the burns, using it as a plaster.

As for the rest of him, he was so dried up that his skin felt like stiff leather. Because of his wont for fasting during whatever rituals he practiced, the frigid weather, even in such a short time, had taken a heavy toll. Even in good weather Skywalker barely had a drop of fat on him. The cold had quickly burned that pitiful amount away, leaving his body defenseless. I could plainly see every one of his bones as well as the joints holding them together.

Sitting Bear's wives were coming in and out, hurrying each time I barked a new request. Those women were the

best nurses I ever knew. They didn't complain or send me
wounded looks when I spoke too harshly. They did what
needed to be done, and I have no idea how I would have
managed without them. They brewed up the tea just as I
directed, and when it was ready, I began pouring it down
Skywalker's skinny throat. What I gave him was a special
concoction of mine. I called it tea, but it isn't an enjoyable
tea. It is made from several herbs and a large dose of salt.
It's dreadful tasting really, but Skywalker couldn't taste, so
flavor wasn't a concern. The importance of this tea, why I
made him swallow so much of it, is that its properties restore balance to the body.

Normally I used this tea for sunstroke patients. Skywalker wasn't sunstroke, but advanced dehydration is the
same no matter how it's caused. Simply giving plain water
to someone in this critical condition never works. The water
just passes on through without benefit. But salt! Salt causes
the liquid to hesitate long enough for the body to receive
the nourishment of the herbs boiled into the tea. In the
patients I've treated, once they've stopped gagging and
vomiting enough to hold the tea inside, they almost immediately began to feel well, their dried-up bodies plumping up again. If ever there was a body that needed plumping
up, it was Skywalker's. He began to recover enough to
argue, and that being the best sign he could give me, I
poured more tea into him.

I have no idea how much time had passed when the
women eventually pulled me away, ordered me to sit and
rest. Every muscle in my body felt weak and trembly as I
watched the women clean Skywalker, change his clothing
and bedding, settle him comfortably. As the women began
to exit, the oldest one paused, tapping me lightly on the
head. When I looked up, she smiled down at me.

"You are a good doctor. If any man can save him, that

man is you. But you can't save anyone if you don't rest. As a mother of sons I'm telling you this. Get some sleep."

She didn't move. She waited until I lay down. Then she covered me up, ran a hand tenderly across my forehead, and left. I lay for a long time just watching him. He was breathing, but not enough to raise the covering blankets. Outside the lodge the hand of darkness was crossing the face of the earth, ending the day. People of Sitting Bear's camp had taken refuge in their lodges and, out of respect for the man they believed to be dying, kept themselves quiet. Watching Skywalker through the flames of the fire, my eyes grew heavier and heavier. Before I knew it, I was asleep.

It wasn't a heavy sleep, and I kept drifting in and out. Finally, feeling uncomfortably hot, I opened my eyes and watched the fire shadows swaying along the walls, touching the many war trophies of a great war chief.

Sitting Bear was a warrior's warrior. Being a chief of the Ten Bravest meant that, during battle, he wore a sash long enough to cross one shoulder and flow down to the ground. The sash was not for decoration. When he took his place on the battlefield, he shot an arrow through the tail end of the sash, literally pinning him in place. This proved to the enemy that he was not a man who would run away. He was fully prepared to fight to the death just where he stood. Sitting Bear was an old man with numerous arrow holes in the end of his sash, the miraculous thing being that he was still alive to recount the battles each hole represented.

From those battles came the relics hanging on the walls of his lodge. He was proudest of the battle axes and lances he'd taken from the Osage, but he also had a varied collection of guns. One, an old musket, had once belonged to an ancient Metal Head (Spaniard). Beside the musket was a shiny silver helmet once worn most probably by the long-ago owner of the musket.

These were interesting things that I didn't mind staring at as I listened to Skywalker's steady breathing. It was the other things I didn't want to look at. Still, I couldn't stop my eyes from sliding in the direction of the masks collected during raids against the Apaches and the Pueblos. The masks were made of wood and painted to depict foreign gods and spirits. In the firelight, the holes cut into the masks for human eyes to look out of seemed darkly alive, the menacing stares boring through me. The masks made my flesh creep, especially as Sitting Bear had framed each mask with human hair, scalps he'd taken with his own knife.

Desperately, I tried to think of something else. In doing so, I listened to the sounds of dry leaves scurrying before a driving breeze. This seemed such a pleasant sound, and I enjoyed it, until I realized that everything beyond the lodge's walls was completely still. That there was no wind, and because of the snow-covered ground, there couldn't be any dry leaves to run before it. I lay there listening, feeling prickles of fear and the hairs beginning to rise up on the back of my neck. I was certain now that the sounds were actually whispers, and the most chilling realization of all was that the whispering was inside the lodge with us. Skywalker's head rolled to the side. He opened his eyes and looked directly at me.

"Cedar," he rasped. With great effort he raised his hand and pointed toward the fire.

Knowing now what he wanted, I scrambled out of the bed. The whispering continued, seeming to become more frantic. Feeling just as frantic, I tore open packed parcels belonging to Sitting Bear. After a desperate search, I found what no person of Kiowa blood could do without—a good supply of cedar chips. Cedar is good for all manner of things, but mostly, for purification. Once I found Sitting Bear's supply, I carried the entire storage box to the fire and dumped all of the chips into the flames.

All at once a fragrant aroma, clean and pleasing, filled the lodge, and the fire became unnaturally bright. I felt an enormous sense of relief, every trace of fear leaving me. And as I stood there watching the curling chips glowing red, I felt foolish. Foolish for having been so afraid of small noises.

I looked back over my shoulder. Skywalker's eyes were still open, his features relaxed. I took the empty box back to where I'd found it, then went to his bedside, crouching down behind my legs, my arms on my knees as I studied him.

"That's what you were doing," I said softly. "You were freeing the dead. And endangering your own life to do it."

Skywalker closed his eyes. "So many," he murmured. "And all of them . . . so frightened." His eyes fluttered open, his gaze fixing on mine. "Does that surprise you?" His poor lips tried to bend in a smile. "That the dead can be afraid? Well, it's true. When a dead person can't accept being dead, he becomes afraid. And stuck. He can't go forward to his new existence. Not without help." Again, he tried to smile. "There are so many . . . here. Helping them has been . . . draining." His cold hand sought mine and I held it. "I'm sorry I worried you." Using the last of his strength, he said slowly, "Get more cedar. Keep it burning with the fire. It's the only thing that will keep them out while I try to regain my strength."

I ran out of the lodge, hysterically beating on every door until the occupants answered, giving me all the cedar belonging to their household. I kept the fire in Sitting Bear's lodge burning cedar throughout the night, the cloying fragrance at times becoming too much for my senses.

Eventually, through the smoke hole, I saw the gray light of dawn. Only then did I relax my vigil, lying down. I must have fainted, because the next thing I knew, many hands were shaking me awake. With a sharp gasp, I sat up so quickly that the men surrounding me had to jump back to avoid our knocking heads. My eyes were open and I was sitting up, but my mind was patchy, dream-streaked. Then I remembered with awful clarity the thing that had whispered in the night.

The living men now around me had no more patience or time to spare. In the seconds it took to exhale, White Bear's face came close to mine and he shouted for me to wake up completely. His broad face was such a welcome sight I wanted to kiss him. But what he said shoved any such notion right out of my head.

"We just got word. Your wife is in trouble."

The day was half gone. I used only the time necessary, before the rush for home, to do the annoyingly time-consuming requirements of the human condition: relieving a swollen bladder, washing myself, and bolting down enough food for survival. White Bear stayed with me, talking nonstop.

"First I was glad when the messenger rode in, reporting that the witch had been rooted out. Then, when he said the name of the witch, I went a little crazy."

Pulling on my winter robe, I shouted, "He said Crying Wind's name?"

"That's right."

"Who accuses her?"

"Red Bird."

"How dare he—"

White Bear raised a silencing hand. "He claims he has proof."

"What proof?" I scoffed.

"The worst kind. A baby became deathly ill just after Crying Wind is said to have touched it."

"That isn't proof," I cried.

"It is to people who have become so afraid of Red Bird's Dark Way talk that they're half out of their minds."

"And you allowed him to talk up their fear."

White Bear raised his mighty arms toward the sky. "I did not! I just didn't know how to shut him up. If you want to blame anyone, blame yourself. If you had been a little faster in finding out who killed The Cheyenne Robber's horses and who killed that poor little woman, then my cousin, your wife, would not be in trouble."

"I've been doing my best."

"No, you haven't." His hands on his hips, he leaned forward, speaking forcefully. "You've been running all over the place with that lump-skull Little War. And don't think I don't know about your little errand to retrieve your wife's necklace, or that you almost froze to death because of it. You could have come to me about that stupid necklace, but, oh, no! You always have to be Crying Wind's hero. Well, while you've been busy being her hero, you've been failing miserably at being mine."

"Sometimes," I fumed, "I wish I could be you."

At first he was startled, then he was pleased, a grin spreading across his face. "I know. It's because I'm so good-looking and powerful."

"No. It's because it must be such a comfort to be able to blame everyone but yourself."

His lips pursed as he thought for a second. "Yes, as a matter of fact, it is. And isn't it just too bad for you that you'll never be me."

After hastily leaving instructions with Sitting Bear's wives on how to brew the tea and care for Skywalker, I left with White Bear, riding just as hard as we could over thawing and boggy ground. We were filthy with mud by the time we arrived, but neither of us cared. What struck me hard was that my home camp looked dejected. Because of the warming shift in the weather, our village suddenly looked as if it had been set up on swampland. Then there was the despondency of the people themselves. They stood silently, all of them grim, even the youngest children. I spotted my child standing by the side of White Bear's eighth wife. Her toddler baby was perched on one hip while on the other side my son huddled, holding her hand. He brightened only slightly as I dismounted and rushed to him. He let go of her hand, raising his little arms up to me. Once I had him, I held him protectively, telling him over and over that everything was going to be all right.

While I was doing this, Red Bird was stating his case, in full voice, to an incensed White Bear. While Red Bird puffed himself up, I turned to the woman who had been so kind to my child.

"Where is my wife?"

"She's in the Grandmother's lodge. She ran there after Red Bird accused her."

Our religion is complex. At the crux is the belief in the Ten Grandmothers. Tal-lee was the supernatural child born from the union of the sun and a human woman. When Tal-lee became a man, he turned himself into ten portions of powerful medicine, which have since become known as the Ten Grandmothers. Each Grandmother has a private lodge. Anyone who feels threatened is permitted to take refuge in a Grandmother's lodge. The persecutor, in this instance Red Bird, is not allowed to follow. The person needing sanctuary can be certain of being fed and well looked after by the married couple assigned as the keepers of the Grand-mother. I was relieved that my wife had both the time and the presence of mind to run to the Grandmother, but that very fact meant she'd felt herself to be in physical danger. Looking back over my shoulder, my face holding hard the expression of pure loathing, I began to listen to Red Bird.

"I appreciate how upset you are," Red Bird said to White Bear. He placed a hand on White Bear's arm in an attempt to be comforting.

It gave me enormous pleasure when White Bear shrugged him off. White Bear's arms crossed his chest as he said, in a tone conveying contempt, "You cannot even *begin* to appreciate how upset I am. Crying Wind is my favorite female cousin. I think so much of her that I wouldn't allow her to remarry until I found a man equal to her."

Compliments from White Bear were few and slow in the offing. I realized he couldn't be thinking clearly to compliment me so publicly, but it made me feel good anyway. My son pulled back from my shoulder, studying my face as if seeing something there he hadn't noticed before. Then his little arms went tightly around my neck and he rested his head in the curve of my neck. I rubbed his back and rocked my body from foot to foot as I again gave my attention to the ignoble Red Bird.

"I swear to you, I would never have made the charge if she hadn't pushed me into it."

White Bear craned his head, studying the man before him the way a hawk studies prey before tearing into it. "Why does this sound to me as if you have been watching her?"

Red Bird paled. "I—I have suspected her all along. She-she's a strong-willed woman, and because of her friendship with Skywalker and her marriage to the herbalist, Tay-bodal, she has access to a great deal of power."

"While this is all true," White Bear sneered, "the men you speak of have never done harm. They use their gifts only for good. For the benefit of all. Why would a woman, admittedly a woman of strong opinions, but a genuinely good woman, debase the powers of a friend and her husband?"

Even from where I stood, I heard Red Bird swallow. "For that, I have no answer."

A soft chuckle reached my ear and I turned my head in the direction of the sound. Owl Man was beaming, thoroughly enjoying himself.

"What man," Red Bird continued, "understands the mind of a woman? They are perverse creatures. All I know is that I perceived a type of danger flowing from her. I didn't understand it, but I knew it was there. I made special charms to keep this danger locked up inside her, but her own husband thwarted my attempt. He brought the amulets to me and then threw them at my feet. Again I tried to warn him, but he wouldn't listen. There was nothing more I could do but wait and watch. Unfortunately, she did exactly as I feared. She used the powers she stole from Skywalker and Tay-bodal and struck again. This time, her victim was an innocent baby. In good conscience, I could no longer keep silent. I'm afraid the woman has proven herself guilty. If she weren't, why would she run away? Why hasn't she faced me with the truth?"

That was the final rip in the thin cloak of patience. Carrying my son, I stomped forward and accused this man to his face.

"She couldn't face you because you are a bully, using what power you supposedly have to incite a riot. You are a person beneath all contempt. Everything you have said is nothing more than a string of half-truths."

I looked around boldly, envisioning the crowd to be with

me on this issue. But faces turned away, heads lowered. I looked quickly at White Bear, expecting more from him than he seemed willing to give. Amazement stole my breath away. I hugged my son more tightly against me as blood throbbed in my ears.

My wife was always a lover of what she called juicy gossip. Most women are, I think, believing gossip to be harmless. It isn't. As a longtime student of human nature, I knew in my heart that people listened to gossiping tongues more than they listened to that small voice of reason dwelling inside all of us. The very fact that no one could look me in the eye let me know that gossip and Red Bird's lunacies were working together to condemn my wife. Once again, I was relieved she'd had the wit to run for safety.

Sensing his success, Red Bird began puffing himself up again, launching a new verbal attack against a defenseless woman. I looked down at my muddy shoes and leggings. The filth served to remind me that verbal mud clings best to the last one to throw it. Trading more public insults with Red Bird would do my wife more harm than good. Hefting my son on my hip, I turned and walked away. White Bear called after me, but with my head high, I kept walking. Had I looked back, I would have been gladdened by the sight of others following my example. White Bear's youngest wife, the one who had been kind enough to care for my son, was the first to drift away. Within minutes, White Bear's other wives followed suit. After them, still more women began to leave. Of course I wondered about the tremor that had crept into Red Bird's voice. Wondered too why it had increased in volume. He was frantically trying to call back the women.

The last voice I heard belonged to White Bear. With all of the considerable lung power available to him, he called for an immediate council of chiefs.

CHAPTER
7

The old couple responsible for the safekeeping of the Grandmother stood outside the little lodge. They were both quite old, both of them white haired and round shouldered. I knew them to be thoroughly good people, entirely the sort who should be trusted with the care of one of our most sacred icons. Relief filled their expressions as they spotted my approach. The woman, known as Medicine Woman, the name she'd taken upon assuming the considerable responsibility of guardianship of one of the Grandmothers, opened her arms to me and my little son. After giving me a hug, she took Favorite Son from my arms.

"How is she?" I asked.

Patting my son's back and bouncing him in her arms, Medicine Woman snapped at me. "How would you expect her to be? She's upset and rightly so. I've never heard of such foolishness in my life. A good and decent woman having to take refuge is unthinkable. Normally we get the men who have proven to be scoundrels or the women who've been caught with men they're not married to. But a woman like Crying Wind—"

"We've done our best to make her comfortable," the old man, known as Deer Trail, quickly said. "We've brought her food, but I don't think she ate it."

"Who can eat when they're crying?" Medicine Woman asked crisply. "I know I can't." She began pushing me. "You get in there and cheer her up. She needs to know that someone loves her and believes in her."

I needed no more pushing. As I opened the door of the small lodge, the dim light from outside touched her. Crying Wind flinched and retreated, trying to hide. From under the cover of blankets a strained and teary face timidly regarded me. This woman was not the wife I adored. My wife did not look pinched and afraid. My wife was a woman of spirit. But this, this pitiful sight, was what Red Bird's ambitions had caused her to become. In those seconds, I experienced such a stab of hatred for Red Bird that it sent me reeling. I wanted to kill him, tear him apart. But before I could do that, I had to comfort the woman I loved, let her know that no matter what, I was still her husband.

She was barely holding herself together. As I softly spoke her name, she lost the last ragged edge of control. Hiding her face in her hands, she began to weep. Rushing to her, I took her in my arms and just held her as she cried it out. Meanwhile, Deer Trail came in, bringing a container of hot tea and two bowls. I mouthed a thank-you and he grunted. He stayed just long enough to replenish the dwindling fire. Then we were alone again, the tea growing cold as Crying Wind continued to weep against my chest. I became impatient. Impatient because I badly wanted the tea before it turned to ice and because I didn't care at all for this weepy version of my wife. I wanted the real woman returned to me, and this flood of emotion was getting us nowhere.

When I moved away, her clawing hands pulled at my

robe and I spoke harshly. "I'm just getting the tea! I'm not leaving you."

She slumped against the backrest, her round, teary eyes studying me with a new attentiveness. I came back, thrusting the filled bowl toward her. She looked from it to me with a tight-lipped expression.

"Take it," I said forcefully.

In a tone that was low, reluctant, she said, "I don't deserve . . . kindness."

Her saying that made me angry. "Yes, you do. Stop feeling so sorry for yourself. You didn't do anything wrong."

She became hysterical. "Yes, I did! It's on account of me that a baby is sick. I made it sick. But I swear, I didn't do it on purpose! I was only trying to help."

Now we were getting somewhere. "Tell me exactly what you did."

Hope glimmered in her eyes. "So you can undo the damage? Make that baby well again?"

"Yes. Take the tea."

She obeyed, eagerly drinking the contents. Once we were both refreshed, I saw both in her face and her quick movements as she handed me back the bowl a flicker of the real Crying Wind. I moved in to sit beside her again, wrapping a protective arm around her.

"All right," I said firmly. "Begin the telling and, please, leave nothing out."

Not one tear or quiver was in her tone as she began at the absolute beginning. Most of what she said was the history of the baby's parents, who their parents were and their parents before them. When she launched herself into the clans and bands these people came from, I had to force myself not to slump into utter boredom, but I dared not interrupt her. Finally, she came to the part that interested me completely.

"They are so young, too young really, and this is their first child. On account of this, they panic over everything the baby does. Anyway, early this morning, so early that the sun wasn't even up, they came to our door, both of them distraught and holding the baby in their arms. They wanted you but you weren't home. I told them I would get word to you, but that didn't suit them. They said the baby had been crying all night and they were certain it was going to die." Crying Wind threw up her hands. "Well, as a mother I certainly knew that wasn't true. It takes a lot to kill a baby and—" She stopped, a trembling hand coming to her mouth as she looked up at me with her brimming and oddly owl-like eyes.

"You didn't mean what you just said," I said softly. "It was just a joke slipping out. The type of joke you're known to make in normal circumstances. And any day but today, it would be funny."

She lowered her eyes, smiled faintly. Briefly, we were both quiet.

"They were so insistent," she said. "Certain that I could do something. That baby was only cutting teeth, but they wouldn't listen to me. They were certain it was crying because of something very serious. I could tell the only thing the three of them needed was some sleep. And, I wanted to get rid of them. They were in my way, ruining my morning, and Favorite Son was being overly noisy in the bargain. When I couldn't stand it any longer, I went to your lodge." She looked at me accusingly. "It's a mess in there. I had to clean up before I could find anything. And the whole time I was doing that, the husband stood outside, throwing a tantrum because the baby was crying again, and he said his wife was too distraught to even nurse it."

"What were you looking for, in my lodge?"

"Some of the stuff I've known you to give Skywalker when he can't sleep."

"What!"

She twisted in my arms. "Well, it always helps him."

"Of course it does," I shouted, "but he's not a baby."

"Well, I only took a pinch of it."

My heart banging in my chest, I asked in a flat tone, "How did you give it to the baby?"

"Just the way I've seen you prepare it for Skywalker. I made a tea and gave a little bit in a spoon. In no time at all, the baby was asleep and both parents seemed relieved. They took the baby home, and within no time at all, men, led by Red Bird, appeared at my door and accused me of putting a curse on the baby. They said it was limp and lifeless and no one could wake it up.

"I panicked. I said I would send for you, but Red Bird said it was too late, that my evil had found me out. People began to gather and listen to what Red Bird had to say. I couldn't outshout him. I tried and tried, but he wouldn't let me speak. Then people began shaking their fists, threatening me with terrible abuse. Someone threw a rock that just missed my head. I had just enough time to tell Favorite Son to hide before I started to run."

She shuddered, sobs coming back into her voice. "I ran and ran, and all of those people were chasing me. As I ran past homes, I heard the men behind me yelling, 'We've found the witch! We've found the witch!' People in the homes I passed came out and joined the chase. I had no idea where I was going. Most probably I would still be running if I hadn't fallen down. Hands grabbed onto my wrists, and when I looked up, I was looking in the face of Deer Trail. I started to struggle but he told me not to fight him. He helped me to my feet and into this lodge. It took me several moments to realize just where I was, and all the time I was in here and Deer Trail held me, that crowd outside was yelling for him to bring me out. They went quiet and I heard Medicine Woman saying that I was under the Grandmother's protection and only the council of chiefs could decide what was to be done about me . . .''

As her words trailed off, I held her tightly, envisioning the howling mob, led by Red Bird, chasing after my wife. Again, I wanted to kill him. As slowly and as painfully as possible. Then, with a jolt, I remembered White Bear's voice calling for the council of chiefs. That meant my wife's fate was being decided at this very moment. If I was to save her, I had no time to spare. Kissing her quickly, I ordered her to get some sleep and moved to go.

"Don't leave me!" she begged.

"My little love," I said in a thick voice, "I must. But I promise, by this time tomorrow, you will be safe in your own home where you belong. With all of your might, trust that I love you. And trust me.''

Stepping outside, I bumped into Little War and my wife's silent cousin, Elk Cry. Little War's marred features were set in a deep scowl. Elk Cry was agitated, his hands swiftly signing the words his crippling stutter would not allow him to speak. Displaying no patience for the time-consuming hand signs, Little War took the younger man's hands in his and spoke to me directly.

"We've been sent by White Bear. He said to tell you that he will stall the council as long as possible, maybe even all night, but that's all the time he can give you. Feelings are high. He says the chiefs want someone to blame in order to bring the people relief from their fears. Unfortunately, your wife is too handy. I'm afraid, although White Bear didn't say it, that her fate has already been decided.

If they don't come for her tonight, they will come for her tomorrow. I'm sorry my friend. I wish I brought you better news."

All I could do was nod. In a voice filled with torment, I said, "I would like to visit the home of the stricken baby."

"That isn't possible," Little War said bitterly. "The Buffalo Doctors are there and they would kill you on sight if you turned up. My good advice is this: Stay just as far away from those grieving parents as you can. It would do Crying Wind no good if that young father attacked and killed you."

It was good advice. My going there would only make things worse. I could only hope that the medicine Crying Wind had given that baby hadn't been so much as to maintain a prolonged sleep. The minute that baby woke up, the Buffalo Doctors would take credit for having cured a drugged child, but that didn't bother me. What bothered me was that the drug might not wear off in time for the child's recovery to save my wife. I couldn't take the chance of waiting. I had to find the supposed true witch before my wife was blamed for every evil these fearful and foolish people could think up.

Backward. That's what Skywalker had said. Everything is backward. Once again I mentally cursed him for being so cryptic. But, all right, I would begin all over again, working backward.

"I would like to speak to He Goes's first wife."

Little War's eyebrow rose. "You can't."

"Why not?"

Little War began to sputter, and because he couldn't get the words out, Elk Cry signed for him: "He Goes is a chief. He is with the council. You can't go in there and ask his permission to speak to his wife."

"Fine," I scoffed. "Then I'll speak to her without his permission."

"But he will be greatly offended!" Little War cried.

"I see," I jeered. "But his sitting in judgment of my wife, deciding if she will live or die, that isn't offensive?"

Both Little War and Elk Cry were at a loss for words.

"Neither of you have to come with me."

"But we will," Elk Cry signed. "You will need good guards. Speaking for myself, I am one of the best guards. I notice everything."

I placed a hand of gratitude on his narrow shoulder. "I know you do."

Elk Cry kept me company while we waited for Little War to return with three horses. While we waited, Elk Cry tried to keep my mind occupied. His swift hands spoke as eloquently as any unimpaired tongue.

"Before the death of his second wife, odd things had been going on over in He Goes's camp." I lifted a brow, indicting my interest, and Elk Cry's deft hands continued. "People were said to be having a hard time sleeping because of the shadows."

"Shadows?"

Elk Cry nodded rapidly, his hands moving faster, almost too fast. "Late at night, and caused by the light of outside fires, shadows moved against lodge walls. At first everyone thought it was funny. Night crawlers, they said."

Night crawlers, a term used for lovers trying to be discreet.

"Then," Elk Cry continued, "two camp dogs died and the people of He Goes's band became afraid. A day later, He Goes's youngest wife died."

"What about the shadows? Have the people seen them again?"

"No. If they had, I would have heard. Just as I've heard

that now the people of that band are convinced that the shadows had been made by the witch looking for someone to kill. Once He Goes's wife died, they say the witch moved on to another camp. Ours.'' This last part embarrassed him and his hands stopped. They didn't move again during the final moments we waited for Little War.

To our mutual relief, the wait wasn't long. Just as we were mounting up, Medicine Woman and Deer Trail came walking toward us, their arms loaded. With a curt nod, Deer Trail acknowledged me and kept walking to the Grandmother's lodge. He stooped and entered while his wife paused to look up and speak to me.

"We're bringing her more blankets and hot food."

"I appreciate your kindness."

She made a sound in the back of her throat. "We only do what the Grandmother requires whenever some poor soul comes to her for shelter. If you truly want to show your gratitude, find a way for your little wife to return to her own home without fear of further threat."

"I will . . . Mother. But still, I thank you."

She lifted her shoulders in a dismissive shrug and walked away. I turned the horse's head and rode off, Little War and Elk Cry following.

He Goes's camp looked deserted. At first I was horrified, afraid that the very woman I was in such a hurry to find was back in the camp I'd just left. This fear was not translated to Little War. He dismounted and ran to the lodge I knew belonged to He Goes. Before he even announced himself, He Goes's widowed sister, carrying the small black pot I'd seen her use while making such fine cigars, stepped out. She was genuinely glad to see Little War, and again I wondered if there wasn't more than a bit of feeling beginning between those two. Theirs was a lengthy exchange.

Impatience filled me, and everything inside me clenched. I was about to rudely shout for Little War to flirt later when the woman pointed off into the distance and Little War came running back, jumping onto his horse.

He spoke rapidly as he adjusted himself in the saddle and took up the reins. "She said the woman we seek, her sister-in-law known as Smiling Woman, moved her lodge to the far side of the camp. She said that to her knowledge, Smiling Woman was at home, but whether she would receive us without her husband's knowledge or permission was something she could not promise. She said Smiling Woman can be . . . difficult. Maybe she will talk to us, maybe she won't."

I lifted a hand in silent thanks, and the woman smiled her sweet-faced smile and waved to me. As we were riding off, I glanced back. She waved again, then went on with her duties, pouring out the contents of the pot into a shallow dug hole.

The lodge belonging to Smiling Woman was a good distance away, almost a quarter of a mile outside He Goes's camp. This was unusual, even for an estranged wife, a woman still dependent on her husband's provision and protection. The second thing I noticed was the many horse tracks around her very recent homesite. The woman herself was outside, beating dust out of rugs that were hung over a line of rope tied between two trees. When she heard our approach, she turned and watched us until we came to a stop.

Like her daughter, she was reed thin, her face birdlike. And there was irony in her name, for the woman glaring at us didn't seem someone easily given to smiling. She threw down the rug-beating stick and with forceful strides came toward us. Her impressively decorated buckskin dress was heavily fringed from the shoulders and hem. With each step the long fringing swayed in counterpoint like the movements of a turbulent river. The hair that was tied behind her was streaked with gray. No lines were on her face. None whatsoever. Which told me that this was a woman of great self-control. She was not one to go about displaying her feelings for all to read in her expression. I couldn't help recalling Little War's view of the dead woman's wedding day, how this woman had publicly mourned, pouring ashes on her head as she begged her husband to reconsider. Only a strong love or strong hurt would prompt a woman like the one walking toward me into such a public display. She stopped less than a yard from where we sat on our horses. Her booted feet planted firmly apart, she folded her arms under her slight bosom and stared blankly at us.

In a voice almost as dry as the desert summer wind, she said, "What do you want here?"

"I am called Tay-bodal. I have come to talk to the woman known as Smiling Woman."

She continued to look at me steadily.

I hastened to continue. "I can only beg your pardon for coming to speak to you without your honorable husband's knowledge or permission—"

She raised a hand. "You're certain he doesn't know?"

"Yes, lady, and I ask you—"

She turned, began walking away. Looking back over her shoulder, she said, "We better talk quick. He will find out."

I was deeply at odds about sitting in a strange woman's private lodge without her husband's consent. It put me in a risky place. Men have been publicly flogged for less. But, if I wanted answers, there was nothing for it but to take the risk. My only consolation was that two understanding friends sat outside on guard. On the other hand, this woman's lodge was in such an open area that our hasty departure would be seen and our identities duly noted. I wanted this woman to talk fast, but she was taking her time in settling down to do it. While I fidgeted, she puttered around, packing or putting out of harm's way the evidence of the things a solitary woman did to fill her hours. She stacked up baskets that were being woven, and items of clothing being decorated with beading. At last she sat down and, without preamble, began to speak.

"Everyone believed the sun rose out of the earth each morning simply to please her," she said, meaning the dead woman. "In the beginning, I thought so too. When she first came to me, she was a girl nearly grown." She lifted her shoulders in an indifferent shrug. "It didn't matter. Even though she was someone almost past the age of mothering, I accepted her as a daughter. She called me Mother and behaved as a proper daughter ought to do. She was very helpful and obedient and learned to speak our language rapidly. My real daughter, Shade, has always been such a shy child. This girl brought Shade out of herself and they became very close, inseparable. Then I began to see through her, and what I saw beneath the surface of that winning smile was not pleasant."

She gazed down at the idle hands in her lap, collecting her thoughts. Her last statement reminded me of a thing my father had said to me once: Never be fooled when the wolf shows its teeth. It isn't smiling.

Smiling Woman looked up and in a dull voice continued, "I tried to ignore what I suspected, that the girl was no more than a schemer, a deceiver. Then came the day when I could no longer close my eyes to her true nature. I found out, by accident, that girl was seriously misbehaving and that she was using Shade to help her. During her first full season with us, I thought she was being generous with Shade, teaching her the most flattering way to wear her hair, paint up her face, wear her clothes. But, on the day I learned about the young man she was slipping out to see, I began to understand more clearly just why she wanted Shade to look so much like her. She was using Shade to lead me on a false trail, following Shade when I thought I was following the other one.''

Her eyes became hard and her mouth a tight line as she said crisply, ''I despise liars. When I realized what she was getting up to and how deeply she was involving Shade, I went to my husband. I told him it would be a good idea to marry that girl off and do it quickly before she brought disgrace to our family and ruined our daughter's reputation.''

She took a deep breath, folded her arms beneath her breasts. I could feel her anger, but other than the coldness in her eyes, the emotion did not touch her face.

''He agreed, of course, but then he would have. Until that night, I'd no idea he planned to marry her himself, that he'd given her over to me only until she reached marriageable age.''

''I understand,'' I said quietly, ''that on the wedding day you publicly grieved.''

Her lengthy gaze was narrow-eyed and her manner impervious. ''Yes,'' she said evenly. ''But I wasn't grieving for her. I'd long stopped caring about her. My grief was for the glaring stupidity of my husband. He was making a complete fool of himself and for a girl-woman who would only play him false. He forced me to go public when he wouldn't listen to me in private. He was convinced my opposition to the marriage was due to my jealousy of her youth and beauty.''

''Were you jealous?''

She snorted derisively. "My husband wanted more children. I am too old to give them to him. For years I have been fully prepared for him to marry a younger woman. As for her beauty," she said with distaste, "it went no further than the paints she applied to her face. Nothing of true worth lay beneath. Her skin was the type the sun doesn't like. She was the kind of woman who would shrivel up before her time. I knew that in a few years, she would come to be mistaken for my mother. So, no, her beauty bothered me not at all. What upset me enough to cause me to make a spectacle of myself was her grip on my daughter and the blindness that seemed to afflict my husband in all things concerning her. I hoped that by shaming him publicly, he wouldn't go through with the marriage. But lust does not understand shame. My husband was a slave to his lust, and he had to have her no matter what I did or how much the people of his own band whispered behind their hands."

She ran a weary hand over her brow. "In the very first months of the marriage, she began teaching my poor simple sister-in-law how to serve him better. This was not done so that my sister-in-law, an impoverished widow, could gain more favor with her provider-brother. No, her true purpose was simply to give herself more free time in order to slip out and meet her lover. While that didn't bother me, I became concerned when I realized that my foolish daughter was still helping her."

Both of my brows shot up. "How was she doing that?"

She glared at me as if I were a simpleton. "They were still dressing alike, still playing the game they'd once used against me. But this time, I had no redress. If I told my husband, I knew that somehow that bent mind of his would find a way to blame Shade, and not her. That's when I decided the best way to deal with her was to remove Shade. Permanently."

● "By marrying her off to The Cheyenne Robber."
She rewarded me with a thin smile.
"But why him? Why not someone else?"

The slight smile vanished. The silence between us was lengthy as she stared at me in that impenetrable way of hers. She was making it clear that this was one question she would not answer.

It took me several moments to gather my thoughts. Then, I went at her with a stream of different questions.

"I see by the many tracks outside that you receive many visitors. Was The Cheyenne Robber a visitor here? Did he come and speak to you about the marriage? How were you, after White Bear was unable to convince him to marry Shade, able to change his mind?"

Looking away from me, she sounded a soft, humorless laugh. She turned her face back to me, giving me a long, careful look. When she spoke, at first I believed the woman had gone crazy, for she began to speak of things that seemed to have nothing to do with the subject at hand. But, knowing with a certainty that this woman was anything but crazy, I didn't interrupt. I forced myself to be patient and hear her out.

"Crying Wind was, at one time, my relative, a member of this very band. Her first husband was my husband's nephew, a young man who lost nearly all of his family to the stomach-cramp sickness [cholera]. My husband took him in, treating him like a son. When that young man married Crying Wind, we were all happy. Crying Wind has always been a worthy person, and she made her husband a good wife, eventually giving him a son. When that poor young man was killed by the Tehans, my husband mourned him the way a father mourns. And then he began doing a very unhealthy thing. He began taking over Crying Wind's baby boy.

"I went to her, warned her that if she did not take her child and go back to her true relatives, my husband would take her son away from her. At first, she didn't want to believe it, but as the child began to walk, He Goes began carrying the boy around, bragging that his son was the smartest baby in the entire Nation. Hearing this finally convinced her. With my help, Crying Wind took her son and escaped to White Bear, placing herself and her child under his protection.

"When my husband realized she was gone, he went into a rage. With a party of men he followed her to White Bear's camp, demanding White Bear give him the child. White Bear, of course, refused, and an animosity began between them. Then you came along, marrying Crying Wind and adopting her son. My husband hates you on account of that, and he has never forgiven Crying Wind."

I was stunned as I listened. Being a man living outside the confines of bands for nearly half my life, I wasn't familiar with my own wife's history. When I first met her, she'd tried to tell me about her first marriage, but because I was jealous of a dead man, I wouldn't allow it. Now her past was grabbing me by the throat. And the peril she currently faced seemed to double in size as I realized that one of the chiefs on the council, He Goes, had so much to gain by condemning her as a witch. In spite of the cold air seeping into the lodge and remaining, because this woman's fire was inadequate, I felt myself begin to sweat. Unaffected by the cold or my noticeable shock, Smiling Woman continued unhurriedly along.

"My husband saw his chance at regaining the child through a stronger tie with White Bear. That tie, of course, is the marriage of his daughter to White Bear's nephew, The Cheyenne Robber. All I had to do was suggest the marriage and my husband did the rest, following White

Bear to this awful place. Because of the ongoing trouble
between White Bear and Kicking Bird, by now White Bear
was more open to forming a blood tie with He Goes. White
Bear in no way considered your son at risk. He has no idea
that regaining the child is my husband's primary intention.
White Bear can be very simple sometimes. Anyway, while
He Goes was busy plotting, his wife,'' she said sourly,
''was cutting loose. Meeting her lover and acting the slut.
And still using Shade to help her. When The Cheyenne
Robber began letting it be known that he didn't want a
second marriage, I became desperate my husband would
find out about his whoring wife and Shade's complicity
before I could get her safely away. It was because I was
so desperate that I contacted Crying Wind, told her what
was really happening.''

Everything inside me froze. Smiling Woman tilted her
head as she stared at length, realizing the effect her words
were having on me. Her tone softened, became sympa-
thetic.

''Crying Wind was frightened for her son, I was frightened for my daughter. In the way of the First Women, we
made an agreement. It would be the two of us together
against the devious minds of the men threatening us. My
part was that I would do all I could to talk my husband out
of his plans for the baby boy while she kept an eye on
Shade and carried messages for me to The Cheyenne Robber. All of the tracks you noticed outside my home are
Crying Wind's. She has been my only visitor, my only
contact with your camp.''

I slumped, becoming lost to memory. Once again I saw
the condition of Crying Wind's pinto mare, sweaty and
shivering in the shelter beside my warm, dry horse. Then I
clearly recalled the last peaceful night she and I had shared,
the night she'd tried to talk to me and I didn't listen. The

agony I felt in these seconds was profound. My wife had been worried, fighting for the survival of her family. She and I were still so new in our marriage that she hadn't known how to approach me with her troubles. And too, I knew she sensed that Favorite Son and I were still coming to terms with each other, that we had a long way to go before he or I felt genuine affection for each other. She had to have believed that she faced yet another danger—that danger being me. As her husband, if I didn't object to White Bear's giving over her son to the little boy's closest blood relative, her hands would have been tied. So, unable to trust my heart on the matter of her son, she hadn't been able to trust my love for her. The only friend she felt she had was this coldhearted woman. A woman who used her to run about carrying messages and, in doing so, placed her under the fanatical eye of the witch-hunter, Red Bird.

A lot of things were beginning to make sense, pieces of the puzzle clicking together. All that was missing was the thing I asked.

"I have been told that your husband's dead wife had a knowledge of plants and their uses."

The abrupt change of subject caught her off-balance. At first she was startled, then relief came into her eyes. With the wave of a dismissive hand she eagerly replied, "What you heard is true. It was that person's one true talent. She learned it from her blood mother. A woman who, if the girl can be believed, was a healer. She bragged too that her blood mother was also a wondrous cook. To prove her claim, she taught my talentless sister-in-law to cook for my husband. Personally, the foods those two used to prepare together were much too spicy for my taste, but my husband greatly enjoyed them."

"And I'm given to understand that she taught your sister-in-law how to make cigars."

"Oh, yes. Cigar making was another of her limitless specialties. However, it took her a long time to teach my dull-witted sister-in-law just how to do it." She sounded a sour laugh. "During the teaching she was known to have reduced my sister-in-law to tears. It irritated her beyond words that she was forced to be so very patient with my sister-in-law. My poor sister-in-law tries very hard, but she's so terribly slow to learn. Long ago I tried teaching her how to make baskets. Even though I have more patience than that other one, I was forced to give up. The baskets my sister-in-law eventually produced were just awful. That other woman, for her own reasons, wouldn't give up. She stayed after my sister-in-law until she eventually learned how to do it just right. But even then, she yelled at her."

"Why?"

Smiling Woman shook her head and said in a lowered tone, "Because she said my sister-in-law was too stupid to understand how important it was to dispose of the flavoring liquid in the right way."

Another image sprang to mind—the image of the woman pouring out the liquid contents of the black pot. Pouring it into a hole, and starving camp dogs coming on the run to investigate what was being thrown away.

"I'm sorry," I said, "I don't understand. What is flavoring liquid?"

Smiling Woman was still speaking when I jumped to my feet and ran out of her lodge.

As I came out in a rush, Little War and Elk Cry bounced to their feet, looking at me anxiously. When I leaped onto my horse, both hastily followed suit. Too excited to spare time to ask Elk Cry and then carefully watch his hands, I put the question directly to Little War.

"Do you know if The Cheyenne Robber attends the council?"

Little War bobbed his head. "Of course he's there. And you should be glad. He's speaking on your wife's behalf."

That did not surprise me. He, more than anyone, knew my wife was innocent of the ridiculous charge. He would know because my wife was not, as Red Bird claimed, rushing about practicing witchcraft. She'd been carrying secret messages back and forth between himself and Smiling Woman.

"The Cheyenne Robber and Shade were seen," Beloved had said.

If that was true, that The Cheyenne Robber had covertly been dallying with a young woman of good family, and Shade's mother through my wife's spying had found out, then Smiling Woman had used this knowledge to force him into the marriage.

I heard my wife's hesitant voice in my head, the words she'd said before giving me the news of The Cheyenne Robber's second marriage. "Now don't be mad."

Once again that statement had me so mad I was grinding my back teeth down to a gritty powder as my two friends and I rode at a gallop straight through the heart of He Goes's deserted-looking camp. I wanted another word with the sister-in-law. Smiling Woman, being a mother, had readily blamed any and all indiscretions on the dead woman, slanting her view of the facts to make Shade seem the complete innocent. But young girls are rarely innocent when they are slipping around.

I should know.

Once upon a time, I was a very young man and did a bit of slipping around myself. And I wasn't slipping alone.

Smiling Woman's tale unnervingly mirrored my early experience. I'd had a friend, Buffalo Heart, who had been hopelessly in love with a girl and she with him. The trouble was, neither family cared for the other and so the young lovers had to meet in secret. To accomplish this, they'd needed understanding friends: a girlfriend who could be trusted, and a male friend who knew how to keep his mouth shut. That male friend had been me. This is the way it went.

The two girls would go off together with no objections made by their mothers because the girls were trusted to act as proper chaperons, one for the other. In the meantime, Buffalo Heart and I walked off together in the opposite direction, arms thrown across one another's shoulders, just two young men enjoying each other's company. As soon as we got to the edge of the village, we quickly doubled back, finding the girls. Once Buffalo Heart was with his girl, we parted company. On that first occasion, I felt lost and at odds with the situation. The girl I'd been left with was nice, but she was a stranger. Frankly, I didn't know what to do with her, but we were trapped with each other for however long Buffalo Heart courted his love.

My girl wasn't overly pretty in the face, but she was exceptionally pleasant. And she turned out to be a good listener. While we walked around, I did all of the talking and she didn't seem to mind at all. Before I knew it, I was lost in conversation with her, going on, as was my habit then, with my fascination of all things living. Now and again, she asked a pertinent question. It pleased me enormously that she was actually listening and seemed interested in the things I was saying. Time just seemed to fly.

I suppose, in its way, the whole thing was fairly innocent. That girl and I didn't even know each other, so we hardly behaved as passionate lovers. We were more like two people becoming great friends. After that, Buffalo Heart didn't have to beg me to help him. I was quite eager to be a party to his subterfuge and so, it would seem, was that other girl.

We met in this way more than a dozen times, and each time we met, we had more fun than the last. The best time was when we found a shallow cave and explored it. Because the cave was dark, her hand slipped into mine. I instantly experienced tingles all up and down my spine, and a riot of butterflies swarmed in my belly. I did not let her hand go, not even when we were safely out of the cave. What pleased me most was that she did not try to take her hand away.

The most ironic thing was that while she and I were getting along so famously, Buffalo Heart and his girl weren't getting along at all. Before the summer was finished, Buffalo Heart wanted no more to do with his girl, while I and the girl who had been forced on me were deeply in love.

How did it end? Quite simply. I married her. Both of our families were greatly surprised by the match, but they were also quite pleased. The two families became one on our wedding day, and she and I were more than happy with each other up until the day she became sick and died. Because of her death, and the subsequent death of both my parents, I became an outsider, remaining content to be alone and live without the restrictions of band or clan ties. Until four months ago, when I saw Crying Wind.

This bittersweet memory put me in mind that the basic natures of young people do not change. If, while acting as an escort, Shade had been placed in the company of the young man acting as the escort to the lover intent on being with a married woman, it was a short walk to the conclusion that Shade and her male counterpart found themselves emotionally involved. At least, if that male counterpart was The Cheyenne Robber, Shade had become emotionally involved. The Cheyenne Robber is irritatingly handsome. He can also be just as irritatingly charming. And while acting as a blind for his foolish friend, it wasn't inconceivable that he was charming to Shade. She may have fallen victim to this charm, but I didn't think so. Not when I remembered my one and only conversation with her and how . . . resigned . . . she'd seemed to the inevitability of the match.

It had been Smiling Woman who had read the situation in error, believed her pliable daughter to have feelings she hadn't. At any rate, she had been right about one thing. She needed to have Shade out of the way before He Goes realized he was being duped. Forcing The Cheyenne Robber to accept the responsibility for a situation he'd helped start seemed the best logical conclusion. And as her daughter's welfare took precedence over anyone else's, it had bothered Smiling Woman not at all that White Otter might be excessively aggrieved or that her unborn child might be placed in jeopardy. How was it possible, I wondered, that such a hard person with such a calculating mind found herself lumbered with the name Smiling Woman?

Despite her statement to the contrary, I believed Smiling Woman had been and continued to be jealous of the dead girl. He Goes, as well as a good number of other people, mourned for that girl. And the more they mourned, the more the girl's attributes were hailed, placing her further and further above Smiling Woman. As saying bad things about the dead is considered evil, Smiling Woman must have felt trapped and rubbed raw. So, she'd moved her lodge to the edge of the camp where she wouldn't have to hear any more praise of the dead woman she'd heartily despised.

With effort, I placed Smiling Woman temporarily out of my mind as we pulled up in front of He Goes's lodge. His sister came out quickly, looking worried as I dismounted. Reading her anxious expression, I knew this woman lived in perpetual fear of her provider-brother. Afraid that if he became angry enough to disown her, she would find herself living among the Dapom. While I appreciated her plight, I needed confirmation of my suspicions—that Shade wasn't quite the innocent her mother would have me believe.

She wrung her hands as she silently wept, tears sheeting her face. "Please," she pleaded softly. "Please don't force me to speak against my brother's daughter."

"Whatever you say," I assured, "will be held in confidence."

She glanced up at Little War, her brimming eyes searching his only eye. Little War dismounted, came to her, planting himself firmly by her side. Now, while I fully understood his protective instincts, I did feel he was being a bit excessive. Especially as his body language seemed to imply that she remain silent. Then his one eye glared at me, silently accusing me of recklessly putting at risk the woman he cared about. But she, being slow in the head, misunderstood. She took his presence as being a comfort, so instead of remaining quiet, information rattled out of her.

"It's true what my sister-in-law said. But the dead woman who was my sister-in-law did not have only one lover. She had several."

Little War visibly bristled. Placing a hand on her arm, he said meaningfully, "You don't have to say anything more. If your brother finds out about your knowledge of these things—"

"He won't!" I shouted, impatient with his protectiveness. "I swear on my life, He Goes will not learn of this conversation." I turned my attention back to the nervous woman. "Please, continue. What you have to say will bring no harm to you and it just might help the woman I love very much."

"Crying Wind?" she asked, confusion in her tone.

"Yes," I sighed. "Crying Wind."

The woman shook her muddled head. It was clear she didn't understand how an old secret scandal could help my wife, but she obliged me. "Shade didn't want to help her. She really didn't. But that girl . . . had a power over Shade. A power so strong that often I found Shade weeping for no reason. When I asked her what troubled her so, Shade just patted my hand and said, 'Not now, Auntie. Not now.'

"That girl ran my brother. Whatever she wanted, he gave, and whatever she said, he believed. Shade and I had to do her bidding. We had no choice. So, Shade helped her slip away whenever the mood took her and I did the chores. Then my first sister-in-law and my brother began to fight all the time. And when they weren't fighting, he was taking himself off to other camps visiting the other band chiefs. He didn't know what was going on in his own home because, when he returned, his second wife would be there and all the meals and all the cleaning had been done."

This struck me as entirely reasonable. He Goes had, after all, left his beautiful young wife in the company of the women of his family. He had no idea that all of them, for separate reasons, were bound by silence. That girl must have felt completely free to get up to all manner of things, knowing full well that the other women would hold their tongues. But this power soon came under threat. Smiling Woman began an overt plan to take Shade out of the household, placing her out of harm's way. And once Shade was free, Smiling Woman would be free. Once He Goes was made aware of his favorite wife's conduct, he may or may not have turned his anger on his sister. She was, after all, a simple person and his young wife quite cunning. It would have served no purpose to punish his sister for his wayward wife's sins. Smiling Woman would have known this, and that meant that, by speaking the truth, this worried woman before me would have been free as well. But Smiling

Woman hadn't told me the full truth because she couldn't see that she had anything to gain from it. Everything was just as it should be. The bad wife was dead, her daughter was safe, and her sister-in-law was as free as a slow-witted person could know how to be.

I changed the subject. "On the day of the girl's death, can you name those present?"

She sent Little War a beseeching look. His response was a nonchalant lifting of his shoulders. She looked back to me.

"My brother had many guests that day. His wife sat beside him as my sister-in-law, my niece, and I served the men who had come to speak with him. Shade was very nervous."

"Why?"

She tilted her head, trying to hide her face. "Because The Cheyenne Robber was there. And White Bear. White Bear did all of the talking, but The Cheyenne Robber kept giving Shade mean looks. His looks upset her. . . ." Her words trailed off.

As time to allow an appreciative moment for her sensitive feelings was limited, I hurried her on with another question. "Who else was in attendance?"

Another look passed between her and Little War. Lightly, her hand touched his arm. "He was here, as well as the one known as Red Bird and the old man, Owl Man."

"What were they discussing?"

Little War took over the conversation. "They were discussing the union between the bands. A union that would be a forever treaty once the blood of the families was mingled."

"Meaning Shade and The Cheyenne Robber."

Little War nodded.

"And The Cheyenne Robber was coming around to this idea?"

"Oh, yes!" the woman cried. "I don't understand why he looked at Shade the way he did, but he seemed quite in a hurry to get the marriage settled. He would have taken her that very day if he'd been allowed."

"What stopped him?"

The woman began to chew the corner of her mouth as her gaze fixed on mine. "That other one. The wife of my brother who died. She got mad about all the marriage talk. She said she had a headache, and because my brother became concerned for her, he sent the men out, saying they would talk again the next day."

I canted my head as I regarded her. "How did your brother seem?"

"About the marriage of Shade?"

"Yes. About that."

A lovely smile graced her face. "Oh, he was so pleased."

I could well imagine he was. Not only was he becoming inseparably linked with the powerful Rattle Band, but he had begun the first move in his concealed scheme to make a claim for my son. Anger building inside me, I asked harshly, "What happened then?"

She retreated a step, finding herself in Little War's protective arms. "I-I gave her a cup of coffee to help ease her headache and . . . she dropped dead."

"You gave her the coffee?" I cried.

"Y-yes," she said timidly. "There were three pots. I don't remember how there came to be three pots. Shade and I only brought in two while my sister-in-law served foods. Maybe when my sister-in-law went out for more food, she brought in the third. I can't be sure. People kept getting up and going out and coming in again. Anyway, that pot was full so I took a cup of coffee from it. My dead sister-in-law was drinking the coffee as she stood close to my brother, arguing with him. Then, she went all white in the face and fainted in his arms.''

The memory caused her to weep, and Little War hugged her as he glowered at me. "Now are you satisfied?" he asked, his whispering tone heavy with menace.

"Not quite. I need to know who else went out and came in again."

The woman looked at me forlornly but seemed content to remain in Little War's arms. "The Cheyenne Robber and . . . Shade,'' she barely said. She looked up at Little War, adoration shining in her eyes. "And this one and I."

"This is enough!'' Little War shouted. "If you wish to continue our friendship, you will leave her alone."

I raised my hand in surrender. "You're right, friend. I have overstepped the mark of good conduct. I can only ask that you remember my wife's peril and judge me with compassion.''

The heartfelt request placated him. Little War looked away from me to the woman. "We must go now. But I will return. When I do, I will speak to your brother.''

Her face began to glow and she placed her hands to her mouth. I turned away from the tender scene. As I mounted, I noticed a taut expression come over Elk Cry's face. Catching my questioning eye, he turned his face away. The most curious thing happened next. As Little War and I took our leave of the woman, Elk Cry rode out. He stayed far ahead of us in our journey to the camp. This left me to understand that he was angry with me. I did a mental review of the uncharitable way I'd behaved toward that simple-natured woman. Being impaired himself, Elk Cry was overly sensitive to the rough treatment of impaired persons. This in no way means to suggest that Elk Cry thought

of Little War as being damaged. Little War had been born
perfect; the scars on his face were the marks of a warrior's
honor. Elk Cry and the woman we rode away from were
the truly damaged. His stuttering tongue and her simple
mind were obstacles they had needed to overcome from
birth. This gave him every reason to be angry with me, and
I every reason to worry that I'd just lost a remarkable
friend.

CHAPTER

8

The day was becoming chilly as late afternoon progressed. I was lost in thought as Little War and I rode together without speaking. Ahead, Elk Cry's form was becoming more diminished. The warmth of the day had caused the spotty patches of snow remaining in this small plain to recede enough in depth so that now it looked like pockets of white burred with the slumping tendrils of brown grass. Tall, bare-limbed cottonwoods thickly lined both sides of a runoff creek of the minor river that bisected the canyon prairie. Cottonwoods are known to be thirsty trees. They always grow alongside a good water source. Our horses needed water, so Little War and I quietly gave them their head. Elk Cry's horse wanted water too, but he controlled his mount with a firm hand, continuing on his determined way, disappearing from our sight as Little War and I veered off.

At the creek, Little War and I dismounted. Our horses moved to the creek for a drink. Still seeking the sanctuary of my own thoughts, I hunkered down, chewing the corner of my mouth as my eyes savored the sight of the tallest and oldest cottonwood. Its trunk was almost as white as the snow clinging to the banks of the creek. This old tree served to remind me that whatever we mortal men might get up to, our frail efforts will never be as lasting or as rewarding as those belonging to this silent witness of our arrogance. It felt good just to sit there for a time considering that tree and nothing else. Little War left the horses and came toward me, squatting down before me, partially blocking the sight of the magnificent old tree and, in doing so, pulling my mind out of that comfortable place.

"Where are we going now?" he asked simply.

I raised a brow as I regarded him intently and at length. When I spoke, it was with carefully phrased words. I was losing too many friends of late. I would not want the loss of another.

"My old friend, I believe I have rubbed down to a blunt edge your supposed indebtedness to me. We are even. I think it would be best if you left me to sort out this business on my own."

With his one eye, he managed to look askance. Then he began to pester me with questions. I had no answers for him. None, at least, that I was willing to share. Not then. Agitated, he put one last question to me.

"Do you believe the sister of He Goes intentionally killed He Goes's second wife?"

I looked at him levelly, answering him in a drawling voice. "No. I don't believe there is a mean bone in that woman's body."

Little War nodded briskly in agreement, then stood. After retrieving his horse, he left me to my musings. I waited a good long time to be certain that he was gone. I wanted no witnesses, no listening ears attuned to what was said during this next visit I had to make.

· · ·

I arrived at the stand of pines that blocked The Cheyenne Robber's homesite from the view of his neighbors and tied the reins of my horse to a thick branch. My horse was content with this and had found a patch of green growing at the base of dead grasses. It was happily crunching at the greenery as I slipped through the trees. At the edge of this small forest, I crouched and surveyed The Cheyenne Robber's camp. Smoke curled from the smoke holes of the huge blue lodge and from the small dull lodge. The lodge belonging to the servant. Nothing else stirred. There were no camp dogs to bark a warning, and The Cheyenne Robber's shield was missing from the tripod set just a few feet off to the left of the doorway of the blue lodge. The missing shield meant that he was most definitely not at home.

As a habit, shields were not carried when the warrior owner was just walking around visiting with friends. The shield sat outside his home lodge, covered by a protective blanket. In this state, the primary wife was responsible for the shield. It could not fall over or be touched by anything restrictive to the warrior's medicine. For example, if while receiving his war medicine he was told to avoid eating from a metal spoon, no metal objects could touch or come near his shield. A warrior's list of other restrictions regarding his shield were so numerous that I have known wives to sit outside their lodges for long hours of watchful guard until their husbands saw fit to come home and relieve them of the burdensome task. That The Cheyenne Robber's shield was missing meant that it was now set out on a tripod in front of White Bear's lodge—a thing that happened whenever a council of chiefs was called. The shields on display allowed ordinary members of the bands to know which men made up the council. The shields also warned people away. A council lodge surrounded by shields belonging to powerful men meant that there would be no

eavesdropping. The men on the council were free to speak
their minds at length while an impatient public awaited the
council's verdict.

Cautiously, I crept out of the wooded area. I made my
way, not to the large blue lodge, but to the servant's lodge.
I was counting heavily on Shade's being in that lodge and
the servant's being in the blue lodge with White Otter for,
as she was nearing so close to her time, I knew The Cheyenne Robber would not allow her to be alone. Ordinarily,
it was the duty of the second wife to attend the first, but I
could not imagine White Otter allowing Shade anywhere
near her. Using all of the stealth at my command, I made
my way silently to the secondary lodge and, once I was
there, without any warning threw open the door. The sight
that greeted my eyes was unbelievable.

The Navaho was naked, and he was on top of an equally
naked Shade.

Looking at my face suddenly filling the door hole, they
were just as shocked as I. Even so, the Navaho recovered
first. He scrambled off of Shade and covered her with a
blanket. When he stood and began to advance on me, I
turned to run.

Hundreds of thoughts went through my mind as I ran for
all I was worth. The principal thought was that The Cheyenne Robber's trusted servant had turned like a mad dog
on his master and that before killing off The Cheyenne
Robber's wives, he was first availing himself of them. I had
no gun, no knife. All I had was the slight advantage of
distance. I poured on more speed knowing my only chance
was to get to my horse and then ride for The Cheyenne
Robber. If it hadn't been for the blasted ankle flaps so
adored by the men of my breed, I would have made it. But,
as it happened, one of the flaps lingered just a bit too long
between strides and I stepped down on it, tripping myself.

Before I could get up again, the Navaho was on me and we commenced to roll around in a highly unsightly fashion.

He had the advantage of weight. All I had was terror. Still, I made a good fight of it until he eventually had me pinned. By this time, both women, Shade wrapped in a blanket, had gotten to us. I was still struggling, still yelling, while the Navaho lay on top of me. The next thing I knew, White Otter's worried face filled my line of vision.

"Stop it!" she cried. "Stop fighting. People will hear."

All I could do was pant and look at her stupidly. White Otter knelt down, speaking directly into my face. "You shouldn't have come here. You've ruined everything."

I put up no more fight as the Navaho hauled me to my feet. At the sight of his nakedness, White Otter primly averted her eyes while Shade hurriedly tied a covering cloth around his hips. Then Shade muttered and White Otter turned to face us all.

"Tay-bodal," she said firmly. "My husband told you to keep away. Why have you disobeyed him?"

My astonished mouth flew open and my words came out in a sputter. "I am not the criminal!" Using my arm like a lance, I pointed to the Navaho. "This man is a rapist. He must be killed."

White Otter rolled her eyes and clicked her tongue. "He is not a rapist. And I will not discuss this out in the open for just anyone to hear." She turned and, like errant children, the three of us tagged behind her, the Navaho and I sending each other scathing looks.

White Otter and I entered her lodge. Shade and the Navaho hurriedly went to the smaller lodge, presumably to properly dress themselves. White Otter, settling herself comfortably, seemed unfazed. I sat down with my head resting in my hands, trying to clear the jumble of thoughts.

When I spoke, my voice was barely more than a strained whisper.

"Would it be too much to ask for food? I'm feeling a bit light headed."

"When those two come in," she assured, "I know they will bring something for us to eat. They always do." She covered her legs with a blanket and leaned against the backrest.

I looked at her, my mood sullen. "How long have you known about . . . them?"

She sighed wearily. "Since last night. My husband is a terrible liar. Once I got over the shock of his having a second wife, cracks in what he said and the way he acted began to appear." She allowed a moment for that to sink in, then continued. "His reasons for marrying her kept changing. That's when I knew he was lying. When he lies, he never remembers what he said last. Then there was the fact that he wasn't spending any time with his new wife. He would leave me, stay away for a few moments, then he would come back to me. No man, not even my husband, is that quick. When I realized this, I stopped crying and became more attentive. The most noticeable thing was that our servant was gone more than he ought to be and my husband was seeing to my needs. It didn't take a lot of guesswork to realize just who was married to Shade. When I threw this in my husband's face, he broke down and confessed."

She shook her head as she gazed off into a distance somewhere behind me. I didn't move, I didn't speak. I simply waited for her to continue. The whole while I waited, I felt my temples throb. Lack of food and trying to solve too many puzzles all at once had joined forces to give me a thumping headache.

White Otter sighed again. "I will tell you exactly what

my husband told me. And this time I believed him because this tale is beyond his abilities to make up. Shade and Good Friend have known each other for almost an entire year. Their acquaintance began when Shade and the girl who became her second mother used to slip out at night so that the other one could meet her admirer. When that other one went off to be alone with whoever it was she went off with, Shade was left on her own. This all happened during the same time my husband was secretly courting me. In order for my husband to look as if he were in one place when he was actually in another, Good Friend wore my husband's clothing and made his hair to seem like The Cheyenne Robber's.''

I looked at her skeptically. The Navaho's hair looked much too short to pass for The Cheyenne Robber's. She guessed what I was thinking.

"Really, Tay-bodal. For a clever man you are being tiresome. Good Friend's hair is quite long when he hasn't got it all tied up the way Navahos tie up their hair behind their heads. All he had to do was untie it. On a darkened night, walking around dressed like The Cheyenne Robber, people thought that was who he was. He was careful never to get close enough for anyone to notice the real difference. Anyway, while he was playing at being my husband, he came across Shade. She was crying and her tears affected him. Without thinking, he went to comfort her. And that's how they made their acquaintance.

"Because of my husband's activities and the dead girl's, it was easy for them to keep on meeting. Then came the time when my husband had his little . . . trouble. My husband became afraid not only for me but for Good Friend. He told Good Friend to run away before the worst happened. If my husband was found guilty by the council, he knew that if Good Friend was still around, he would

be claimed as a slave by someone else and what would
happen to him after that. My husband, being a lusty male,
could not stomach the thought of that happening to a man
he greatly cared for. Good Friend then told him that he
couldn't leave and why. He was in love with Shade but
he didn't know if she loved him enough to run off with
him. Until he knew for certain just what she felt in her
heart for him, he couldn't leave. Not even if the risk meant
castration and permanent enslavement. My husband understood how he felt. He should have. It was on account of
his feelings for me that he faced death himself. So my husband advised him to hide.''

This explained why, during The Cheyenne Robber's dark
days, a time when he faced the ultimate sentence of banishment, I had not seen so much as a glimpse of his trusted
servant.

''The plan then became that, if my husband and I were
sent out from the people, Good Friend and possibly Shade
would join up with us. The way my husband tells it, if you
hadn't come along the way you did, it would have been the
four of us against the world. In his mind, it would have
been quite the jolly little adventure. But fortunately for me,
you did come along. My husband is too much the romantic
to see the gloomy side of a tribe consisting of only four
people, one of them pregnant.

''Thanks to you, life greatly improved for my husband
and me, but Good Friend and Shade were still up to their
necks in difficulty. Most especially after the dead woman
was forced into marriage with Shade's father. The intrigue
that took place after that is almost too mind-numbing for
words. Because of my condition, my husband kept all of it
from me. But the way it was working out was the dead
woman was still up to her tricks of meeting lovers. According to Shade, there were several. Shade continued to

help this odious girl deceive her father, but during this time, Shade was being forced. I am told it was because the dead woman hinted broadly that she knew Shade's secret. That if Shade refused to help her, she would tell Shade's father that his high-born daughter was consorting with someone beneath her. Shade believed this terrible woman knew everything, and if she told what she knew, it would mean certain death for Good Friend. Shade loved him too much by this time to risk his life, and so she continued to help her second mother. Yet, when she met with Good Friend, she could not hide her torn emotions from him. Good Friend didn't know what to do for her. We were all already in this place, and with so many camp guards and only one sure way out of the canyon, escape was impossible.

"Next came the demand from Shade's parents that my husband marry their daughter. My husband refused. And he continued to refuse until Good Friend confessed that the girl he loved was none other than the one everyone wanted my husband to marry. This knowledge made my husband stop shouting and begin thinking. Next came your wife. Crying Wind spoke to my husband out of my hearing, but I could plainly see that Crying Wind was agitated, extremely worried. My husband came to me, saying that he had to marry Shade. He said that the marriage was purely political and that I shouldn't worry about it, that it had nothing to do with the two of us. I didn't believe him on account of my mother. She had already paid me a visit, said she'd been hearing talk about The Cheyenne Robber. So, after my husband told me that he had to marry Shade but that the marriage was political, I went to her and tried to convince her of the very lie I didn't believe myself. My mother has a sharp mind. She could tell I didn't believe anything I said, and so my visit to her made everything worse.

"The next thing I knew, my husband's herd was attacked, a young woman I'd never heard of was dead, and my husband showed up with Shade. The sight of her pretty face and her slender body inside a beautiful wedding dress broke my heart. I took to weeping without being able to stop. You turned up during the worst of it, and I do apologize for my unseemly behavior."

"You told me then," I said softly, "that your husband was doing something dangerous."

She wanly smiled as she nodded. "I was clinging to the lies. My husband told me that the marriage was a fake. That as soon as spring came and we were able to leave this canyon, he was throwing Shade away. That was the dangerous part. He Goes Into Battle First is not the sort of man to sit and say nothing while his only daughter is treated so poorly. I knew there was going to be trouble, trouble worse than what he'd faced not so long ago. I begged him not to do it. I said I would accept her as my sister wife but he wouldn't listen to me. I poured all of that out on you, and again, I can only apologize."

"But the plan remains the same," I said, "even now that you've learned that Shade's real husband is Good Friend. The plan is, after we all leave the canyon, Shade and the Navaho will disappear."

She took a deep breath as she gazed up at the crossed poles of the smoke hole. "Yes," she said thinly. "It's a terrible plan. He Goes will never accept a feeble tale of his daughter simply running off all on her own. But it's too late for any plan of reason. My husband's actions have made it too late. The truly terrible part of this was that as I began to suspect my husband's lies and he eventually confessed, I was unable to confide this truth in my parents. I badly wanted to because you know my father, Hears The Wolf, is a highly intelligent man. If anyone could think of a way out of this, he could. But, my first loyalties are to my husband. He'd sworn me to secrecy. After I knew that the bride and groom were Shade and Good Friend, it seemed only fitting to me that they honeymoon in the better lodge. My husband was so happy that I seemed to be going along with this insanity that he barely grumbled about giving up his personal comfort. He thought of his sacrifice as his gift to the young lovers. We were forced to rethink that when my father showed up at the door."

She placed her hands against her face and stared blankly. "I will spend the rest of my life trying to blot that ugly scene from my mind. My father stood at the door, yelling for me to come out. Good Friend guarded the door, risking a beating because he could not allow my father to pass. If my father had, he would have seen Shade, not me. My father would have then concluded that I had been reduced in status, and he would have killed my husband. The Cheyenne Robber and I were in the smaller lodge when we heard the yelling. The Cheyenne Robber ran out and the situation went from bad to worse. My father called The Cheyenne Robber all manner of awful things, and when he wasn't doing that, he was yelling for me to come out. Knowing that this was the worst thing I could do, I stayed put."

"I heard about it."

Her hands came away from her face and her eyes flared. "You did?"

"Yes. Your father approached me, wanting my help to get you out of here. He's fully prepared to fight The Cheyenne Robber in order to free you."

"Oh, no," she groaned.

"But take heart," I said bitterly. "My wife's troubles seem to have bought you time from your own."

Her answer was a deep, cleansing breath.

We both became quiet as we heard the outside approach

of Shade and Good Friend. White Otter sent me a worried glance. In spite of her bulk she leaned forward and whispered hurriedly.

"Be kind. They are both such shy people. And as much as it shocked you to find them the way you did, I know in my heart it mortified them."

To my delight, when the two entered, they brought in food. Neither said a word and the three of us studiously avoided eye contact as they served White Otter and me. I said nothing as I accepted a platter of foods, the aromas causing my mouth to water and my empty stomach to growl. Shade and Good Friend sat somewhere behind me as I ate ravenously.

When White Otter and I finished, I said gently but firmly, "I need to question the woman Shade. I ask your permission to do this."

White Otter beckoned, and the frightened girl-woman came to sit by her side. Shade kept her head lowered, her hair shielding her face.

"I need the name of your dead second mother's lovers."

Her head still lowered, Shade's slight body stiffened. "Please," she meekly begged, "please don't ask me."

"Young woman," I said, my tone stern. "The time for secrets has passed. I need the answers only you can give."

There was movement behind me. From the corner of my eye I saw the Navaho walk around to where I sat. He joined his wife, and as he sat down, she huddled against him. His defiant eyes bore into mine. I stared right back, knowing full well that he would not chance the safety of the women with an attack on me. I continued to wait for Shade to answer. After an interminable amount of time, White Otter placed a gentle hand on Shade's.

"You must tell him whatever he asks. He is a good person. He is someone we all can trust."

At that point I could not readily agree with White Otter. Deep in my heart I knew that if saving my wife meant exposing these two, then that's just what I would do. So, I made no promises one way or the other. I continued to wait. Finally, Shade raised her head slightly.

"I-I didn't know them all. She was very vain about men, believing that all who saw her fell instantly in love. Once, when a young man spoke to me, she said out of her own mouth that the only reason he spoke to me was so that he could get close to her. To prove it, she went out of her way to attract that young man's attentions."

"And who was that man?"

Amazingly, Shade giggled. "Someone who, if he hadn't spoken to me in a friendly way, she would never have looked at even once."

My irritation began to mount. "His name, please."

I had startled her so that involuntarily she looked at me. Quickly looking away again, she muttered, "The one known as Little War."

The information rocked me. The girl-woman continued on in a flat, soft voice. "It was sad really, the way he was so flattered by her sudden interest in him. They met twice that I know of, then, once she was certain that she had his heart, she refused to speak to him again. She took up with someone else."

"And that name?" I rasped.

"Elk Cry." She looked up, this time forgetting her former embarrassment. "I believe that she honestly cared a great deal for him. He can't talk but he is very handsome. I suppose the shame of consorting with another man's wife became too much for him. He just stopped coming around and she wouldn't speak of him to me again."

"But Little War," I said dully. "He continued to come

around, visiting your father and knowing that he had committed an offense against him.''

She shook her head adamantly. ''No. That wasn't why Little War visited. He saw her for what she was, and I know that he was genuinely sorry in his heart for having been fooled by her. In his way, he tried to warn my father.''

''Were there any others?''

She became quiet, as if mentally scouring a lengthy list. ''None,'' she finally said, ''of any importance. One was a man who threw her over before she ever got her hooks into him. After him, there was another she wouldn't talk about. She was seeing him a lot. More than she had anyone else. Then there came a man that she really wanted, but he rejected her and that made her angry. She could be very ugly when she was angry.''

''I need those names as well.''

She hesitated, canting her head to look at White Otter through her hair. Then her hand sought her husband's and held on tight. ''The first one I spoke of was Big Tree.''

I experienced a roll of nausea. Big Tree, the warrior with the pretty girl's face and a man of high war honors, was the very type who would attract the eye of such a scheming female. That he had even toyed with her sickened me.

''I really don't know who the other one was, but the last one . . .'' She looked at me with brimming eyes. ''Please,'' she begged again.

''I must know.''

Defeated, she whispered, ''The Cheyenne Robber.''

White Otter gasped sharply. My eyes slew from her to the trembling Shade. There was thunder in my tone as I said, ''She set her sights on a newly married man?''

''Yes,'' Shade mewled. ''But he wouldn't even talk to her. That made her angry, but not half as angry as what he said when she finally got him to talk to her.''

The three of us were stone silent, all eyes on her. Shade looked around worriedly, then rushed to assure White Otter. "Your husband wasn't even tempted. He laughed at her. He told her to run home to her husband quick before he turned her over his knee and spanked her for being naughty."

White Otter's lips trembled, then she laughed. "He's said that before to other women. He probably forgot all about it the instant she ran away."

"But she didn't forget," Shade said. Yet the two women seemed to be forgetting the two men in their presence easily enough as they faced each other and shared the juicy tale. "She went into a rage. The worst I ever saw. She tore up everything in the lodge, and I and my poor auntie were running about trying to repair the damage. My mother came in during that time, demanding to know what all of the noise was about. My auntie is such a sweet soul, kind but a little bit innocent in her view of things. Before my father's dead wife could stop her, my auntie blurted the cause of the fuss."

Shade leaned in close to White Otter. They looked for all the world like two friends lost in the glow of salacious gossip. "You should have seen my mother's face. Oh! She looked so pleased. My second mother of course began to deny all of it. She said she was nearing her woman's time and couldn't control her temper the way she ought to do." Shade waved a hand and made a face. "My mother didn't believe a word of it. She knew my auntie wasn't a liar and that my father's second wife was. My second mother read my mother's face. That's when she threatened my mother."

"How did she do that?" White Otter asked a bit breathlessly.

"Unfortunately, it was very easy for her. She told my mother that if she repeated what my auntie said, she would tell my father that I had been out spreading my legs with someone he would never accept as a son-in-law."

White Otter gasped.

"She didn't name him, but I was terrified she meant Good Friend. My mother didn't really care who it was. The only thing she cared about was that I was accused of having a lover and that I wasn't saying anything to deny it. My mother left the lodge, refusing to say another word. I ran after her, trying to make her listen to me, but she shook me off. After that, the only time she spoke directly to me was when my father was present. In those times, she acted as if there were nothing wrong between us, and my father didn't question it. But my mother knew how to get revenge on her sister wife. She went to my father and suggested the match between me and your husband. My second mother became livid when my father readily agreed. Then my mother sat back and watched her sister wife fume. It was perfect revenge really. I would be given in marriage to the man my second mother still wanted. And once I was married, my second mother wouldn't have dared to speak a word against me, while my mother would be free to tell my father what she knew. It didn't matter to my mother that I would be unhappy because she saw me as a ruined woman. My mother has a very strict way of thinking. Ruined women got what they deserved and they should bear their shame in silence. Fortunately for all of us, my husband wasn't ashamed. He spoke to your husband, and now, here we all are."

Before Shade and White Otter could lose themselves in the delusion that all had come right in the end, I sounded a sour note. "Yes. Here you all are. In worse trouble than before." I looked at the Navaho. "You face death, your wife faces a life of being shunned, and The Cheyenne Robber and his wife face the loss of high rank." I looked nar-

rowly at White Otter. "Do you suppose your proud
husband will ever find peace and contentment as a Kaan?
That the son you might be carrying inside you will never
be an Onde?"

White Otter visibly withered. "Oh, Tay-bodal," she said,
tears coming into her voice. "Whatever are we going to
do?"

I had to think. My elbows on my knees, my hands
shielded my eyes as my beaten brain drew a blank. Tension
was rife in that lodge, all three people looking hopefully to
me. The only thing I could think to do was tell White Bear.
I did not dare say this, for the shrieks and wails from the
three would have been terrible. Plus, the possibility was
high that the Navaho would never allow me to leave this
place alive.

Looking up, I stunned White Otter with what to her was
a meaningless question. "Do you know anything about a
man known as Bear Shadow? I am given to understand he
is a friend of your husband's."

White Otter batted her eyes rapidly. "I-I haven't formally met him. I only know that they've had a falling out."

"About what?"

She chewed her lower lip. Then, in a resigned tone she
said, "What else? About a woman. Women seem to be the
cause of all of my husband's problems."

Wanting her to stick to the point, I pressed, "Just tell
me about this one woman."

White Otter sighed. "Oh, very well. I'm told her name
is Spring Rains. She was just one of many girls he was
going around with before he met me. She visited him a lot
when he was in the prison lodge, but then again so did
many others. Which is why I moved in with him against
my mother's good advice and White Bear's order for me
not to do it. I was The Cheyenne Robber's true wife and I

was carrying his child. It galled me that other women didn't know this and visited him so openly. Anyway, once I was with him, the women didn't come around anymore. Both he and I forgot all about them. Then, just as he was freed by the council, he heard that his friend Bear Shadow had married. Happy for his friend, my husband paid the new couple a visit, bringing them a wedding gift. It became apparent to Bear Shadow during this visit that his wife still had feelings for my husband. Becoming quite jealous, Bear Shadow ordered my husband out of his home and refused the gift. To my knowledge, they haven't spoken since.''

A lot of things became apparent to me in that moment. One of those things was that I was in the presence of Raven Woman and her lover from the ledge. Needing undeniable proof, I said to Shade, ''May I see your foot?''

Her eyes widened in profound surprise. She glanced first at the other two and then back to me. ''My . . . foot?''

''Yes. Be so kind as to hold it out.''

After another worried glance at White Otter and the Navaho, she scooted her thin bottom off the backs of her legs and stuck out her foot. I placed my hand against the sole, measuring it against the remembered measurement of the prints on the ledge. It was a perfect match. Next, I looked at the Navaho.

''May I see your foot, please?''

With a shrug, he showed me his foot. The thing that had been missing from the male's prints on the ledge now stared me in the face. The Navaho's shoe did not have an ankle flap. Mentally, I cursed myself for not having had the wit to realize this when I studied the prints. Then, I had only concerned myself with size, committing each to memory. Had I been a little more committed to the task of studying the prints, it would have come to me that the telltale drag of the flap was absent, that the male's print was too clear for a masculine Kiowa foot.

In the long ago, the flap had been more than what it became, grandiose decoration. During the time before we Kiowa gained horses and warriors were on foot, the ankle flaps obliterated tracks when traveling through enemy territory. The Navahos had never had to worry about that, as they live in a country of shifting sand and blowing winds, which nicely wiped out their tracks for them. This man, while he had gone around disguised as The Cheyenne Robber, had worn his own shoes.

White Bear was right. I am not a good tracker.

Another thought occurred—the thought of so many young people skulking around in the night and all of them disguised as other people. The two before me had gone around, one looking like her dead second mother, the other, like his master. Meanwhile, the dead woman disguised herself to look like Shade. But what guise had her lovers worn? I asked this directly of Shade.

Her thumb and forefinger pulled at her lower lip as her frightened eyes locked with mine.

"All I know," she said just above a whisper, "is this man would not leave her alone. She's stopped caring about him, said he wasn't what she'd been hoping for, but he wouldn't stop pestering her. I think she first went after The Cheyenne Robber just to frighten this other man off. But then she started thinking about him again. I think she wanted him to speak up, challenge my father for her. She hated my father."

"She was looking for a hero," I offered.

"Yes," Shade quickly agreed. "And she used those very words. She said a real hero would come for her soon. She made a mistake, thinking The Cheyenne Robber was just the person, but when he laughed at her, she went back to thinking about the man she saw the most. And she let him think that she was seeing The Cheyenne Robber.''

"How did she do that?"

Shade made a face. "It was too easy really. This man mistakenly followed me one night, thinking I was her. He saw me meet Good Friend and believed him to be The Cheyenne Robber."

"How do you know he followed you by mistake?"

"I saw him. Once I was with Good Friend, the following man no longer tried to hide. In fact, he waved to me, trying to coax me into coming away from Good Friend." She looked up at her husband. Their hands became locked. In a tight voice she said, "We were frightened. We ran away. We heard him yell that we would pay for our deceit."

The couple became lost in silent emotion. My heart began to appreciate their plight. Hastily, I shrugged that off. "Did you get a good look at this man?"

Shade spoke in a defeated tone. "It was dark. I never saw his face, only his outline. The thing I could see clearly was his shield."

"He carried a shield!"

"Yes," she whimpered. "It almost shined in the moonlight. And I could see that it was painted with the design of the Eagle Shield Society. A blue eagle and two blue guns."

On a yellow background. The color yellow would shine in moonlight because it was meant to. I sat for a moment in stunned silence. I now knew without a single doubt the identity of this man. And knowing his identity, I rushed more questions at the couple.

"When the two of you were on the ledge, did you see this same man among the horses?"

The Navaho's eyes flickered. "How did you know we were on the ledge?"

I waved an impatient hand. "That doesn't matter. Tell me what happened when you were on the ledge."

The Navaho spoke for himself and his wife. As he spoke, I was mildly amazed by his command of Kiowa, a command of the language he'd disguised from me during our first meeting, speaking in a broken, childish manner. He wasn't hiding from me now, and for that, I was appreciative.

"We knew we had been seen when we heard the cries of the herders. What we didn't know was that they thought they'd seen a witch. We were trying to hide from their further view as we said our farewells. What we had to do was make certain Shade was safe with her mother, who would vouch for her whereabouts if the herders had recognized her.

"But just as we were beginning to make our way down from the ledge, we heard terrible screaming. I told Shade to remain where she was as I ran to the edge and looked down. I couldn't see very much. The horses were all in a state, some of them running, and the hobbled ones bucking, trying to free their front legs so that they could run too. Then I heard another scream and realized the sound was made by a horse. But the sound wasn't right. It was the chesty sound that angry or frightened horses make, but this sound was more like . . ." He made a face and shook his head. "I don't know—like the chesty sound wasn't coming out of its mouth."

"It wasn't," I said meaningfully. "The sound was coming from a slashed throat."

The Navaho nodded vigorously. "That's right. That's just how it was. But I didn't know it then. All I knew was that something was terribly wrong and I had to get Shade away from there. We didn't dare meet again. It hurt me to leave her alone when there was so much trouble, but I couldn't get to her.''

"This is why you risked Ghost Sickness. You were in He Goes's camp to let Shade see you, let her know that your love for her was still strong.''

"Yes," he said weakly. Then he tilted his head to the side as he gave me a long and considered look. "The Cheyenne Robber said you were a smart man and that we would have to be very careful about you. Forgive me for saying this, but I didn't believe him. You just don't look very smart.''

Remembering all of the disguises so many had worn of late, I said with a touch of irony in my tone, "Appearances are too often misleading.''

He sent me a bashful smile and lowered his head.

CHAPTER

9

I had more questions. Those I directed to a now more relaxed Shade. She regarded me with the same open expression I had observed on the very first day she and I had spoken. The day she'd sat outside the death lodge guarding Owl Man and me as we examined the dead woman's remains.

"Did your second mother ever instruct you in the art of making cigars?"

The question seemed harmless. Shade relaxed even more, leaning against her husband's side. "Yes. It wasn't a difficult thing to learn."

"But it was for your auntie."

Shade lowered her eyes and blushed. "Well," she began, then hesitated. I could tell she was trying to find a way to be kind. "My auntie has always needed more . . . time to learn things."

"I had the privilege of watching her work. She seemed quite expert to me."

Shade brightened, sitting up fully. "Oh, yes. Once she's learned a thing, it stays with her forever."

"I noticed that she dipped the tobacco before rolling it up. I've never seen anyone do that before."

Shade became completely at ease. "Oh, that's flavoring liquid. The one who died said that Mexican people did that all the time. Coffee or white man's crazy water are the best flavors. The liquid must be boiled three times and with tobacco leaves added during the cooking. She called those 'throw-away leaves' because, during the cooking, they melt away. When cigar leaves are dipped into the cooled liquid, they feel sticky. Which is good, because then the leaves are easier to roll up."

"You blood mother said that your second mother was most impatient with your auntie because she didn't throw out the liquid just right."

Shade nodded solemnly. "This is true. She told my auntie again and again to be careful with it, but my auntie would forget."

"On the day your second mother died, your auntie said that there were three pots of coffee."

Shade frowned slightly as she thought. "No," she said in a soft drawl. "That can't be. My mother and I made the coffee. We only made two pots."

"You're certain?"

"Oh, yes," she said quite brightly. "I remember my mother saying she didn't want to waste any more coffee on my father's visitors than she had to. We made two pots. I don't know anything about a third pot."

"Do you remember those who went out and came back in on that day?"

She was thoughtful again. "A lot of people did. Mostly the men, to relieve themselves." She shook her head sadly. "I'm afraid I didn't pay any attention. I just wanted to finish serving and leave. The Cheyenne Robber was sending me mean looks that made me nervous—nervous because by then he knew that I was in love with his servant and that he would have to marry me if he hoped to keep Good Friend safe. He was very angry.''

I fully appreciated how she must have felt. With a man like The Cheyenne Robber lancing her with his eyes, it would have been unnatural if she'd been able to notice anything else going on around her. Still, her lack of knowledge frustrated the liver out of me. There was nothing more to be gained here. I thanked the three people for their candor and the trust they had placed in me. Caught up in this munificent oratory, a thing I'm afraid custom demands whenever a guest is served food, I went a bit too far, rashly promising to do what I could to aid the lovers' cause. I failed to realize the blunder until, excited by the promise, Shade threw her arms around my neck and hugged me while her husband blathered heartfelt thanks. Now I was trapped. And whenever I feel trapped, my first response is anger. As there was only one person I could vent this anger against, I determined in my heart to seek him out. But as I left the lodge, I instructed all three people to remain together, looking meaningfully at the Navaho. Understanding this was hardly the night for love, he muttered assurances that he would faithfully guard both women. Outside, I stomped off into an early evening, which was becoming quite cold as darkness quickly settled.

My horse was happy to see me, anxious to return home. Even as I mounted up, my horse was already making the dash for home. A person I did not expect to see on my arrival there was Elk Cry. He was just a few yards in front of my dark and deserted-looking lodge. To keep himself warm during the wait, he'd made himself a fire and was crouched before it as I rode up. Recognizing the rider coming out of the darkness as me, he stood. Even in the dim light I plainly saw that he was still wearing that piqued expression. I felt my heart harden. If he wanted to be mad at me, that was all right. I was mad at him too. Mad because I knew now that he had yielded to the temptations of an amoral woman. I said nothing to him as I dismounted and he approached. In fact, intentionally, I kept my back to him as I lead my horse to the shelter. When I came out, he boldly planted himself in front of me, forcing me to read what his rapid hands had to say.

"Looters," he signed. "I've had to keep them out. They say my cousin is a dead woman. That it is their right to take away her things."

I hadn't thought about that. Grudgingly, I thanked him for guarding our few possessions. Then, hands on my hips, I went on a highly vocal attack. "I understand that you are angry with me, but know this. I have just learned a few things that have given me cause to be angry with you."

The hands remained still as Elk Cry bird-eyed me.

Pushing my face close to his, I said in a growl from behind clenched teeth, "I am told that you had relations with a married woman."

Elk Cry reeled, his hands going to his face as he staggered about. It took him awhile to recover. When he did, he came to face me again, those hands moving so quickly I had to concentrate with all my might.

"Not relations. Talk. That is all. Just talk. She asked questions, I answered."

"What questions?" I snapped.

"About rank, the way it worked. She wanted the names of the men of the highest rank."

I mulled that for a second or two. That seemed to fit with what I knew of the dead woman. That she was looking for a man to save her from a marriage she detested. But it couldn't be just any man. He had to be a man more powerful than the man she was married to. I was also greatly relieved to know this young man I thought so highly of had not behaved with the dead woman in an untoward fashion.

"You gave her the names?" I asked without rancor.

Even though there was no trace of anger in my tone, Elk Cry continued to look tense. The hands began to move, slowly. "Yes. And, because she was interested, I explained the rank and importance of societies."

"Beginning," I said as I thought, "with the Ten Bravest and working down."

"Exactly." Elk Cry sighed deeply, his hands falling to his sides.

He and I stood in silence, he gazing longingly at the fire we were too far away from to feel its heat, I lost in thought. Thoughts he startled me out of when he began tugging the sleeve of my shirt, pointing toward the fire. I followed his lead and we settled on our haunches close to the high flames. Elk Cry carefully added more wood from the stock-pile laid at the side. The large amount of wood made it evident that he was prepared to guard my home throughout the whole night. His generosity and devotion to my wife, his cousin, touched my heart. I still did not understand why he was angry with me, and now I wanted him to explain so that I could properly apologize. When I voiced this, his mouth twisted in a frown. He tossed the last piece of wood in his hands into the flames, then those hands were on the swift move again.

"I am angry about what was said to that woman."

Thoroughly perplexed I cried, "I have no idea what you're talking about. What did I say that was so wrong?"

Impatience caused those hands to snap out a lengthy explanation.

The instant I understood, I fell heavily on my rump.

•   •   •

Many torches were stuck into the ground just outside White Bear's lodge. Up to halfway, the lodge was dark. Where the interior insulating ringing wall ended, the lodge was lit, the fiery red paint on the outside wall seeming to glow. I could see the shadows caused by the men inside. I was much closer to the lodge than I was supposed to be. The shields on display were meant to warn off those like me. A torch had been stuck before the tripod bearing the shield of its owner. I walked slowly, taking note of each. The slow inspection finally brought me to the closed door. Taking in a lungful of air, I shouted for White Bear and The Cheyenne Robber to come out.

Both men were sincerely glad to see me. White Bear did all the talking.

"Things are not going well in there," he said frankly. "Red Bird won't shut up and I can't talk him down. The only person able to stall the council is Owl Man. Just before any vote, he makes a grand display of holy ritual, and by the time he's finished, everyone has forgotten what was being voted on. I hope you have some answers, because I can't promise how long that old man can keep it up. He's looking tired."

"He's not the only one who's tired," I complained. "But, yes, I have the answers we need. Before I get to those, there is something we need to discuss in complete confidence." I glanced at The Cheyenne Robber and added, "All three of us."

White Bear returned to his lodge, and judging by the muted groans, the men inside were happy to be given a reprieve from all that sitting. After they filed out, White Bear motioned for The Cheyenne Robber and me to come inside.

"If you don't mind," White Bear said as he tied the door

closed, "my nephew and I would prefer to stand. Speaking for myself, my buttocks are numb."

The Cheyenne Robber grunted in agreement, so we stood in a small circle as I spoke softly, mindful that the wrong ears might be just outside the walls. As I talked, White Bear turned ashen while The Cheyenne Robber busily turned vibrant shades of red. Just as I finished, The Cheyenne Robber opened his mouth to defend himself. His words were ended before they began when the heel of White Bear's beefy palm struck him between the eyes.

"Stupid!" he cried. Before The Cheyenne Robber could duck, the hand clobbered him again and again, emphasizing each declaration. "Stupid, stupid, stupid!"

"Enough!" I shouted. My hands grabbed on to steady a now wobbly-legged The Cheyenne Robber. "You're beating his brains out."

"He doesn't have any brains," White Bear spat. "He's an idiot."

"If we all keep our heads," I tried, "perhaps there's a way out of this mess."

White Bear began to pace, throwing his arms wide. "I don't see any way out of this. I'm ruined. My nephew has ruined me. And if that isn't enough, my cousin Crying Wind is accused of being a follower of the Dark Way." He stopped pacing and looked at me, his expression stricken. In a lowered tone he said, "Maybe I can run away. Become one of those white-man-clothes-wearing Cherokees and change my name."

"The Cherokees wouldn't have you," I said flatly. "So please calm down and listen to me."

The Cheyenne Robber jerked away from me, glowering down into my blanching face. "I'm going to get you for this, meddler. I told you to stay away from my home. You should have listened to good advice."

The anger I felt for having made such a rash promise to the people of his household returned in full force. Drawing from that inner strength, I yelled right back at him.

"Be glad I meddled," I sneered, "for your . . . plan . . . wasn't worth two fingers of salt. If you really believed you could keep a thing like that secret until the warm weather comes, then you truly are an idiot."

The Cheyenne Robber raised his fist. White Bear caught his arm at the wrist, saving me from the blow. "He's right," White Bear seethed. "And well you know it. That's why you want to hit him."

The Cheyenne Robber shook himself loose and glared at both of us. In his defense he said in a low, menacing tone, "I did what I had to do. Good Friend is not my servant. He is like a brother to me. It's just our bad luck that he fell in love before I could send him safely back to his true people."

I advanced on him, almost needing to stand on tiptoe to speak directly in his face. "Do you really mean that?"

The Cheyenne Robber's chin snapped back. Then he bellowed, "Of course I mean it!"

"Good. Then tomorrow you can prove it." I looked back to White Bear. "Tell the council members that I will speak before them in the morning."

I turned to leave, the highly dramatic exit becoming botched when I could not untie the tight knots holding closed the door. White Bear made a disgusted sound in the back of his throat and came to help me, shoving me out of the way as he freed the knots.

Just as I was passing through the door hole, he said, "If what you have to say to the council in the morning is no better than the news you brought me tonight, I will become a Cherokee."

I looked back over my shoulder. "As I said, they wouldn't have you."

Coming outside, the first thing I noticed was the absent shields. The torches still burned, but the tripods were empty. The council members had taken their shields and themselves home. I did not go off in the direction of my home. There was no point. My wife wasn't there and Elk Cry was on guard. My brains thumping, I trudged off for the Grandmother's lodge. Halfway there, I noticed a darkened lump standing directly in my path. The lump moved and I stood frozen in fear. Then I heard the voice that could only belong to one person.

"I've been waiting for you," Owl Man said as he came near.

I let go a breath I hadn't realized I had been holding. Owl Man stopped directly in front of me.

"I thought you would like to know that Skywalker is making a rapid recovery. He's sitting up and eating solid food. He instructed me to ask you this question. He wants to know if you are still looking backward."

The way it was said, it didn't sound like a question. It had the sound of a challenge.

"Yes," I replied. "And he was right. The answers were all behind me."

Owl Man mutely nodded. I began to move and he fell into step beside me. "So, you have all the answers now."

I grunted. "I have too many answers. I need to sort them through."

Owl Man patted my shoulder. "I know a trick that will help you." He fell silent as he tottered along beside me. We were almost at the door of the Grandmother's lodge when he stopped, his hands firmly grasping my upper arms. "Lay down with your wife."

"That's the trick?" I hooted.

His old eyes blinked quickly as he answered in a near wounded tone, "Yes, it is. Sex clears the mind as nothing else can. Sometimes it takes more than one woman to clear the mind completely. Now you know why Owl Doctors have more than one wife."

The revelation was a bit startling. Skywalker had two wives, and of late I'd heard him mention that he was on the lookout for a third. None of that had meant anything to me. I'd simply thought that like White Bear, Skywalker was a bit oversexed. Imagine my surprise to learn that Skywalker's needs could almost be described as medicinal.

"I have to find out about that baby—if it's all right."

"It is," Owl Man answered. "The Buffalo Doctors cured it."

Grunting disgustedly, I left him.

Crying Wind was wonderfully receptive. I hoped her passion was for me but suspected it was because she was more determined to be loved one last time before she died. At any rate, our lovemaking was incredibly intense, and once we were both too physically spent to move, I realized my mind was indeed wonderfully clear. Lying on my stomach, the side of my head resting against my folded arms as I listened to Crying Wind's cute little whistling snore, the events of the past days clicked neatly and firmly into place.

I was sitting in front of the doorway when, just a little after dawn, White Bear came out of his lodge to relieve himself. Because he was still groggy, he didn't notice me until he nearly tripped over me. This immediately set him off and he began yelling. I neatly ducked an awkward blow meant for my head as I hastened inside his lodge. He came back directly, still fuming about tripping over me and almost landing on his face. The episode had been inelegant, and knowing that even for a few seconds he'd looked foolish, White Bear's colossal pride was bruised. He sat down without speaking. Before I could speak, there came the parade of his wives, bringing in food, coffee, and the large pot of hot water White Bear would use to clean himself. As I had already taken a chilly bath, I declined the offer to share the bathing water. Instead, I gratefully accepted bowls of coffee and food. White Bear was giving his upper body a good scrub when his youngest wife knelt down and whispered against my ear.

"Don't worry about Crying Wind. The others and I will guard her. The old woman known to you as Duck says to tell you that she will die before she allows the council to take Crying Wind."

My heart felt glad that my wife still had such good friends, that the recent blackening of her name had not swayed them from what they knew to be true—that she was a good and blameless woman.

"Tell Duck," I whispered in return, "that I would be forever obliged if she would remain inside the Grandmother's lodge until this danger has passed."

The young woman's eyes rounded. "You're certain it will pass?"

I offered her a smile. It felt false, heavyhearted, but I tried. "No member of the council will come to call my wife out of the Grandmother's protection. But Crying Wind must stay where she is until I call her out. Will you make certain the women who are my wife's true friends understand this?"

As she rose, she answered, "You may depend on us."

Knowing without any hesitation that I could, I turned my thoughts to the things I would be forced to say before the council. My sober attitude got the better of White Bear. As

his wives left, he came to sit before me, his big face eager
and troubled.

"You're not going to talk about my nephew, are you?"

"Yes, but not a lot. The part you're worried about is not
important."

"You're sure?"

"Yes," I cried.

I retreated into a deep silence. For once, White Bear respected this, saying nothing more as we waited together.
Within the lapse of a few moments we heard the sound of
men approaching. My lowered head shot up when I recognized The Cheyenne Robber's voice. Instantly I stood up
and dashed out. The Navaho was with him, hobbling the
horse's legs, and The Cheyenne Robber was carefully placing his shield on a tripod. When both saw me, a sour look
came over each face. Ignoring it, I approached The Cheyenne Robber.

"Before the other men on the council arrive, I have a
favor to ask."

The Cheyenne Robber's face became more sour. "And
why would I want to do a favor for you?"

Tired of his petulant attitude, I got right up in his face.
"Because after today, you will owe me many favors and
because the one I'm asking of you now is for your benefit."
Lifting my chin in the direction of the Navaho, I finished,
"And his."

The Cheyenne Robber considered this. Finally he said,
"All right. I'll do it, but only because I have never known
you to be a liar. Nosy and presumptive, yes, but a liar, no.
Now tell me what you want."

Seconds after I finished speaking, the Navaho untied the
horses and he and The Cheyenne Robber rode away. I went
back inside to wait, my stomach beginning to flutter so
badly I felt ill. In no time at all, White Bear and I heard

the sounds of many men outside the lodge. As they entered, my nervousness increased. None of them noticed for they were greeting White Bear and taking their assigned places. Then came the tedious formalities, each man declaring his clan and war society, the formal lighting of the council pipe, the passing of the pipe from hand to hand, each man drawing smoke. As I sat behind the council circle, I was not given the pipe. Just as the pipe reached White Bear again, there came the sounds of a commotion outside. Everyone tensely waited, and presently a voice hailed, the voice of The Cheyenne Robber.

"You may come in," White Bear thundered.

The Cheyenne Robber ducked through the door hole. Behind him followed Elk Cry, Bear Shadow, and Little War, men I had requested him to bring to the council. The Cheyenne Robber took his rightful place beside his notable uncle, while the other three came to sit beside me.

White Bear stared flintily at The Cheyenne Robber. "You're late," he said accusingly.

The Cheyenne Robber shrugged indifferently. "I had an errand."

"Well," White Bear grunted. "Now we must start over."

"Not yet," The Cheyenne Robber said. "I saw Owl Man. He said you have to wait for him."

Red Bird threw up his hands in disgust. "Oh, not again! That old man made us crazy nearly all of last night. Surely we don't have to put up with any more of his foolishness."

My tongue ached to shout him down. Fortunately, White Bear cut him down to proper size, and as White Bear spoke, his narrowed and hard eyes pinned Red Bird.

"That old man has a right to be here. He has earned his place at this fire. You are only my cousin's accuser. If it weren't for that, you would have no place here."

Red Bird turned his head, his features pinched as he
looked for support among the other chiefs. Faces turned
away. The only one that didn't belonged to He Goes. Red
Bird's spine straightened as he believed he'd found an ally
on the council. The spine began to curve when he realized
why He Goes had not turned his face away. He Goes was
staring straight ahead, his eyes locked with mine. I could
almost hear his thoughts. I knew without question that as
soon as my wife was condemned as a witch, He Goes
would claim her son and denounce me as a coconspirator
in the evil.

I wasn't nervous anymore. I could barely wait for Owl
Man to arrive. I wanted to have my say and take revenge
on this man who planned so much grief for my wife. The
wish was granted. No sooner had I thought this than Owl
Man's gravel voice sounded outside and a lot of tussling
was heard. The unusual sounds became self-evident as Owl
Man opened the door. Sitting Bear and three men helped a
remarkably stable looking Skywalker inside. Then came the
great to-do with getting him seated, a suitable backrest ob-
tained for his use. While all of this was going on, Skywalker had the temerity to look over his shoulder at me
and grin.

Even from where I sat, I could plainly see his vastly
improved condition. Healthy flesh showed beneath the dead
skin peeling from his face. And he had filled out, which
meant he'd been a good boy, eating without complaint and
drinking gallons of the salty tea. In taking the place prepared for him, he hobbled on thickly bandaged feet but did
not wince when taking a step. All of this told me that my
friend had the constitution of iron, that he wasn't going to
lose anything to frostbite, not even a little toe. I should have
felt happy about that. What I felt instead was irritation that
he had the power to worry me half to death. But that's

friendship. That's the way it works. Change even the most irritating portion of it, and you lose it completely. And now it was Skywalker's turn to worry about me, which was why he'd left his sickbed too soon. I was in trouble, and sickness would not keep him from my side.

He settled next to Hears The Wolf. Both looked back to me, this time worry clearly etched on Skywalker's face. I smiled. I held the smile until a grin eventually turned the corners of his mouth. During the seconds of this silent communication, I felt my confidence increase. I no longer felt alone, unarmed. I had my friends, I had the truth.

These things were enough.

The lengthy opening procedures began all over again. I used these moments to step outside, listening to the voices from within as I walked the row of displayed shields. I knelt down before a covered shield that had been left to lean against the lodge wall. Lifting the cover, I stared at it until I heard Red Bird's voice. Using a tone so rich and full-bodied in timbre that it could not fail to impress every listener, he accused my wife. During his concluding remarks, I went back inside. As he sat down, I walked straight into the circle of seated chiefs. White Bear lifted a questioning brow as he regarded me. He wanted me to get on with it, so I complied.

"The man you have heard," I said without the normal preamble of proclaiming my birth clan, war honors, and class, "is a fraud. And I am not speaking of his claims of power. I challenge instead his right to present himself as a morally righteous person. Especially as this false presentation is for the purpose of denouncing a thoroughly virtuous woman. The man known as Red Bird does not have this right to judge the woman Crying Wind, because he is a proven adulterer."

Heads turned as chiefs muttered among themselves.

"This man who calls himself a friend to He Goes seduced and was the longtime lover of the young woman who, unfortunately, is now in her grave."

Red Bird screamed "Liar!" again and again. He was so enraged that two men on either side of him had to hold him down. I wasn't paying any attention to him. My gaze was fixed on the tight-expressioned, completely silent He Goes.

"This winter camp," I continued, "has been an encampment of profound discontent. But the unhappiness all around us has not been caused by this canyon or its recent history. The unhappiness I found everywhere I've turned in the past days was unhappiness that was brought to this place, carried in by still-beating human hearts."

I looked meaningfully at Bear Shadow. "Your jealousy against The Cheyenne Robber rode in with you, and yours has been a jealousy you have nursed despite all assurances from The Cheyenne Robber that he is your friend, that he has no designs on your wife. As for your pretty wife, I saw with my own eyes the hopeful smile she gave you when you brought me to your home as a guest. Then I watched as you stomped that frail hope into the dust. If you are looking for a reason as to why she keeps running home to her mother, look no further than yourself. But the most amazing thing is that you've missed the vital fact that she keeps coming back to you. Realize now the real truth of your situation. Your little wife is a high-born woman. If she didn't want to be your wife, she wouldn't be. If she did not sincerely feel the affection for you that you have quite determinedly failed to believe, she would divorce you and marry someone else."

Bear Shadow's eyes crawled to the corners. The Cheyenne Robber smiled faintly and nodded. Bear Shadow looked back to me, his rounded eyes pleading.

"Understand now," I said more gently, "that your wife cares deeply for you. You have never had any need for Red Bird's charms, and you most certainly had no need to slaughter two of The Cheyenne Robber's horses."

"What!" The Cheyenne Robber bellowed. "That was you?"

Bear Shadow threw up his hands in surrender as he spoke in a rush. "I didn't want to do it. But Red Bird said that for the love charms to work, I needed to show power over the one holding my wife's affections. The only thing I could think of that you love more than women are your horses. I give you my word, here and now, that you may have six of my best horses to repay your loss of the two."

The Cheyenne Robber's face was murderous. "Ten," he said flatly.

Bear Shadow blanched, then after a moment's thought said defeatedly, "Done."

"Shake hands," Skywalker's frail voice commanded. Grudgingly, the two obeyed.

The instant his hand was freed from The Cheyenne Robber's knuckle-crushing grip, Bear Shadow looked up at me. In a voice barely above a whisper, he asked, "H-how did you know?"

"You told me yourself. In your home as you gazed into the fire. I asked if you saw the man on the cliff top. You said no. That answer put you in a place you should not have been, among The Cheyenne Robber's herd." As Bear Shadow lowered his ashamed face, I scanned the assembly. "So there you have it. The horses were not killed by any witch but by a tormented young man. I have revealed this shameful deed merely for the purpose of exposing the lie in the first half of Red Bird's claims. The second half is more complicated. For this I must beg your further indulgence."

Worry flitted across White Bear's broad features. This second half included too many things capable of bringing White Bear's notable family to ruin. I looked at The Cheyenne Robber. He was still scowling darkly at Bear Shadow, still more concerned with his lost horses than aware of his present jeopardy.

With a deep sigh and shake of my head, I ventured on. "A lot of young people have been slipping around in this camp."

The bluntly put statement eased a small amount of the tension in the lodge, with some of the older chiefs even fighting off smiles. Finally, we had entered a subject these men could readily understand, night-crawling lovers.

"Most of the creeping was done by innocent lovers, but two among them weren't innocent at all. One happened to be a married woman. A woman, because of her lack of identity of a birth clan, was without the power to divorce her husband. Indeed, she had little knowledge of clans and ranking societies." I glanced, sadly, at Elk Cry.

"From one of the most gentle-natured men I have ever had the privilege to know, she gained this knowledge. Once she had what she needed from him, she threw him over. A thing which was this woman's way, for she was a woman without loyalties. As a captive, her natural instinct was for her own survival and betterment. She went on the hunt, then, for a man more powerful than the husband she didn't want. A man she could only regard as a foster parent. And because she thought of him this way, it twisted her mind each time he took her to his bed."

He Goes's face tightened more. His stare was so intent that I almost withered.

Almost.

"She approached several more men. The names of many of these men are not important. Only two stand out from this list. The first man on this list truly loved her, but unfortunately for him, he wasn't powerful enough to challenge her husband. The second seemed for a time to be just the man she needed. Until she began to see through him.

"This woman was a fake, causing everyone to think of her as beautiful, sweet, and of good character. As the woman known as Smiling Woman can readily attest, she was none of those things. Her beauty came from paints and her lovely nature was a guise she wore to protect herself. As long as she behaved as the helpless maiden, an attitude which had been most beneficial during the first frightening days of her capture, she felt safe. But the flower of youth is a seasonal thing. To protect herself against the days of her own middle age, she needed to advance her situation while she was still in her youth. This well-thought-out scheme meant that she was no one's fool. Especially not Red Bird's. Even if he did carry a shield belonging to the highest order of the Owl Doctors' society during the last days of his trying to win her back."

Loud gasps of disbelief sounded. Red Bird sprang to his feet, again screaming that I was a liar. With a nod from me, Elk Cry stood and went out, coming in again, carrying a shield. A shield painted yellow and emblazoned with a blue eagle and two blue guns. Solemnly, Elk Cry handed the shield to me.

"This is the shield Red Bird carried. Obviously, it isn't the shield he has outside on display. This shield was taken from inside his lodge just after he left to come here. This is the shield he had made for himself years ago when he believed he had successfully tricked his way into the society of Owl Doctors. The very same shield he should have burned when membership to this society was denied him.

But, as you can see, he didn't burn it. Instead, he took it with him into the Colorado, where he could safely walk around with it without fear of being challenged. The trouble he faced returning to his own people was that he had to hide the shield while he made another attempt to join the Owl Doctor society.''

Red Bird was still standing, his face bloodless, his body shaking. I felt no pity for him.

''Circumstance put him in the way of a young woman searching for an important man. At first, by his carriage and exceptional looks, she thought she'd found just the man. But his disguise wore thin. Desperate to hold on to the awe and affections of this seemingly impressionable young woman, he brought out and dusted off the shield. Just as this vain effort was beginning to fail, the secretive misconduct of others seemed to rush out of nowhere, salvaging this man's badly wounded pride. Then came the episode of the woman becoming a raven and the death of the horses.

''As you now know, the horses had nothing to do with witches, and neither did the woman on the ledge. She was just another creeper, her identity unimportant. When she went to the ledge to meet her lover, she opened her shawl to greet him. And that's what the herders saw. Not raven's wings, a shawl.

''But Red Bird jumped on both of these occurrences in order to build himself up. These things and Skywalker's disappearance provided him the opportunity not only to prove himself to the Owl Doctors but to rebuild the dead woman's esteem. And he was beginning to feel desperate on this last issue because he had come to believe that she had turned to The Cheyenne Robber, a man Red Bird knew he could never compete with. What he did not know was that the woman he thought was He Goes's wife was, in fact, He Goes's daughter, Shade. And the man he thought was The Cheyenne Robber was someone dressed up like The Cheyenne Robber.''

"Who?" came the combined cry. "Name this deceiver!"

I raised both hands and gradually the council returned to silence. "His identity isn't important either. He is only a foolish young man. What is important is the way The Cheyenne Robber conducted himself once he learned of the mischief played against him. As a chief, The Cheyenne Robber fully accepted the responsibility brought on by someone's impersonating him. After the woman married to He Goes died, as a chief The Cheyenne Robber took the woman known as Shade, placing her under his protection. He took her not as a wife, but as a companion to his lawful wife. His intention throughout has only been to keep Shade until he felt it was safe for her to return to her rightful home. He did this solely on my assurance that Shade's second mother had been killed by an unknown hand and that Shade herself might be in danger.''

I drank a bowl of water during the time the ring of chiefs vocally thanked and praised The Cheyenne Robber for being such a wise and selfless person. Looking over the rim of the bowl, I caught the twinkle in Skywalker's eyes and read his smirking lips: *Liar.*

Setting the bowl aside, I could only answer this irrefutable charge with an embarrassed roll of my eyes and a weak shrug. Owl Man brought the assembly back to the moment.

"What killed the woman married to He Goes?"

"A tobacco leaf."

To say that the assembly was stunned stupid is to glance over their true response. Tobacco has always been seen as a good thing among our people. Not at any time has it been known as harmful. My declaring it a murder weapon, a poison, went beyond their powers of comprehension. They were all so mortified that even Red Bird sat down, joining the others in a totally baffled daze.

"Anyone within the sound of the recently dead woman's voice heard the way she fussed at her sister-in-law about the reckless way this innocent woman disposed of the flavoring liquids used for making cigars. Hearing this, the killer knew the liquid was dangerous. That fact was further impressed on him when He Goes's sister again forgot and threw out the liquid to the dogs. Right after those hungry dogs lapped up some of the brew, they fell dead."

"I still don't understand," White Bear growled. "A flavoring liquid that's only had a few tobacco leaves dipped into it can't be that harmful."

"Yes, it can. But the real harm isn't from the dipped leaves. The danger lies in how the mixture is prepared. The liquid is boiled three times, each time with a throwaway leaf. A leaf that gets melted down. After three boilings like this, the liquid becomes strong enough in flavor to penetrate the tobacco that will become a cigar, and sticky enough to bind the rolled leaves together. This is a Mexican trick. A trick the dead woman taught to the women of He Goes's family. But it was only He Goes's sister, because she is slow in her head, who could not understand why she mustn't throw out the liquids in the normal way. The dead woman tried to teach her sister-in-law to bury the liquid, but the most the poor woman managed to remember was that it should be poured into a hole. Which she did. And she never put it together that the two dead dogs had anything to do with the liquid."

I turned my head in his direction. "But you did."

His face became chalky, but he did not avert his gaze. I began to move inside the circle, coming to stand before him. The chiefs in front of him, Big Tree and Dangerous

Eagle, moved to either side, glancing back over their shoulders.

"As an accustomed guest in He Goes's home, you saw and heard everything. Just as I am certain that, as a man usually known for being careful, your visits were foolhardy and served no purpose—not after she'd rejected you as brutally as I'm certain she did. Nevertheless, you couldn't stay away from her. You were miserable, but that was all right. Just as long as you knew that she was miserable too. But then, there came a man you believed to be The Cheyenne Robber. A man more than capable of taking her away. A man who would make her happy while you continued to live in misery. You couldn't have that, so you killed her. And how ironic that she should die by taking a fatal drink from the brew she'd taught the other women to make."

"You can't prove this," Little War said quietly.

I sighed deeply, the sadness in my heart overwhelming. Years ago, I'd worked hard to save this man's life. Now, I was taking that life away.

"Unfortunately," I said gravely, "I can. You visited He Goes on the pretext of courting his sister. Elk Cry knew this wasn't true. He knew because, until the day the three of us spoke to her, you hadn't shown that woman any interest. Within Elk Cry's hearing, you told this innocent woman that you would keep your promise. This caused Elk Cry considerable anger. As an afflicted man himself, he has a genuine concern for others who are afflicted. Hearing you lie to an impressionable woman threw him into a rage. He brought that rage to me. And doing that, he inadvertently revealed a murderer."

Little War's battle-scared face twisted, becoming an ugly sneer.

"There was a lot of coming in and going out," I continued, "on the day White Bear and The Cheyenne Robber

came to discuss the joining of the two bands. You knew
The Cheyenne Robber did not want to marry Shade, but
more than anyone, you wanted this marriage. You believed
it would put an end to any plan of He Goes's second wife
of running off with The Cheyenne Robber. What upset you
was the way this second wife talked against the marriage.
Worse than that, He Goes seemed to be listening to her.
He wasn't. He was merely indulging her, as was his very
bad habit where she was concerned. He Goes wasn't listening because he had designs of his own, designs that
could only benefit by the marriage of his daughter to The
Cheyenne Robber. But in your intense jealousy, you didn't
see that He Goes was only pretending to be listening. You
knew you had to do something. Something final. Because
you had come to the decision that if you couldn't have her
and be happy, neither could anyone else. Not even her
rightful husband.

"So, when the sister went out for more food to serve the
gathering, you went with her. She was so flattered and so
flustered by your sudden interest in her that she didn't notice when you carried in a third pot of coffee. A pot that
was never intended to be drunk from. What I don't know
is how you knew she would give coffee from that pot."

Strangely, my lack of knowledge in this final but crucial
detail made Little War enormously proud. His smile became genuine. A smile I'd known many times when we'd
shared a joke or simply enjoyed each other's company. Seeing that smile wounded me deeply.

"All I had to do," he said, "was mention that she looked
as if she could do with a bowl of coffee. That coffee might
make her headache feel better. He Goes's sister still believes the idea was her own."

Behind me, in the otherwise unearthly silent lodge, I
heard He Goes weeping. I badly wanted to weep myself.

"I'm not sorry she died," Little War said defiantly. "She wasn't a good person. She made fools of her husband and me. She would have made a fool of The Cheyenne Robber too, if I hadn't stopped her. And she wasn't a human being, one of us. She wore Kiowa dress and spoke our language, but she was really just a Tehan." A quivering hand lightly explored the scars on his face, the patch covering the empty eye socket. "Tehans did this to me. All Tehans should die."

In the moments it took me to recover my voice, Little War's remaining eye never broke contact with mine. Finally, I turned away, knowing full well that I would never look at his face again.

In a shaking voice I finished what I had to say to the assembly. "Red Bird, still trying to impress a woman no longer impressed by him, still trying to prove himself as a powerful Owl Doctor before Skywalker returned and accused him of being a fake once more, was desperate to find a witch. Doing this, of course, meant that he would reopen her eyes as well as be seen as the savior of a frightened people. The trouble was, he couldn't find a witch because he knew there wasn't one. But he did see my wife dashing about suspiciously. What my wife was doing was trying to save her family—more to the point, her son. Crying Wind learned through Smiling Woman that He Goes intended to make the treaty with White Bear and, after this was done, claim my wife's baby. My son," I said forcefully enough to cause He Goes to raise his head, "is the only child born of He Goes's nephew, my wife's first husband. He Goes has long wanted that child, but Crying Wind blocked him when she took her baby and ran to White Bear, placing herself and her child under his protection.

"Next, I came along, marrying Crying Wind and adopting her son. All of this meant that He Goes simply couldn't ride in and demand the child. He would have to be a bit more crafty. Smiling Woman warned Crying Wind that there was still a danger from He Goes and gave Crying Wind the empty promise that she would do all she could to dissuade her husband if Crying Wind did a favor or two for her. Bluntly put, Crying Wind was made to carry messages from Smiling Woman to The Cheyenne Robber, stressing the urgency of Shade's removal from a dangerous environment.''

I paused, looking at Skywalker, rolling my eyes wearily. He smirked again, working hard to stifle the laughter he felt as I began to lie like a dog.

''The Cheyenne Robber came to me for advice, and I of course said he was completely right to take Shade out of there. That once the supposed marriage was revealed to be false that any offense this caused He Goes would be forgiven on the grounds that, as a chief, The Cheyenne Robber was bound by an oath to protect those weaker than himself.''

Heads vigorously bobbed in complete agreement. The Cheyenne Robber was once again a hero. The applause was almost deafening. (And somehow through all of it, The Cheyenne Robber was able to maintain a straight face.)

''So now you know why my wife was accused,'' I said. I was tired of talking now, wanting badly to sit down before I fell down. ''Out of everyone Red Bird looked at as a possible candidate for witchcraft, only my wife's dashing madly about seemed suspicious. When he questioned her, while cheating her out of a necklace worth ten times more than everything he owned, and she didn't answer to his satisfaction because she couldn't, he was excited. Then, when she tried to help a teething baby and gave it too strong a sleeping potion by mistake, Red Bird had found his witch. It's just too bad for him that his next mistake was not knowing just how much I care for her or how I would fight to save her. But then he wouldn't have any idea about that because Red Bird is a man unable to love anyone but himself. Even the woman he was trying to impress was only useful to him for a while. Which is why he took up with a married woman who hadn't the power of a birth clan to free herself through divorce. He didn't want her to be free. He only wanted to use her body and bask in the light of her awe of him. But once she knew him to be an impostor and said this to his face, he wanted to make her regret throwing him over. And once she was again groveling at his feet, he would throw her over.''

All of this became too much for He Goes. He made a lunge for Red Bird, almost strangling him to death before the others were able to pull him off. While the chiefs grappled to contain him, He Goes made dire threats against Red Bird and against Little War. But Little War was gone. He'd slipped out during the scuffle.

EPILOGUE
1924

The summer day was sultry, even in the cooler shade of the covered front porch belonging to a dispirited, gray-colored clapboard house. The house was in the country, miles outside of the bustling town of Anadarko, Oklahoma. The young white man wearing a good white summer suit was from somewhere back East. A place where they wore nice suits, starched shirts, and hats all the time. Here in this mostly casual country, he still wore suits, but lately he had learned to relax a little, removing the coat and rolling up the shirtsleeves. He was a man known to the old man Tay-bodal simply as Keith.

Keith sat on a chair in the mildly relieving porch shade, writing frantically in a thick notebook. He had come a long way just to collect stories folks in and around these parts considered fairly useless. But Keith didn't think they were useless. He wanted every story the old man had in him.

In an all-out effort to collect these stories, he had traveled by car from his home in Brooklyn, taking a room in a hotel in Anadarko. Tay-bodal lived nearly five miles out of An-adarko. Every morning Keith made the drive from the hotel to the old Indian's house, tucked in a hollow of dry, hot wallowing prairie. There was a little creek that ran close to the house, and where there was water there were cotton-wood trees. Tay-bodal's march of trees lended blessed shade to one side of his house. Keith remained on the porch of that house for as long as the old man allowed. Which was generally around sundown, when the old man would get up from the chair, go inside his house without a word of farewell, and close the door.

On the first day Keith arrived at the storyteller's house, following directions that had gotten him lost several times, he'd been hot, tired, and impatient. These things caused him to blunder rather badly. After the old Indian shuffled to answer the knock, Keith began to speak rapidly and in broken English, believing this type of dialect the thing the old man would understand. Artfully, Keith slipped in a few *ughs* and prefaced more than one sentence with *me-want-um*.

Clad in a pair of baggy britches held up with suspenders, a plaid shirt, and a fine black hat perched on a white-gray head, Tay-bodal stood patiently behind the screened door while Keith blundered on in a clipped Eastern accent. Then, as he had learned from fairly accurate history texts dealing with the various customs of American aborigines, Keith redeemed himself marginally by remaining silent as he waited for the old Indian to speak. And what the old Indian finally said struck Keith right between the eyes just as swift and sure as any bullet.

"Young man, I appreciate how far you've come and how hot the day is. I'm sorry you got lost so often in this heat, and it upsets me to know that what I am about to say to you will most certainly hurt your feelings, but the truth must be told. If you can't speak English any better than

you're speaking it now, I don't believe anyone would benefit from your trying your hand at writing a book."

As Keith profusely apologized, the old man behind the
screen chuckled.

Tay-bodal came out of the house carrying two glasses of
tea. Keith grunted, not looking up from his writing. Tay-
bodal set the glasses down on a rickety table, then sat down
in a rocking chair that wouldn't rock because it couldn't.
Years before, he had knocked the rockers off the legs. The
chair permanently leaned back, but that was all right. It
wasn't moving and would never again make him feel
queasy because of the rocking movement. He would have
thrown the thing away if it hadn't been a gift from his
friend Hawwy. Usually, the cats sat in this chair and Tay-
bodal in the good chair, but Keith was a guest. Tay-bodal
suffered the uncomfortable chair in silence.

Keith looked up from the scratching of pen against page.
He crinkled his nose as ink-stained fingers adjusted the
glasses sliding down a thin, finely shaped nose. Through
the glasses, pale blue eyes stared at Tay-bodal's ancient
profile.

"What happened to Little War?"

Tay-bodal sipped at the tea, shrugged indifferently. "He
lived on the edge."

Keith shook his blond head as if clearing it. "I don't
understand."

Tay-bodal set the glass down next to his slippered feet.
As he leaned back in the chair, a huge orange-and-white
cat jumped into his lap. Tay-bodal absently stroked the cat.

"Because Little War hadn't killed a recognized Kiowa,
he wasn't banished. But killing that girl-woman the way he
did made people understandably wary of his presence. So,
he followed the bands, living outside one and then another.

He remained a useful warrior, distinguishing himself time and time again, especially in the last days of our nation. In the end, he was one of the warriors chosen by Kicking Bird to ride the prison train to that real hot place far away from here.''

"Florida," Keith supplied.

Tay-bodal nodded and grunted.

"Did he survive that?"

"No." The sadness in Tay-bodal's voice was more final than the spoken word.

A lengthy silence ensued. Keith drank the tepid, too sweet tea. Setting the glass on the table, he asked, "What happened to Shade and the Navaho?"

Tay-bodal chuckled heartily. "Oh, The Cheyenne Robber adopted that Navaho. Made him a full brother. To seal their brotherhood, let everyone see that the Navaho freely accepted his new life as a Kiowa, The Cheyenne Robber gave him Shade. The bands, even He Goes's band, approved of this, and the last weeks we stayed in the canyon were filled with warm feelings and a lot of feasting. It was a good way to leave that place, the canyon. Everyone felt better.

"On our last day down there, though, a thick mist came and settled in. Above the canyon, the prairie was bright and sunny, but deep in that hole it was hard to see your own nose. The people took that as a sign that it was a good time to go, and they were pretty quick about it. Families were already leaving while my family was packing up. All around us I could hear horses and the drag of travois. We were taking too long to get going because my little son had found a puppy from somewhere and was crying that he wanted to keep it. In the meantime, my wife and I were having an argument about just how to pack up our possessions. I didn't want her touching my medical supplies, and she said I couldn't pack up right if my life depended on it. Favorite Son was bawling about that puppy, and Crying Wind and I were bickering back and forth in this manner when The Cheyenne Robber, Good Friend, White Bear, and Skywalker came riding by. They did not pause. They simply looked back over their shoulders and laughed.

Crying Wind was still fussing as she took care of everything just the way she wanted to, and Favorite Son was begging her to pack the puppy, while I just stood there, staring after the men I cared for so much, until that thick mist just swallowed them up. When I think of them now, I see them just that way, all of them young, strong, and confident that the world would always belong to them as they disappeared into the mist. I find it fitting that this same mist has come to settle permanently over my eyes."

Minutes slowly ticked by on Keith's pocket watch while Tay-bodal sat, staring off almost sightlessly, and because of the filmy blue cataracts, into a middle distance. Gradually, Keith's attention returned to the notebook lying open on his lap, and Tay-bodal listened as the pen scratched hurriedly against rustling paper.

"You gonna put all I said in a book?"

Startled, Keith looked up, staring intently for a moment at the craggy profile. "Yes," he said softly. "I'm putting all of it in a book."

Tay-bodal considered this at length, then said, with dry humor in his tone, "If I'm gonna get to be in your stories, you think maybe you could make me a bit taller and . . . handsome?"

Keith smiled warmly. "I promise, I'll do my best."

Listening as the pen once again scratched at the paper, Tay-bodal lifted his homely old face to the sun.

MARGARET COEL

THE EAGLE CATCHER

When tribal chairman Harvey Castle of the Arapahos is found murdered in his tipi, the evidence points to his own nephew. Father John O'Malley, head pastor at nearby St. Francis Mission, does not believe the young man is a killer. In his quest for truth, O'Malley gets a rare glimpse into the Arapaho life few outsiders ever see—and a crime fewer could imagine...

___0-425-15463-7/$5.99

THE GHOST WALKER

Father John O'Malley comes across a corpse lying in a ditch beside the highway. When he returns with the police, it is gone. Together, an Arapaho lawyer and Father John must draw upon ancient Arapaho traditions to stop a killer, explain the inexplicable, and put a ghost to rest...

___0-425-15961-2/$5.99

THE DREAM STALKER

Father John O'Malley and Arapaho attorney Vicky Holden return to face a brutal crime of greed, false promises, and shattered dreams...

___0-425-16533-7/$5.99

Prices slightly higher in Canada

DANA STABENOW

EDGAR AWARD–WINNING AUTHOR

__BREAKUP   0-425-16261-3/$5.99

April in Alaska is the period of spring thaw, what the locals call *breakup*. First, the snow uncovers a dead body near Kate's home. Then a woman is killed in a suspicious bear attack. Kate is drawn further into the destruction of breakup—and into the path of a murderer...

__BLOOD WILL TELL   0-425-15798-9/$5.99

When a member of the Native Association dies mysteriously, Kate is thrown into the thick of tribal politics. The more she learns, the more she discovers how deeply she is tied to the land—and to what lengths she will go to protect it.

__PLAY WITH FIRE   0-425-15254-5/$5.99

Kate must break the silence of a close-knit community to find out who would want one of its members dead.

__A COLD DAY FOR MURDER   0-425-13301-X/$5.99

Kate returns to her roots to find out if a national park ranger lost to the harsh Alaskan snowscape was killed by more than the cold.

__A FATAL THAW   0-425-13577-2/$5.99

Nine bodies lay dead in the snow. Eight are victims of a crazed killer. But it's the ninth, a woman with a tarnished past, that's troubling Kate Shugak.

__DEAD IN THE WATER   0-425-13749-X/$5.99

Kate goes to work on a crab fishing boat to try to find out why part of its crew disappeared on the Bering Sea.

__A COLD-BLOODED BUSINESS   0-425-15849-7/$5.99

Kate goes undercover to investigate drug trading on the TransAlaska Pipeline that's causing overdoses and deadly on-the-job errors.

Payable in U.S. funds only. No cash/COD accepted. Postage & handling: U.S./CAN. $2.75 for one book, $1.00 for each additional, not to exceed $6.75; Int'l $5.00 for one book, $1.00 each additional. We accept Visa, Amex, MC ($10.00 min.), checks ($15.00 fee for returned checks) and money orders. Call 800-788-6262 or 201-933-9292, fax 201-896-8569; refer to ad #441

Penguin Putnam Inc.	Bill my: ☐Visa ☐MasterCard ☐Amex _____ (expires)
P.O. Box 12289, Dept. B	Card#_____
Newark, NJ 07101-5289	
Please allow 4-6 weeks for delivery.	Signature_____
Foreign and Canadian delivery 6-8 weeks.	

Bill to:

Name_____

Address_____ City_____

State/ZIP_____

Daytime Phone #_____

Ship to:

Name_____	Book Total	$_____
Address_____	Applicable Sales Tax	$_____
City_____	Postage & Handling	$_____
State/ZIP_____	Total Amount Due	$_____

This offer subject to change without notice.